Accident⋯⋯⋯⋯⋯⋯⋯⋯⋯⋯⋯⋯ has always ha⋯⋯⋯⋯⋯⋯⋯⋯⋯⋯⋯ and losing herself in a good book. Husband…yes. Children… two boys. Cooking and cleaning…sigh. Sports…no, not really—in spite of the best efforts of her family. Gardening… yes. Roses, of course. Kelly was born in Australia and has travelled extensively. Although she enjoys living and working in different parts of the world, she still calls Australia home.

Visit Kelly online at www.kellyhunter.net

the trouble with Valentine's

Kelly Hunter

MILLS & BOON

Published in Great Britain 2013
Mills & Boon, an imprint of Harlequin (UK) Limited,
Eton House, 18-24 Paradise Road, Richmond, Surrey TW9 1SR

THE TROUBLE WITH VALENTINE'S
© Harlequin Enterprises II B.V./S.à.r.l. 2013

Originally published as *Wife for a Week* © Kelly Hunter 2006

ISBN: 978 0 263 90578 6

26-0113

Harlequin (UK) policy is to use papers that are natural, renewable and recyclable products and made from wood grown in sustainable forests. The logging and manufacturing processes conform to the legal environmental regulations of the country of origin.

Printed and bound by
CPI Group (UK) Ltd, Croydon, CR0 4YY

To generous hearts

CHAPTER ONE

H<small>ALLIE</small> B<small>ENNETT</small> H<small>AD</small> B<small>EEN</small> selling shoes
for exactly one month. One long, mind-numbing
month working solo at the exclusive little shoe
shop in London's fashionable Chelsea, and she
really didn't think she'd last another. Back in the
storeroom she'd sorted every pair of shoes by
designer, then model and finally by size. Out here
on the shop floor she'd arranged the stock by colour and, within the colours, by function. Dusting
and vacuuming? Done. Serving customers? Not
yet but hey, it was only midday.

It was also Valentine's Day, and Hallie had
been charged with convincing all her non-existent customers that high-end shoes were the new
chocolate. Ruby-red heart-shaped helium balloons
bumped across the ceiling. Two dozen heart-
shaped shoe boxes sat on the counter ready for

the filling. The shop window boasted two dozen long-stemmed roses. Good things happened on Valentine's Day. Unexpected things like, for instance, a sudden rush of customers.

A shoe shop girl could hope.

Hallie added a few of the heart-shaped shoe boxes to the shop window. Who said she didn't have marketing initiative? All those gentlemen looking for the perfect gift – the ones who actually knew their beloved's shoe size – they'd be here any minute now.

Because there were so many of them.

Hallie picked up the nearest shoe, a pretty leopard-print open-toed sandal with an onyx heel, and tried to figure out why anyone would actually pay three hundred and seventy-five pounds for a pair of them. She dangled the dainty shoe from her fingertips, turned it this way and that before finally balancing it on her palm.

'So what do you think, shoe? Are we going to cram a sweet size six like you onto a size eight foot today?'

A quick jiggle made the shoe nod.

'I think so too but what can I do? They never listen. These women wouldn't be caught dead in a size eight shoe. Now if they were men it'd be different. As far as men are concerned, the bigger the better.' The door to the shop opened, the bell tinkled, and Hallie hurriedly set the shoe back on its pedestal and turned around.

'Darling, what a thoroughly delightful shop! Why I've never noticed it before, I have *no* idea. And then when you started talking to the shoe I just knew I had to come in.'

The woman who had spoken was a study in contradictions. Her clothes were pure glamour and her figure was a triumph over nature considering that she had to be in her late fifties. But her wrinkles were unironed, her hair was grey, and her 'darling' had been warm, possibly even genuine.

'Please do,' said Hallie with a smile. 'Look around. Trust me, they never talk back.'

'Oh, you're an Australian!' said the woman, clearly delighted with the notion. 'I love Australian accents. Such marvellous vowel sounds.'

Hallie's smile widened, and she spared a glance for the woman's companion as he followed her into the shop, a glance that automatically upgraded to a stare because, frankly, she couldn't help it.

As far as women's fashion accessories went, he was spectacular. A black-haired, cobalt-eyed, dangerous-looking toy who no doubt warned you outright not to bother playing with him if you didn't like his rules. He was like a Hermès hand-bag; women saw and women wanted, even though they knew the price was going to be astronomical. And then he spoke.

'She needs a pair of shoes,' he said in a deep gravelly baritone that was utterly sexy. 'Something more appropriate for a woman her age.'

'You're new at this, aren't you?' muttered Hallie before turning to stare down at the woman's shoes, a stylish pair of Ferragamo man-eaters with a four inch heel. They were a perfect fit for the woman's perfectly manicured size-six feet. They were fire-engine red. 'There is *nothing* wrong with those shoes,' said Hallie reverently. 'Those shoes are gorgeous!'

'Thank you, dear,' said the woman. 'Why a woman turns fifty and all of a sudden certain peo-ple to whom she gave birth start thinking she should be wearing orthopaedic shoes is completely beyond me.' The woman seemed to age ten years as wrinkles creased and unshed tears leached even more colour from eyes that would have once been a bright sparkling blue. 'Your father would have loved these shoes!'

Ah. It was all starting to make sense. He of the indigo glare was the woman's son and right now he was in big trouble. 'Right,' said Hallie brightly.

'Well, I'll just be over by the counter if you need me.'

He moved fast, blocking her escape. 'Don't even think of leaving me alone with this woman. Give her some shoes to try on. Anything!' He picked up the open-toed leopard-print sandal. 'These!'

'An excellent choice,' she said, deftly plucking it from his hand. 'And a steal at only three hundred and seventy-five pounds. Maybe your mother would like two pairs?'

His eyes narrowed. Hallie smiled back.

'If only I had something to look forward to,' said the woman with a sigh that was pure theatre as she sat on the black leather sofa and slipped off her shoes. 'Grandchildren, for instance. I need grandchildren.'

'Everyone needs something,' said her son, looking not at his mother but at her. 'What do *you* need?'

'Another job,' said Hallie, kneeling to fit the sandals. 'This one's driving me nuts.' She sat back on her heels and surveyed the sandals. 'They fit you beautifully.'

'They do, don't they?'

'How do you feel about travel?' he asked her while his mother preened.

'Travel is my middle name.'

'And your first name?'

'Hallie. Hallie Bennett.'

'Nicholas Cooper,' he said and gestured towards the woman. 'My mother, Clea.'

'Pleased to meet you,' said Clea, her handshake warm and surprisingly firm. 'Nicky, she's darling! She's perfect! You need a wife, you said so this morning. I think we've just found her.'

'Wife?' said Hallie. *Wife?* That'd teach her to shake hands with strangers. Nicholas Cooper's smile was lazy. His mother's was hopeful. Probably they were both mad. 'Is this a Valentine's Day prank?'

'Of course not,' said Clea. 'It's fate.'

'Fate,' echoed Hallie. 'Of course. My mistake.' Rule number one of customer service – the customer was always right.

'He's loaded,' said Clea encouragingly, getting back to the matter at hand –which clearly wasn't the buying of shoes.

'Well, yes.' Hallie could see that from the way he dressed. He was also far too amused for his own good. 'But is he creative?'

'You should see his tax return.'

'I don't know, Clea. I think I prefer my men a little less…' What? She slid Nicholas Cooper another quick glance. Sexy? Wild? Gorgeous? 'Dark,' she came up with finally. 'I prefer blonds.'

'Well, he's not a blond,' conceded Clea, 'But look at his feet.'

Everyone looked.

He wore hand-stitched Italian leather laceups. Size 12. Wide.

'Of course, as his mother I can't let you marry him unless you're compatible so maybe you should just kiss him and find out.'

'What? Now? Ah, Clea, I really don't think—'

'Don't argue with your future mother-in-law, dear. It's bad form.'

'No, really, I can't. It's not that, er, *Nicky*, doesn't have a lot going for him—'

'Thanks,' he said dryly. 'You can call me Nick.'

'Because clearly he does. It's just that, well…' She cast about for a reason to resist. Any reason. Yes, that would do. It wasn't quite the truth, but little white lies were allowed in sticky situations, right? 'I wouldn't be very good wife material right now. I have a broken heart.'

'Oh Hallie, I'm so sorry,' said Clea in a hushed voice. 'What happened?'

'It was terrible,' she murmured. 'I try not to think of it.'

Clea waited expectantly.

Obviously she was going to have to think of something. Hallie leaned forward and tried to look suitably woebegone. 'He was secretly in love with his football coach the whole time we were together!'

'The cad!' said Clea.

'Was he blond?' said Nick. 'I'm betting he was blond.' He was standing beside her, close, very close, and she was kneeling there, her gaze directly level with his...oh...my!

'Are you *sure* you're not interested?' asked Clea.

Hallie nodded vigorously and dropped her gaze, looking for carpet and finding feet. Big feet. 'It's this job,' she muttered, more to herself than anyone else. Probably he was bluffing. Probably he had regular size eight feet tucked into those enormous shoes. Her hand shot out of its own accord, spanning the soft leather of his shoe, testing the fit for width and finding it tight. Uh, oh. She pressed her thumb down and felt for toes, found them at the very top of the shoe. 'Phew!' She felt breathless. 'It's a tight fit.'

'Always,' he said, amusement dancing in his eyes. 'But I'm used to it.'

Hallie smiled weakly and scrambled to her feet as warmth spread rapidly through her cheeks. It was his eyes. His voice. Possibly his feet. Any one of them was a guaranteed temptation, but all three together? No wonder she was blushing.

'What my mother meant to say was that I need someone to *pretend* to be my wife for a week. Next week to be precise. In Hong Kong. You'd be reimbursed, of course. Say, five thousand the week, all expenses covered?'

'Five thousand pounds? For a week's work?' There had to be a catch. 'And what exactly would I have to do to earn that five thousand pounds?'

'Share a room with me but not a bed, which is fortunate considering your broken heart.'

Was he laughing at her? 'What else would I have to do?'

'Socialize with my clients, act like my wife.'

'Could you be a little more specific?'

'Nope. Just do whatever it is wives do. I've never had one, I wouldn't know.'

'I've never been one. I wouldn't know either.'

'Perfect,' said Clea, bright-eyed. 'I'm believing it already. Of course if the kiss isn't convincing it's just not going to work.'

'No kissing,' said Hallie. 'I'm heartbroken, remember?'

'There has to be kissing,' he countered. 'It's part of the job description. Who knows? You might even like it.' There was a subtle challenge to his words and lots of amusement.

'Kissing would cost extra,' she informed him loftily. What did she have to lose? It wasn't exactly the sanest of conversations to begin with.

'How much extra?'

Hallie paused. She needed ten thousand pounds to finish her Sotheby's diploma in East Asian Art; she had five of it saved. 'I'm thinking another five thousand should do it.'

'Five thousand pounds for a few kisses?' He sounded incredulous, still looked amused.

'I'm a very good kisser.'

'I think I'm going to need a demonstration.'

Uh oh. Now she'd done it. She was going to have to kiss him. Fortunately common sense kicked in and demanded she make it brief. And not too enthusiastic. One step put her within touching distance; a tilt of her head put her within kissing range. She stood on tiptoe and set her hands to his chest, found his shirt soft and warm from the wearing, with a hard wall of muscle beneath. But she digressed. With a quick breath, Hallie leaned forward and set her mouth to his.

His lips were warm and pleasant; his taste was one she could get used to. She didn't linger.

'Well, that was downright perfunctory,' he said as she pulled away.

'Best I can do given the circumstances.' Hallie's smile was smug; she couldn't help it. 'Sorry. No spark.'

'I'm not sure I can justify paying five thousand pounds for kisses without spark.' His lips twitched. 'I'm thinking spark is a must.'

'Spark is not part of the negotiation,' she said sweetly. 'Spark is a freebie. It's either there or it's not.'

'Ah.' There was a gleam in his eyes she didn't entirely trust. 'Turn around, Mother.' And, without waiting to see if his mother complied, Nicholas Cooper threaded his hands through her hair and his mouth descended on hers.

Hallie didn't have time to protest. To prepare herself for his invasion as he teased her lips apart for a kiss that was anything but perfunctory. Plenty of chemistry here now, she thought hazily as his lips moved on hers, warm, lazy, and very, very knowledgeable. Plenty of heat as her mouth opened beneath his and she tasted passion and it was richer, riper than she'd ever known. She melted against him, sliding her hands across his shoulders to twine around his neck as he slanted his head and took her deeper, tasting her with his tongue, curling it around her own in a delicate duel.

If this was kissing, she thought with an incoherent little gasp, then she'd never really been kissed before. If this was kissing, imagine what making love to him would be like…

His smile was crookedly endearing when he finally lifted his mouth from hers, his hands gentle as he smoothed her hair back in place. 'Now that was much better,' he said in that delicious bedroom voice and she damn near melted in a puddle at his size twelve feet. 'We'll take the shoes.'

Right. The shoes. Hallie boxed the sandals with unsteady hands, swiped his credit card through the machine, fumbled for a pen and waited for him to sign the docket before she risked looking at him again. His hands were large like his feet, and his hair was mussed from where *her* hands had been.

What would it be like to pretend to be this man's wife for a week? Foolish, certainly, not to mention hazardous to her perfectly healthy sex drive. What if he *was* as good as his kiss implied? Who would ever measure up to him?

No. Too risky. Besides, she'd have to be crazy to go to Hong Kong for a week with a perfect stranger. What if he was a white slave trader? What if he left her there?

What if he was perfect?

He was halfway across the room before she opened her mouth. Almost to the door before she spoke. 'So you'll get back to me on the wife thing?'

At five thirty-five that afternoon, Hallie counted the day's takings. It wasn't hard; she'd only made three sales and that included the shoes Nicholas Cooper had purchased for his mother. Next, she shut the customer door, turned the elegant little door sign to 'closed', and was about to set the alarm system when a breathless courier rapped on the display window and held up a flat rectangular parcel.

Not shoes, thought Hallie. Shoes did not arrive by courier in flat little parcels, even designer ones. But the courier's credentials looked real, the address on the parcel was that of the shop, and the name on the paperwork was hers so she opened up with a sigh, signed for the parcel, and locked up behind him before turning back to the parcel.

It was a brown-paper package tied up with string. Hard to resist, what with it being a favourite thing and all. Besides, it was Valentine's Day. Good things happened on Valentine's Day. Unexpected things. Hopefully it wasn't a bomb.

Hallie snipped and ripped to reveal a slim travel guide to Hong Kong and Nicholas Cooper's business card. The card said he was a gaming software developer. Good to know. She flipped it over and discovered a message on the back.

'Marco's on Kings', it read in bold black scrawl, and beneath that, '7 pm tonight, Nick'.

Presumptuous, yes, he was certainly that. His kiss had been presumptuous too.

Not to mention annoyingly unforgettable.

So what if Marco's was one of the best seafood restaurants this side of heaven? So what if raindrops on roses might conceivably be in Nick Cooper's repertoire? No sensible woman would even consider his proposal. Pretending to be a complete stranger's wife for a week was ridiculous, even by her standards.

And yet…

Hallie reached for the travel guide and smoothed it open, first one page, and then another.

Hong Kong; gateway to the Orient. Money and superstition. Heat and a million camera shops. A squillion neon signs.

'An enchanting blend of East meets West,' read

the travel guide. Half a world away from this shoe shop, whispered her brain. Ten thousand pounds.

So there were a few drawbacks.

Lies. Deception. Nick Cooper's kisses. Hallie tucked a stray strand of hair behind her ear and closed the book with a snap.

Big drawbacks.

And yet…

Twenty minutes later, Hallie let herself in through the front door of her brother's Chelsea flat and dumped her handbag on the sideboard. Why Tris had bought the little two-bedroom apartment when he never stayed more than a year in any one place was a mystery, but she certainly appreciated the use of it. No telling what Tris would make of Nicholas Cooper's offer.

Probably best not to tell him.

Ten thousand pounds, whispered her brain as she slipped off her shoes and padded down the hallway.

No.

Dinner at Marco's, then. It's only dinner.

No it's not. If you go to dinner you'll ask him why he needs a wife for a week and then where will you be? Next thing you know, you'll be agreeing to go to Hong Kong with him.

So?

Travel was her middle name.

Oh, boy. Hallie stumbled over the hallway runner and wondered just what it was about Nicholas Cooper that made her lose her mind.

He had a wicked smile. No doubt about it.

And his offer was definitely intriguing.

A rueful smile tugged at her lips. Best not to even think about his kisses.

Come ten to seven, Hallie had finished her argument and was in the bathroom, hurriedly applying makeup, when she heard the front door open and close, followed by the sound of a man's long, loping strides down the hall. Moments later Tris appeared in the doorway, little more than a vague shadow at the edge of her vision. 'You're back,' she said, busy with the mascara. 'I wasn't expecting you until tomorrow.'

'Plans change,' he said. 'Going somewhere?'

'Dinner at Marco's on Kings Road.'

'Classy.' Was it just her imagination or was Tris a whole lot more preoccupied than usual? 'Who with?'

Ah. That was more like it. 'Nick.'

'Nick?'

'We met today. At the shop.'

'He wears ladies' shoes? Is this supposed to be reassuring?'

'He came in with his mother. He *bought* her some shoes.'

'Run,' said Tris. 'Run the other way.'

'Nope. I've made up my mind. It's Valentine's Day and I'm embracing the unexpected. I'm having dinner with him.' She finished with the mascara, reached for a smoky grey eyeliner.

'So…' said Tris. 'Does *Nick* have a last name?'

'Of course he does but if I tell it to you you'll run a check on him at work and come home and tell me what kind of toothpaste he uses. Where's the fun in that? Besides, it's not even a date, exactly. More of a business opportunity.'

'What kind of business opportunity?'

'I'm not sure yet.' No need to bore him with details. 'Something involving travel.'

Tris sighed, heavily. 'And you believed him.'

Time to change the subject. 'There's leftover lasagne in the fridge,' she said as she dropped her lipstick into her evening bag and turned to leave the bathroom, halting abruptly as she took her first good look at her brother. 'Whoa.' His dark, shaggy hair was filthy, his left hand was carelessly bandaged and his clothes looked like they'd been dragged through a sewer with him still wearing them but it was his eyes that bothered her most. Because they were full of frustration and pain. 'You look terrible.'

'I'm fine.'

'Liar.' He was holding himself so stiffly. Ribs, maybe. He sagged against the doorframe, his shoulder hunched and Hallie revised her opinion. 'Shoulder?'

Tris nodded. Every so often he dislocated his left shoulder. The first time he'd done it he'd been six and their father had rushed him to the hospital. These days Tris opted to do without the six hour wait in A&E and sort it out himself.

'Have you ever considered a different line of work?' asked Hallie, mainly because it needed to be said and who better than a sister to say it? 'Because seriously, this undercover gig isn't doing you any favours.'

'You'd rather I sold shoes?'

'Well, yeah,' she drawled, and then forgot all about the insult to her current occupation when Tris leaned his head against the doorframe and closed his eyes. 'You want me to put your shoulder back in?'

Tris nodded, opened his eyes, pushed off the doorframe and went and sat on the edge of the bath. Hallie got up into his space, put the heel of her hand to his shoulder and lined up her weight behind it, ready for the hard, sharp push she was about to deliver. Better she put the shoulder back in than Tris trying to fix it himself using the doorframe. That never ended well. 'On three, okay?'

Tris leaned into her, as relaxed as he was going to get. 'Just do it.'

'Patience, grasshopper. Ready?' Time to count off. 'One.'

Hallie shoved hard and in it went. Tris groaned and almost landed in the tub.

'Thanks,' he muttered hoarsely.

'Not my pleasure.' Hallie found painkillers in the bathroom cabinet, tipped three of them into her brother's palm and watched him swallow them dry.

'You done in here?' he asked. 'I could use a shower.'

'No kidding.' She hated to see him hurting. She was also reconsidering her dinner plans. 'You want me to stick around?'

'What? You're going to cancel a free feed at Marco's to stay here and fight me for the last of the lasagne?' Tris summoned a faint smile. 'Touching, yet stupid.'

'The job went bad, didn't it?'

'I don't want to talk about it, Hal.'

Hallie sighed. He never did. Tris didn't talk about his work. Ever.

'Go,' he said, waving her away with his bandaged hand. 'I'm gonna take a shower and get cleaned up. There's nothing you can do. Eat. Be merry.'

And from within the confines of the bathroom as he shut the door behind him, 'Don't talk toothpaste.'

Nick Cooper always gave a woman fifteen minutes' grace. Any longer than that and he was inclined to leave or start without them. Fact was, women enjoyed keeping men waiting. They did it deliberately to heighten anticipation and make a man wonder. To make a man want. All part of the game, but then games were Nick's specialty. For every attack, there was a counterattack, no matter how good your opponent. And Hallie Bennett's fifteen minutes were almost up.

Not that Nick was even sure she was dining with him – as she hadn't called – but he'd headed for Marco's regardless. A man had to eat. And call it a hunch but he thought she'd show. He browsed the blackboard specials, scanned the printed menu, looked around for a waiter and saw, instead, the delectable Hallie Bennett heading his way.

Botticelli's Renaissance, her colouring; she of the Titian hair, creamy complexion and golden-brown eyes. But her hair was cropped to chin length and her face was pure arthouse Animae; all big eyes, clean lines and memorable mouth.

His body stirred and he narrowed his eyes in an attempt to conceal the fierce rush of anticipation that accompanied her arrival as he stood to greet her. Kissing that smart mouth of hers into submission had been an absolute pleasure. Getting to know the rest of her was tempting, very tempting, but the truth was he couldn't afford the distraction. He didn't need a bedmate this coming week; he needed a partner. Someone with an opportunistic streak, a quick wit, and a deft touch with the ridiculous.

So far, Ms Bennett had impressed him on all counts.

'Sorry I'm late,' she said when she reached him. 'I wasn't sure I was coming until the last minute.'

'What made you change your mind?' he asked as he saw her seated and tried to ignore the quickening of his breath and of his blood.

'Hong Kong and ten thousand pounds,' she said, her accompanying smile drawing his attention to the generous curve of her lips, currently painted a deep, luscious rose. Her lip colour matched her

dress, a sleek, cling wrap of a dress that empha-
sized the perfection of the body beneath.

'I like your dress,' he said with utmost sincerity.

'Thank you,' she said, her eyes lightening with a
humour that was hard to resist. 'I like it too. Have
you ordered?'

'After you.'

She chose the clam chowder. He chose the reef
fish and, at her nod, a bottle of white to wash it
down.

'I'm curious,' she said once that was all settled.
'You're rich, you're handsome, you're healthy –
you are healthy, aren't you?'

'Perfectly,' he said, enjoying her candour.

'So why do you need a pretend wife for a week?'

'I'm negotiating distribution rights to a computer game my company has developed. Unfortu-
nately, the distributor's teenage daughter took a
liking to me and I found it extremely difficult to,
er, dissuade her.'

'You mean you couldn't fend off one fledgling
female? You? You're kidding me, right?'

'Wrong.' Nick sighed. He could handle preda-
tory women, honest he could. But a semi-naked
eighteen-year-old Jasmine Tey had cornered him
in his bedroom late one night and the sheer
unexpectedness of it coupled with more than one

glass of his host's most excellent rice wine had rendered him momentarily incapable of sensible thought. 'She was very young,' he muttered defensively. 'Very sweet. I was trying to let her down gently.'

'You invented a wife,' guessed Hallie. 'And now you have to produce her.'

'Exactly. Will you do it?'

'Why not ask a woman you already know to help you out? She'd probably do it for free.'

'Because then I'd have to dissuade *her*. Whereas you and I will have a business arrangement, a contractual obligation if you like, and once you've fulfilled that obligation, you leave.'

'Ah.'

It was a very expressive ah.

'Will you and your *wife* be staying with your associate and his family?'

Nick nodded. 'They have a guest suite. And it's only John Tey and his daughter. He's a widower.'

'Dining with them? Socializing? Getting to know them?'

'All of that,' he said.

Hallie Bennett leaned back in her chair and regarded him steadily. 'That's a lot of lies, Nick. Why don't you just tell your distributor the truth? Maybe he'll understand.'

'Maybe.' Nick didn't have a good enough measure of the man to know. When it came to business, John Tey was cutthroat sharp. When it came to his daughter, the man was putty. 'As far as I can see, John Tey gives his daughter everything she wants.'

'I was raised by my father and four older brothers,' countered Hallie. 'Trust me, giving her what she wants won't apply to men.'

She had a point.

'Unless of course, your distributor decides that marrying his daughter off to you makes good business sense.'

'Exactly. I can't risk it.' He didn't want to marry Jasmine. He didn't want to marry anyone just yet. And then the bulk of her earlier remarks about her family registered. '*Four* older brothers, you said.'

'Not you too.' Her voice was rich with feminine disdain. 'Would it help if I told you they were all pacifists?'

'Is it true?' he asked hopefully.

'No. But we were talking about you.'

'You're right. I need a wife for a week. It'll be over so fast your brothers will never know. Will you do it?' Nick waited as the waiter set their meals in front of them. Waited while she thanked the man, reached for her napkin and set it across her lap, her features relaxed, her expression non-committal. She was more than he remembered from the shop. More vibrant. More thoughtful. Four brothers.

'I'd need to know more about you than I do now,' she said finally.

'I'll send you a fact file.'

'I'm not a fact file person.'

Why was he not surprised?

'No,' she continued. 'I'm more of a hands-on person. You're going to have to show me where you live, where you work and what it is you do all day. That kind of thing.'

Nick groaned.

'You can send me the fact file as well,' she said with a placating smile. 'I don't suppose it can hurt. And we're going to need some rules.'

'What sort of rules?' He wasn't very good with rules. Probably not worth mentioning.

'I want physical contact limited to public places,' she said firmly.

'No problem.' His lips twitched.

'And only when we have an audience.'

'You're absolutely right.' At this rate she'd get through every sexual fantasy on his list before dessert. 'What else?'

'I'll follow your lead but only within reason. I won't be a simpering "yes" wife.'

'But you will simper a little?'

Her chin came up, her eyes flashed warningly. 'Can't see it happening.'

'Okay, I can see that simpering might be a stretch for you. Forget the simpering.' He wouldn't. 'Can you do possessive?'

'That I can do,' she said. 'You want the whole "hands-off-my-man", slapping routine?'

'No slapping,' he said. 'Ladies don't slap.'

'You never said anything about being lady-like.'

Fantasy number three. *Damn* she was good.

'Oh, and there's one more thing…'

'There is?' Every man had his limits and Nick had just reached his. His brain fogged, his blood headed south and he was thinking leather, possibly handcuffs, although where he was going to get handcuffs from was anyone's guess. Silk then. No problem finding silk in Hong Kong.

'Earth calling Nick?' said Hallie in exasperation. She'd seen that glazed look before. Knew that Nick Cooper was definitely *not* thinking business. Men! They could never multitask. 'Nick! Can you hear me?'

'Oh I'm listening.'

He had the damnedest voice. The laziest smile. But this was a business arrangement. Business, no matter how tempting it was to think otherwise. 'My return ticket stays with me.'

CHAPTER TWO

HALLIE COULDN'T QUITE REMEMBER whose idea it had been to tour Nick's workplace after dinner, only that it had seemed a sensible suggestion at the time. Business, she reminded herself as they stepped from the restaurant out into the cool night air and he slipped his jacket around her shoulders. Strictly business, as she snuggled down into the warmth of his coat and breathed in the rich, masculine scent of him. The fact that his chivalrous gesture made her feel feminine and desirable was irrelevant. So was the fact that he was quirky and charming and thoroughly good company. This wasn't a date, not a real one. This was business.

Nick's office was only a couple of blocks away, familiar territory, this part of Chelsea, and they walked there in companionable silence.

'I need to make a phone call,' she said as

Nick halted in front of a classy office block and unlocked the double doors that led through to a small but elegant foyer. 'I'm sharing a house with one of my brothers at the moment. He's a touch protective; he likes to know where I am if I'm out with someone new. I used to get annoyed with him. Nowadays I just tell him what he wants to know. No offence.'

'None taken. It's a smart move. Makes you a smart woman,' said Nick.

Nice reply. Hallie pulled out her mobile and dialled Tris's number, grateful when he picked up on the umpteenth ring. He told her he was fine and not to nag. She told him where she was and that she'd be back before midnight and disconnected fast, before he could give her the be careful speech.

Hallie slipped her phone back into her handbag. Nick ushered her into the lift, the doors closed, and it was intimate, very intimate in there. She cleared her throat, risked a glance. Impressive profile. Big feet. And an awareness between them that was so thick she could almost reach out and touch it, touch him, which wouldn't be smart at all. He turned towards her and smiled that slow, easy smile that bypassed brains and headed straight for the senses, and then—

'We're here,' he said, and the lift doors slid open.

Nick's office suite was a visual explosion of colour and movement. Cartoon drawings covered every inch of available wall space; computers and scanners crammed every desk. There was a kitchenette full of coffee and cola; a plastic trout mounted above the microwave. The whole place was organised chaos and completely intriguing. 'So how many people work here?' she wanted to know.

'Twelve, including me.'

'Let me guess, they're all men.'

'Except for Fiona our secretary. Sadly she refuses to clean.'

'I like her already.'

'Figures,' he said. 'So does Clea. This is my office,' he said, opening a door to a room that was surprisingly tidy.

'What's the basketball hoop for?'

'Thinking.'

Right. 'And the flat screen TV and recliner armchairs?' There were two chairs, side by side, a metre or so back from the wall-mounted television.

'Working.'

Ah. Why she'd expected a regular office with

regular décor was beyond her. There was nothing the least bit ordinary about Nicholas Cooper. 'So tell me more about this game of yours. Is it something I'd know all about if we were married?'

'You'd know about it.' Nick's voice was rich with humour as he slid a disc into the gaming console and gestured towards an armchair. 'If we really had been married these past three years you'd have banned all talk of it by now.'

That didn't sound very wifely. 'Couldn't I have been supportive and encouraging?'

'Sure you could. I was thinking realistically but we don't have to do that. We can do fantasy instead.'

'Hey, it's your call. You're the fantasy expert. By the way, how long did you tell your distributor you'd been married for?'

'I didn't.' He slid her a glance. 'I'm thinking a couple of months, maybe less. That way if we don't know something about the other it won't seem so odd.'

'Works for me.' And then the game came on. The opening music was suitably raucous, the female figure on the screen impressively funky. 'Very nice,' she said politely. 'What does she do?'

'Mostly she fights.' He handed her a gaming handset. 'Press a button, any button.'

Hallie pressed buttons at random and was rewarded by a flurry of kicks, spins and feminine grunts. Not, Hallie noted, that the figure on the screen even came close to raising a sweat. 'Are those proportions anatomically possible?' she wanted to know.

'Not for earth women,' said Nick. 'Which she's not. Xia here is from New Mars.'

'New Mars, huh? I should have guessed. The clothes she's almost wearing are a dead giveaway. Does she have a wardrobe change option?'

'You want to change her *clothes*?'

'Well, she can hardly kick Martian butt in six inch stilettos, now can she?

He stared.

Hallie sighed. 'You're losing credibility here, Nick.'

'What did you do before you sold shoes?' he wanted to know. 'Bust balls?'

'I worked a blackjack table at a casino in Sydney for a while.'

'Why did you stop?'

'I never saw sunlight.'

'And before that?'

'A brief stint washing dogs in a poodle parlour.'

The memory was dim but still worthy of a shudder. 'Too many fleas.'

'So are you actually trained in anything?'

'I have a fine arts degree, if that counts for anything. And I'm halfway through a Sotheby's diploma in East Asian Art. That's why I came to London.'

'Why East Asian Art?'

'My father's a history professor with a particular interest in dynasty ceramics and I hung out in his workshop when I was a kid, read all his books.' It had been the crazy-cracks in the glazes that had first captured her interest. The rich history behind each of the pieces had held it.

'So you're following in your father's footsteps. He must be proud of you.'

'No, mostly my father ignores me. I learn anyway. I can spot a fake dynasty vase at fifty paces. In fact I'm absolutely certain the Ming in the Museum of London's a fake.'

He stared.

'All right, ninety percent certain.'

'So why aren't you finishing your diploma?'

'I will be. Just as soon as I earn enough money for my last two semesters.'

'By selling shoes?'

'It's a job, isn't it?' she said defensively. 'Interesting, well paid jobs are hard to come by when you're a student. Employers know you're just filling a gap.'

'Couldn't you ask your family to help out?'

'No.' Her voice was cool; he'd touched a nerve. Her brothers would have lent her the money. Hell, they'd wanted to *give* her the money and so had her father for that matter, but she'd refused them all. Little Miss Independent, and it galled her that they hadn't understood why she'd refused. None of her brothers had taken money from anyone when *they'd* started out. She was staying with Tris because there was more than enough room for her in his home and because London rentals were outrageously expensive. That was all the help she was prepared to accept.

No, money for nothing wasn't her style at all. But ten thousand pounds for a week's work… a week's fairly unorthodox and demanding work… Well now, that was a different matter altogether.

'How much do you need to complete your studies?' he asked curiously.

'Ten thousand pounds plus money to live on. But I've already saved five so with your ten thousand I figure I've got it covered.'

'And then what?' he said. 'Then will you roam

the world in search of ancient artefacts and long lost oriental treasure?'

'Yeah, just like Lara Croft and Indiana Jones,' she said, heavy on the sarcasm. 'You know, maybe you need to get out more. You might just be spending too much time in fantasy land.'

'See? I knew it wouldn't take long before you started sounding like a real wife,' he countered with a grin. 'Don't you want to be a Tomb Raider?'

Sure she did. She just didn't think it very likely. And as for sounding like a nagging wife… Hah! Wait till she really put her mind to it. 'Right now I'm thinking I want to be Xia here because she's really good at this alien butt-kicking business, isn't she? What does she get if she wins?'

'Points.'

'Points as in money? Does she get to shop afterwards?'

'Only for a new weapon.'

'What, no plastic surgery? Because I really think a breast reduction is a must here.'

'Our target demographic is teenage boys.'

'I'd never have guessed.'

'Besides, there's nothing wrong with her breasts; those are excellent breasts. Fantasy breasts.'

Hallie sighed.

'Not that yours aren't very nice too,' Nick added politely.

'Mine are real,' she said dryly, slanting him a sideways glance. 'Completely real. Just in case anyone should ask.'

'I'm very impressed.' His eyes were blue, very blue, and his smile was pure pirate. 'Because they look to be in excellent shape. I should probably take a closer look; acquire a real feel for them so to speak. I'm not a fact-file person either.'

'Is your distributor's daughter watching?' she countered smoothly, even as her breasts tingled and her nipples tightened at the thought of him touching her. 'Are we in a public place?'

'Sadly, no.' And through eyes half closed, his attention back on the screen, 'Man I love kinky women.'

Oh, boy. 'So what's in this game for us girls?' she said hastily. 'Other than this very cool vibrating controller.'

'Shang.'

'Excuse me?'

'Shang. Paladin princeling.'

Nick flicked back to the main menu and a male figure appeared on the screen. He had dark, carelessly cut hair, an exotic face, a tough lean bod, and was no slouch in the ammunition department either. 'Is that a gun in his pocket or is he just glad to see me?'

Now it was Nick's turn to sigh. 'You're not taking this seriously.'

'It's a game, Nick. I'm not meant to.'

'You're right, you're not. My mistake. *I'm* the one who has to take it seriously. My people have spent three years developing this platform, Hallie, and now it's up to me to market it. I can't afford to make mistakes. Not with John Tey, not with his daughter. That's where you come in.'

'Call me naive when it comes to big business but I think lying to a potential business partner about your marital status is a mistake,' Hallie felt obliged to point out.

'You sound like my conscience,' he muttered. 'If you have a plan C let's hear it.'

'Ah, well, I don't currently have a plan C.'

'Pity.'

He looked tired, sounded wistful. As if having to deceive John Tey really didn't sit well with him. Sympathy washed over her and all of a sudden she wanted to slide on over to his recliner and comfort him. Weave her hands through that dark, tousled hair, touch her mouth to his and feel the passion slide through her and the heat start to build as she feasted on that clever, knowing mouth and – Whoa! Stop right there. Because that wasn't sympathy.

That was lust.

'What?' He was looking at her strangely.

'Indigestion,' she said. 'I think it was something I ate. Probably the clams.'

'Probably the situation,' he said. 'What's it to be Hallie? Are you in or out?'

Hallie hesitated, tempted to say yes. Not for the adventure, the excitement, or the money but so that she could spend more time with Nick. The same Nick who was prepared to pay her ten thousand pounds so that at the end of the charade she'd *leave*.

A sensible woman would refuse him now and save herself the heartbreak, the *genuine* heartbreak, that was bound to come if a woman was careless enough to fall for him. A smart woman would sigh over that Hermès handbag, maybe even spend a minute or two imagining what it would look like on her arm, but in the end she'd turn away. That was what she *should* do.

What she said was, 'Do you believe in destiny, Nick? Do you believe in fate?'

'Only as a last resort. Why?'

'I think we should let the game decide. Xia and Shang against the Martians. If we win we go to

Hong Kong as man and wife. If we lose, you throw yourself on the tender mercies of Mr Tey and spill your guts.'

'You're serious, aren't you?'

She was.

'Deal,' he said, and the fighting began.

Two murderous hours later it was decided. They were going to Hong Kong.

CHAPTER THREE

JASMINE TEY HAD ALMOST conquered her habit of stiffening with apprehension every time someone mentioned Nicholas Cooper's name. It had taken a while. Two weeks, to be exact, and it had been a month since she'd last seen him. So much could happen in a month. New memories could replace excruciatingly embarrassing ones. Selective amnesia could happen, not that it *had*…

Not that it *could* with Kai standing in the kitchen telling her that Nick was coming back next week to finish his business dealings with her father.

And bringing his wife.

Jasmine would *never* have done what she did had she known about his wife.

'So, are they staying here or downtown?' she asked in what she hoped was a disinterested voice.

'Here.'

'Oh.'

'You enjoyed Nick's visit last time,' said Kai mildly.

Yes, she had. Nicholas Cooper had been fun to have around. His eyes had so often been crinkled and smiling. He'd been careful to include Jasmine in his conversations and he'd paid attention to her opinions whenever she'd voiced them. She'd taken it as encouragement.

So heady, Nick's attention.

So stupid, what she'd done next.

She'd gone to Nick's room one night and waited for him. Not naked, nothing so shameful as that, but she'd waited, hands twisting, breathless with anticipation. She wanted to know what a man's lips would feel like against hers. She ached for the slide of warm hands around her waist. She'd wanted *someone* to want her and there were so few some-ones in her sheltered world to choose from.

She'd wanted *Kai* to notice that Nicholas Cooper had treated her like a woman rather than a girl.

She'd been such a fool.

Nick had stepped into the guest room, taken one look at her standing to one side of the window and blanched.

He'd stammered something about leaving his computer downstairs and needing to go and get it.

'*Wait*,' she'd said. 'I didn't *mean*— I don't mean to offend.' She'd looked pleadingly at him. 'I thought—'

She'd thought he might like to take their friendship further.

'Jasmine.' Nick's voice had cut across hers, low and urgent. 'God help me if I've given you the wrong impression, I never meant to, but if it's romance that you want from me… I'm sorry, but I can't.'

Humiliation had coursed through her, fierce and all consuming.

'You're a lovely girl,' he'd continued. You are. And I'm honoured. And flattered. *Very* flattered. Really.'

He hadn't looked flattered. He'd looked completely aghast and Jasmine had felt the hot prick of tears behind her eyes. 'Is there something lacking in me?' she'd found the courage to ask and he'd shaken his head and gone two shades paler.

'No,' he'd said. 'No. Don't go there; it's not you. Don't ever think that. I just—can't. Jasmine, I'm *married*.'

Jasmine had fled his room after that and Nick

had left the following day on urgent business, with enough speed to make her father frown and wonder about the merits of doing business with flighty Englishmen. Kai had just looked at her, one eyebrow raised, and Jasmine had blushed hard and looked away.

Kai didn't know what she'd done. He merely suspected that she'd done *something*.

'Jasmine?' Kai's voice came to her, soft, as always, and threaded through with steel. As always. 'Something bothering you?'

'No. Nothing,' she said and followed through with a restrained nod and a half-smile. Too much reaction and Kai would know there was something wrong. He knew her reactions, all of them.

And she knew his.

'Your father would like you to entertain Mrs Cooper while she's here.'

'Of course,' she said. It wasn't the first time her father had called on her to help entertain his guests. 'You have the dates?'

Kai gave them to her and she nodded again and turned back to the stir fry she was preparing. 'Would you like some?' she asked, knowing that once upon a time Kai would have helped her with the cooking and thought nothing of sitting down to a meal with her in her father's kitchen. Not so these days, and with Kai's retreat came a loneliness that went bone- deep.

'No, I'm going out.'

'Oh.' Oh, of course. 'It's Valentine's Day.' Of course he would be going out. All the beautiful people went parading on Valentine's Day. Just because Kai had never brought a woman back to his apartment over the garage…just because he'd never introduced Jasmine to anyone… that didn't mean he didn't have a special friend. 'I hope you brought her a big bunch of flowers.'

'What?' Kai looked momentarily puzzled.

'Flowers. For your date. For Valentine's Day. I hear it's best to give them in public, and then you walk somewhere with her, while she's holding them in her arms so that everyone can see how highly regarded she is. And you need a really big bunch.' Kai was looking at her strangely. 'What?'

'How do you *know* all this?'

The question stung, mainly because of all the things he didn't say. *You've only ever been on one date, and that was arranged by your father and the boy in question never asked for another,* he could have said. *And you've certainly never been given a gift on Valentine's Day.* He could have said that too. Instead, he'd gone with 'How do you know all this?' and shamed her anyway.

'I see what people do,' she offered tightly. 'I know what's expected. Just because—

Just because she'd never had a proper boyfriend and barely knew kisses…

'Just go,' she said.

But Kai had never been one to take orders – at least, not from her. He stood there watching her; so many secrets behind those beautiful black eyes. Kai had been her bodyguard for eight years now, ever since she was eleven, and there'd never *not* been secrets in those eyes.

Nicholas Cooper's laughing blue eyes had been refreshingly devoid of secrets.

Well…except for the fact that he had a *wife*.

'It's not a Valentine's Day date,' Kai offered finally. 'I don't have a Valentine. I'm not buying flowers. I'm going to watch a martial arts demonstration. Wing Chun style versus Aikido.'

'Oh.' The bean shoots were burning. Jasmine turned down the heat and gave the food another stir. 'May I accompany you?'

'It'll be hot and crowded.'

This was Hong Kong. It often was. 'I don't mind. I wouldn't treat it like a Valentine's Day outing, or anything. I mean—that's not how I think of you. At all.'

Much.

Kai just looked at her and then with a flicker of something in his beautiful black eyes, he looked away.

'No, Jasmine,' he told her quietly. 'The answer's no.'

Hallie's bedside phone was ringing. She rolled across the bed, arm outstretched, groping wildly. Because no way on earth were her eyes going to open at this hour. She'd spent most of last night watching bad action adventure movies with Tris. She'd planned on a ten a.m. wake-up time, minimum. It wasn't ten a.m. It was still dark, not even dawn. She found the phone, found her ear. ''Lo,' she mumbled.

'Can you get some time off work this afternoon?'

'Nick?'

'Yes, Nick.' He sounded impatient.

'Couldn't this have waited till morning?' she mumbled.

'It is morning. Were you still in bed?'

Hallie slitted her eyes open to glance at the glowing red numbers of her bedside clock. Five-fifty! A.m! Ugh, he was a morning person. The notion was going to take some time to digest. She held the receiver to her breast and took several deep breaths before putting it back to her ear. 'Nick, it's the weekend. I have one day off a week and this is it and there'd better be a good reason for this call. What do you want?'

'To let you know we have an appointment at Tiffany's at two this afternoon to get your rings.'

'Rings?' Hallie's eyes snapped open. 'Tiffany's? As in Tiffany and Co. the jewellers?' She was wide awake.

'Wedding ring, engagement ring. It'll be expected. The manager of the store on Old Bond Street's a friend of mine; he's going to let me borrow some pieces,' said Nick. 'After that we'll go shopping. You'll need suitable clothes as well.'

Shopping for clothes? This coming from the lips of a man? 'You're gay, aren't you?'

'No,' he said, with a smile in his voice that curled her toes.

'Cross dresser?'

'Nope.'

'Have you been drinking?'

'Nor am I drunk.' Exasperation in his voice this time, giving her toes a chance to relax. 'The way we present ourselves in Hong Kong is going to be important and I'm guessing there's nothing in your wardrobe that's suitable.'

'Suitable how?' she snapped as visions of

tailored suits and pillbox hats floated through her mind. 'You're going to dress me up like Jackie Kennedy, aren't you? You're having make-over fantasies!'

'I wasn't until now.' The smile was back in his voice; yep, there went her toes. 'And I'm not thinking First Lady exactly but we can't have you looking like Marilyn Monroe either.'

She should have been insulted. Would have been except that this was a sex goddess he was comparing her to. 'Who's paying for these clothes?'

'I am. Consider it a perk.'

'I love this job,' said Hallie. 'I'm in. Two o'clock sharp at the jewellers. Oh, and Nick?'

'What?'

He sounded complacent. Indulgent. As if she'd reacted exactly as any good little plaything would. 'Bring your mother.'

'How'd the big date go last night?' asked Tris when finally she made it to the kitchen for breakfast. He was standing by the counter waiting for toast to pop. Hallie was all about getting to the coffee pot. 'I didn't hear you come in.'

'That's because you were totally out of it. I checked on you when I came in.'

Tris poured her a coffee without further comment. Hallie added milk, blew gently on it for good measure and finally took a sip.

'He's a nice guy,' she said. 'Funny. Good company…'

'Name?'

Hallie reached for the Hong Kong travel guide sitting on the counter, flipped to the back of the book and retrieved Nicholas Cooper's business card. She held it up, rolling her eyes as Tris not-so-deftly plucked it from her outstretched fingers. 'How's the shoulder?'

'Bruised.' Tristan studied the card. 'Seriously?' His tawny, golden gaze pinned her once more, bright with amusement. 'You're dating a computer geek?'

'Well, it beats dating a cop. Imagine if I brought home someone like you?'

'No cops,' growled Tris.

'Amen.'

'Brat.'

'Boor.' She took in the scrape high on his face and the discoloured skin that ran from shoulder to neckline. 'You still look like hell.'

'Perks of the job. Speaking of, I'm going to be in Prague most of next week. Maybe longer.'

As far as Tris destinations went, Prague was a new one. 'What's in Prague?'

'Vice.'

'Tris, this job you do—'

I wish you'd walk away from it, she wanted to say. I don't like the distance you put between yourself and other people these days and I can't bear to see the bleakness in your eyes when you think no one else is looking.

But the Bennett family never said things like that and Hallie was nothing if not one of them.

'Be careful, won't you?' she said, and took comfort from his smile.

Hallie arrived at the jewellers at exactly two o clock, only to find Nick and Clea waiting for her outside, Clea looking thoughtful, Nick looking just plain smug.

'We got here a little early so we've already been in,' said Nick. 'Henry's given me some pieces on loan. I'm sure you'll like them.'

'What do you mean you're sure I'll like them? You mean I don't even get to go into the shop and ogle the pieces for myself?' Hallie stared at him, aghast. Surely he was kidding. 'Don't you need to measure my ring size or something? I mean, what if they don't fit?'

'Here, dear, try this on.' Clea handed her one of her own rings, a wide band of square- cut diamonds set in platinum. 'We used this one for size. I usually have a good eye for these things.'

Hallie slipped the band on her wedding ring finger and stared at it in dismay. It was a perfect fit.

'Does it fit?' asked Nick, all solicitousness. 'It looks like it fits.'

'It does. But we're still going inside. I for one will be far more amenable once I get to see all the pretties, even if I *don't* get to choose anything.' Hallie placed a dramatic hand over her heart. 'Nick, I'm your future pretend wife. You need to humour me.'

'This really isn't going to plan,' said Nick as Hallie handed Clea's ring back to her and headed towards the plate glass doors of one of London's landmark jewellery stores. 'Why isn't this going to plan?'

'I have no idea,' offered Clea dulcetly as she too headed back inside. 'Coming?'

Henry, Nick's Friday night poker buddy and current sales director of the jeweller's UK branches, smirked when Nick stepped back inside. He'd said nothing when Nick had chosen the pieces earlier with Clea's help, but he'd smirked when Nick had said that Hallie was meeting them here. Henry caught Nick's gaze, highly amused about *something*, and then Henry adjusted his tie, turned and bestowed a charming smile on Hallie and on Clea. 'Let me guess,' he said smoothly. 'You'd like to see the pieces again?'

'Just the rings,' said Nick quickly, otherwise they'd never get out of here.

'And maybe a tiara,' said Hallie.

'And the animal brooches,' added Clea.

'Good call,' said Hallie.

'Certainly, ladies. This way, please.' Henry's amusement was definitely not part of the regular Tiffany's jewellery buying experience. Henry needed a refresher course. 'Nicholas, my friend. Is there anything else I may show you?'

'The door in half an hour would be excellent.'

'I live to serve,' said Henry. 'And I do love a challenge. Shall we take it over to the chairs?'

'No need—'

'Henry, you angel,' said Hallie. 'I need a seat, a tiara and possibly a beverage. Give me the whole Tiffany's excellent service experience. I'm currently in retail. I'm taking notes.'

'I'm up to the part where I'm making you feel special,' said Henry as he gestured towards a cluster of seats and a table set in a perfectly lit alcove. 'Are you feeling the opulence all around you yet?'

'And beneath my feet,' said Hallie as she sashayed forward. 'I'm loving the lighting.'

'So am I,' said Clea. 'My wrinkles are gone.'

Clea and Hallie moved forward. Henry held Nick back.

'I thought you said you *didn't* need a distraction in Hong Kong,' Henry murmured. 'I thought you wanted to focus on the deal.'

'All true,' said Nick. 'Hallie can entertain Jasmine. John and I can get on with business. Why are you looking at me like that?'

'Oh, my friend. I knew fantasy was your speciality. I didn't realise you'd added delusion to your play deck. Nick, *look* at her. That is not a woman you are going to be able to ignore. She is *exactly* your type. She's going to wrap you around her little finger. *You*, my friend, are going to come back from Hong Kong completely smitten, and then you're going to come in and buy every last piece you've just borrowed and I am going to dine out on your commission for months.'

'Want to bet?'

'Don't bet,' cautioned Henry. 'You need to save your money to pay for the tiara.'

'I'm pretty sure the tiara request is a joke. Hallie doesn't want a tiara.'

Henry's smile was full of pity. 'Yet.'

Henry went into organising mode after that, calling two more staff members over and sending them off to fetch the requested jewels.

Ten minutes later the tiaras had been perused and discarded, a dazzling sapphire peacock brooch was still on the table, and the brilliant-cut solitaire diamond engagement ring Nick had picked out earlier was shining away on Hallie's wedding-ring finger as she tilted it this way and that.

'I mean it's beautiful,' said Hallie. 'And it's huge. But I'm not sure it's me.'

'Think of it as a prop,' he offered. 'A reminder that you're pretending to be someone else.'

'Look at this one,' said Clea, holding up a Celtic-inspired swirl of platinum, studded with rubies.

'Nick, look!' said Hallie, her eyes bright with laughter. 'It looks like something Xia from New Mars would wear. Surely the wife of a world-class computer game designer could have *this* engagement ring instead of the boring one?'

'The boring one signals your status more clearly,' he countered. 'That one could be a dress ring.'

'Or a belated Valentine's gift,' offered Henry.

'Not helping, Henry,' muttered Nick.

Hallie slipped Xia's ring on her finger and Nick watched her fall in love.

'Tell her it's not as expensive,' said Henry.

'It's not as expensive.'

'Who cares?' said Hallie, holding her hands up and looking from one ring to the other. 'You're not buying. I'm not keeping. Clea, which do you prefer?'

'The diamond solitaire *is* the more traditional option.'

'Is John Tey an observer of tradition?' asked Hallie and Nick nodded.

'Damn.' Hallie sighed and slipped Xia's ring from her finger and set it back on the table. 'Goodbye, baby. It was fun while it lasted.'

'That's the spirit,' said Nick. 'Keep practising those words.'

Clea's laughter bubbled through the air. Hallie smiled guilelessly and Nick wondered – not for the first time – about the sanity of continuing on this particular path with the not-so-angelic Hallie Bennett in tow.

It still wasn't too late to back out.

Henry glanced at Nick and narrowly avoided snorting.

'Your sales manner is atrocious,' Nick told his old schoolfriend.

'Fortunately, my bullshit detector is as well honed as ever,' said Henry. 'I can set the Valentine ring aside for you for a couple of weeks. You can think about it.'

'I don't need the "let me set it aside for you" offer,' said Nick. 'I feel special enough.'

'Old friend,' drawled Henry. 'Let me do it for you anyway.'

'Did you get the week off work?' Nick asked her as they exited Tiffany's a short time later.

'Yes. The owner's niece is going to fill in for me,' said Hallie, recalling the conversation she'd had with her employer earlier that morning. No need to tell Nick that if the niece liked the job, Hallie was out of one. If everything went to plan she wouldn't need the job anyway.

'What about your brother? The one you're staying with. Does he know you're going to Hong Kong?'

'Not yet. It turns out he's also going to be away next week.' And wasn't that a fine piece of timing. 'I'll leave him a note.'

'That'll go down well,' muttered Nick.

'Trust me. It's as good a plan as any.' Hallie smiled brightly. She really didn't want to dwell on what Tris would have to say about this. 'So where to now?'

Ten minutes later they were standing outside

one of the most exclusive clothing boutiques in Knightsbridge. 'Are we sure about this?' asked Hallie hesitantly. Buying an outfit or two from a mid-range clothing store was one thing, dropping a bundle on a week's worth of designer clothes was quite another. 'I'm all for being well dressed but do we really need to shop somewhere quite this exclusive?'

'Don't worry, dear,' said Clea. 'I get a very good discount here.'

'You want to hope so,' Hallie muttered to Nick as she stared at the sophisticated power suit in the display window. 'I think it only fair to warn you that I still have nightmares about the first time my oldest brother took me shopping for clothes. Pinafore dresses that came to my ankles. Sweaters up to my chin. Wide brimmed straw hats…'

'And very sensible too dear, those hats, what with the harsh Australian sun and your skin type,' said Clea.

Hallie groaned. And here she'd been hoping that Clea would be an ally when it came to clothes. 'My point is I battled for years for the right to choose my own clothes and I'm not about to relinquish it now.' She pointed a stern finger at Nick. 'You can tell me what kind of look you're after but I won't have you choosing clothes *for* me. Are we clear on that?'

'Well, I—'

'Having said that, I will of course ask your opinion on the things I've chosen. I'm not an unreasonable woman. You can tell me if you like something.'

'And if I don't?'

Hallie considered the question. She could be a bit contrary at times. 'Probably best not to say anything,' she said and, squaring her shoulders, sailed on into the shop.

The boutique was streamlined and classy, the coiffed and polished saleswoman just that little bit daunting, never mind that she greeted Clea with friendly familiarity.

'Size eight, I think,' said the saleswoman after turning an assessing eye on Hallie.

'Ten,' said Hallie.

'In this shop, darling, you're an eight.'

Hallie liked the woman better already.

'Do you have any colour preferences?' the woman asked.

'I like them all.'

The saleswoman barely suppressed a shudder. 'Yes, dear. But do they all like *you*? Let's start with grey.'

Hallie opened her mouth to protest but the woman was having none of it. She pulled a matching skirt and jacket from the rack and held them out commandingly. 'Of course, it relies on the wearer for colour and life but I think you've got that covered.'

'Umm…' Hallie took the suit from the woman and held it up for Nick's inspection. 'What do you think?'

'I'm confused,' he said. 'If I tell you I like it you may or may not decide to buy it, depending on whether *you* like it. However, if I say I don't like it you'll feel compelled to buy it whether you like it or not. Am I right?'

'Yes.' Hallie felt a smile coming on. 'So what do you think?'

'Try it on.'

And then when she did and his eyes narrowed and his face grew carefully impassive. 'No?' she asked. 'It's probably not the look you were after.'

'Yes,' he said firmly. 'It is.'

Still she hesitated. 'It's very—'

'Elegant,' he said. 'Understated. Just what we're looking for.'

Elegant, eh? Not a term she'd normally use to describe herself. She'd won the right to choose her own clothes in her late teens and in typical teen-

ager fashion she'd headed straight for the short-
est skirts and the brightest, tightest tops. Okay, so
she'd matured a little since then—she did have
some loose-fitting clothes somewhere in her wardrobe but truth was they didn't often see daylight.
She had never, *ever*, worn anything as classy as
this. The suit clung to her every curve, the material
was soft and luxurious beneath her hands, like
cashmere only not. Even the colour wasn't so bad
once you got used to it. And yet…

'It's not really me though, is it?' she said.

'Think of it as a costume,' said Nick. 'Think corporate wife.'

'I don't know any corporate wives.' Hallie
turned to Clea, who was busily browsing a rack of
clothes. 'Unless you're one?'

'No!' said Nick hastily. 'She's not!'

'It's very grey, isn't it, dear,' said Clea, who
glittered like a Vegas slot machine in her gold trousers and blood-red chiffon shirt with its strategi-
cally placed psychedelic gold swirls.

'Greyer than a Chinese funeral vase,' agreed
Hallie glumly. 'Do you have anything a bit more
cheerful?' she asked the saleswoman.

'What about this?' said Clea, holding up a
boldly flowered silk sundress in fuchsia, lime and
ivory. 'This is pretty.'

'Why *my* mother?' muttered Nick. 'Why couldn't we have brought along *your* mother?'

'She died when I was six,' said Hallie, and waited for the silence that always came. She didn't mind talking about it, honest. She barely remembered her mother but the memories she did have were good ones.

'Sorry,' said Nick quietly. 'You said you'd been raised by your father and brothers but I didn't make the connection. Try it on.'

And when she did…

'She'll take it,' he told the saleswoman, and Clea nodded her agreement. 'That's non- negotiable,' he said to Hallie.

So much for the rules of shopping. The dashing Nicholas Cooper had a bossy streak she was more than familiar with. 'Lucky for you I happen to agree.'

'His father had excellent taste in clothes as well,' said Clea. 'Bless his soul.'

But Hallie wasn't listening. She was looking at herself in the mirror and her reflection was frowning right back at her as she turned and twirled, first one way and then the other. Finally, hands on hips, she turned to Nick.

'Does this dress make me look fat?'

***

Two hours later, Hallie and Clea had purchased enough clothes for a six-month stint on the QEII and as far as Nick was concerned he was neither the boring geek Hallie had accused him of being when he made her get the dove-grey suit, nor the skinflint his mother claimed. No, for a man to endure so much and complain so little, he was quite simply a saint.

'So where to now? Are we done?' said Hallie after they'd seen Clea to her Mercedes and watched her drive away. 'Is there anything *you* need?'

'A bar,' he muttered with heartfelt sincerity.

'Good call,' said Hallie. 'I'll come too. I never realised boutique shopping was such thirsty work. Mind you, I've never bought more than a couple of items of clothes at any one time before either. Who knew?'

'You're not going to rehash every dress decision you just made, are you?'

'Who, me?' She was grinning from ear to ear. 'Only if you insist.'

Nick shuddered, spotted a sports bar a few doors up and practically bolted for the door. He needed a drink, somewhere to sit. Somewhere with dark wood, dark carpet, dim lighting, good Scotch and no mirrors. He needed it bad.

'Ah,' said Hallie as she slid into the booth beside him. 'Very nice.'

'You don't find it a little too…masculine?'

'Nope. Feels pretty homely to me. I have four brothers, remember?'

'Trust me, I hadn't forgotten. Where do they live?'

'Wherever their work takes them. Luke's a Navy diver midway through a three-year stint in Guam, Pete's flying charter planes in Greece, Jake runs a Martial Arts Dojo in Singapore, and Tristan lives here in London. He's the one I'm staying with while I do my course.'

'Tristan?' After Pete, Luke and Jake, a brother named Tristan sounded somewhat incongruous. 'What does Tristan do?'

'He works for Interpol.'

'Paper pusher?'

'Black ops,' she corrected. 'Somewhere along the line Tris was seconded by some special law enforcement group. I forget the name.' Not quite the truth. Truth was, Hallie had never been told who Tristan worked for these days. She tried not to let that bother her. 'But he's a pussycat really.'

Sure he was. All black ops specialists were pussycats. It was such a caring, non-confrontational profession. 'You know, maybe I need a different type of wife for Hong Kong,' he said. 'Maybe I need a brunette.'

'I was a brunette once,' said Hallie. 'The hairdresser was a young guy, just starting out and we decided to experiment. He left the salon not long after that.' She sighed heavily. 'I'm sure Tris wouldn't really have castrated him.'

Maybe he was doomed. 'Or a blonde,' he muttered. 'I could always replace you with a blonde.'

'Ha. You can't fool me. You're not going to replace me now; you'd have to go clothes shopping again.'

Nick shuddered. She was right. Replacing her was out of the question.

'Besides,' she continued blithely, 'It's not as if I'm going to be telling any of my brothers the finer details of our little arrangement. They wouldn't understand.'

On this they were in total accord.

'So tell me about *your* family,' she said, deftly changing the focus back to him and his. 'When did your father die?'

'Two years ago. He was a property developer.'

'And Clea? You said she wasn't a corporate wife. What does she do?'

'Many people find it hard to believe but she's an architect. A very good one.'

'Is that how they met? Through their work?'

'No, they met at a birthday party. Clea was in the cake. I try not to think about it.'

'What about brothers and sisters?'

'There's just me.'

'Didn't you ever get lonely?' she asked.

'Nope.' She looked like she was struggling with the only child concept. ' I had plenty of friends, plenty of company. And whenever I had any spare time there was always a computer handy and a dozen imaginary worlds to get lost in.'

'And now you create fantasy worlds for a living. I guess that means you always knew what you wanted to do, even as a kid.'

'I always did it. Is that the same thing?'

'Probably.' Hallie's smile was wry. 'With me it was different… every week a new idea… astronaut, race car driver, professional stuntwoman… My family's still not convinced I won't change my mind about wanting to work in the art business.'

'And will you?'

'Who knows?' she said with a shrug. 'I love the thrill that comes with finding something old and beautiful and I love discovering its history and the history of the people behind it. Hopefully I'll find work with a respectable dealer in Asian antiquities and it'll be fascinating but if it's not…well…I'll do something else. At least I'll have given it a try.'

'You want to make your own mistakes.'

'That's it!' There was fire in her eyes, passion in her voice. 'Do you have any idea how hard it is to make your own decisions with four older brothers all hell-bent on guiding you through life? I mean, honestly, Nick, I'm twenty-four years old and I'm not a slow learner. So what if I make a mistake or two along the way? I'll fix them. I certainly don't need my brothers charging in to straighten me out every time I step sideways.' Hallie's chin came up; he was beginning to know that look. 'I can take care of myself. I *want* to take care of myself. Is that too much to ask?'

'Not at all. What you want is freedom.'

'And equality,' she said firmly. 'And it wouldn't kill them to show me a bit of respect every now and then too.'

Right. Nick quelled the slight twinge of sympathy he was beginning to feel for her brothers and concentrated on the bigger picture. Freedom, equality, respect. He could manage that. It wasn't as if she was asking for the sun, the moon and the stars to go with it.

'I want you to know that even though I'm paying you a great deal of money to deceive my future business partner you have my utmost respect,' he stated firmly. 'We're in this together as equals.'

And to the drinks waiter who had appeared at his side, 'Two single-malt Scotches. Neat.'

CHAPTER FOUR

PREPARING THE HOUSE FOR the arrival of Nicholas Cooper and his wife wasn't a difficult task. Jasmine often acted as hostess for her father. Anything from arranging dinner parties to organising tickets and dealing with invitations. Personal assistant, Kai had called her more than once, but it was only to humour her. Jasmine contributed so very little to the running of this household, what with the housekeeper who came in three times a week, and the gardener who worked every morning and Kai who saw to the cars and the dozens of other things her father requested of him.

Bodyguard, her father still called him, only Kai had never been just that.

She really didn't know what he was.

Eleven years old, she'd been, when her father had brought Kai home one night shortly after her mother's death. It had been Jasmine's bedtime and she'd been worried because her father wasn't home yet. She'd worried about everything in those days.

Her father had called her into his home office and she'd stopped in the doorway, not dressed for visitors but unable to look away from the young man standing so straight and still beside her father. In profile, he'd been the most beautiful boy she'd ever seen, and that included on the television. And then he'd turned to look at her and his face had been so pale and he'd looked so incredibly lost. As lost as she felt.

'Meng Kai's going to be living here with us,' her father had said, and Kai's lips had twisted into a bitter smile, even as he offered her a small bow. Jasmine bowed back, lower, because Meng Kai was older, maybe eighteen, and Jasmine knew her manners.

She'd looked up at him again, wanting to ask why he was staying with them and for how long, and maybe she *would* ask her father those things when they were alone, but not now. Her father wouldn't like it if she asked those questions now.

'He'll be staying here indefinitely,' her father said quietly, as if reading her mind, and the utter silence that had followed had been clouded with an emotion that to this day Jasmine couldn't quite define. Maybe it had been despair.

'Did they take Meng Kai's mother too?' she'd asked, and her hushed voice had rippled across that silence and made the boy flinch.

'Something like that,' her father had offered gruffly – her father didn't like to talk about what had happened to her mother, Jasmine knew that, but household staff gossiped and Jasmine had big ears and silent feet and she knew full well what had happened to her mother. She knew what loss felt like. And so too – it seemed – did this Kai, who still hadn't spoken and whose eyes skittered away from hers every time she looked at him.

'It's okay,' she said and stepped hesitantly forward, first one step and then another until she reached his side. She slipped her hand inside Kai's and frowned when Kai tensed and sent her father a panicked look. Her father looked tense too, but he said nothing, so Jasmine filled the gap. 'They can't get us here. We just have to stay away from the windows and not go outside without permission and do exactly what the guards say. You're safe here. No monsters can get at us here.'

Kai had looked down at her and there'd been a world of pain in his beautiful black eyes as he'd replied, 'I know.'

'Kai's a bodyguard,' her father had said finally. 'He'll see to your protection.'

There had been bodyguards on the grounds and in the house for weeks – at least half a dozen of them at any one time. Jasmine didn't know why they would need any more, or why her father would choose a bodyguard so young.

She did know – instinctively – that Meng Kai was special. 'Are you like Bruce Lee?'

'No one's like Bruce Lee,' Meng Kai said.

'Jackie Chan?'

'No.'

Jasmine eyed him speculatively. 'Maybe if you smiled.'

But Kai hadn't smiled. Not during those first few months. Not for a very long time, and then only rarely.

Meng Kai had moved into the apartment above the garage, he'd had free rein of the house. It hadn't been long before the housekeeper and the gardener and Jasmine's tutors all answered to him. Jasmine had answered to him too – such a timid little thing she'd once been. No thought of disobedience – if Kai or her father told her to do something, Jasmine did it. So eager to please. So damn lonely, only Kai hadn't wanted to be friends with her. Not at first.

And then the levee had given way and all of a sudden Kai had unbent – though only with her – and Jasmine had taken full advantage of his change of heart. Kai become her confidante, her sounding board, the big brother she'd never had. Kai was comfort, he was protection, and most of all he was *hers*.

To all intents they'd been family, Jasmine thought grimly, returning to the now just long enough to place new toiletries in the guest bathroom. Father, older brother, younger sister.

And then Jasmine had turned sixteen and Kai twenty-four, and Kai had fought hard for Jasmine to have more freedom, more friends. 'She's too sheltered,' Kai had said bluntly, during one of his rare arguments with her father. 'You have to give her room to grow. You *can't* make her world this small.'

'She has everything money can buy,' her father had countered.

'She needs *freedom*. We both do. She can't continue to look to me for all those things you don't allow her to experience any other way. Send her to school. Let her make friends. Widen her focus.'

Part of her had applauded Kai's words. Part of her had been fearful. To this day, Jasmine didn't know which emotion would have won out, because her father had been immovable.

Jasmine's home-schooling would continue as usual. Her strictly regulated social outings would continue, as usual.

And no matter what Kai had said about needing *his* freedom, Kai had stayed too.

On the morning of Jasmine's seventeenth birthday, Kai had taken her to the flower market. She'd thought of the trip as a birthday outing, at first. Thought that Kai had wanted to please her, and he *had* pleased her. He'd bought her street-stall food and given her one of his rare, unguarded smiles when she'd purchased a fake jade turtle on a leather band and slipped it over her head.

She'd been truly happy in that moment; and Kai had reached out to untwist the little turtle and his knuckles had brushed her skin and his eyes had met hers and then he'd withdrawn his hand slowly, almost casually, and put his hand to the back of his head as he'd turned away.

Such a fleeting touch shouldn't have had the power to throw Jasmine's world into chaos. Kai had always been beautiful to her. He'd always been her hero.

But just for that moment in time she hadn't thought of him as a brother.

She'd bought flowers for the household after that and had them delivered, and she'd tried not to dwell on Kai's touch and the awkwardness that followed. Such an innocent, everyday touch. Kai had meant *nothing* by it. Nothing at all.

Kai hadn't wanted to go to the nearby bird market but Jasmine had persisted and finally got her way. Walk it off, she told herself. Focus on something else, something other than Kai. She'd heard that sentiment just days earlier, when Kai had confronted her father, and all of a sudden she saw a *reason* behind Kai's impassioned words on her behalf.

A reason she barely knew how to acknowledge.

Morning had flowed around them, warm and bright as they'd made their way on foot to the bird market. Early morning, full of bright-eyed songbirds in their tiny bamboo morning cages. Plain little things, some of them, until she closed her eyes and listened, and then the beauty of the sound had taken her breath away.

So many birds, so many cages; all sorts of birds and everything one could possibly think to feed them. Expensive, the best of these birds. Doting owners who lavished their attention upon them. It had been such a welcome distraction from the memory of Kai's touch. Something else to think about besides the smooth weight of the little plastic turtle against her skin. Jasmine had loved strolling through the bird market.

Kai, upon reflection, had not.

'What do you see?' he'd asked as they reached the end of one crooked alley way and turned to step into the next. 'Why do you like it?'

'I like it because there's life here, and celebration, and beauty and sound and old men whose smiles fill their faces when their favourite songbird sings. There's colour here, and frenzy. A social structure built around these alleyways. Why wouldn't I like it?'

'Have you ever wondered,' he said, and his voice was low and rough and he would not look at her, 'what they'd sound like if they were free?'

Three days after the marathon shopping trip, Hallie boarded a plane to Hong Kong. She'd been manicured, pedicured, pampered and polished and was corporate-wife chic in her lightweight camel-coloured trousers and pink camisole. Her shoes matched her top, her handbag was Hermès, and Nick was at her side, thoroughly eye-catching in a grey business suit and crisp white business shirt minus the tie. She was the woman who had it all and it was all pure fantasy.

That didn't mean she couldn't embrace the moment.

Wispy streaks of cloud scattered the midday sky, their seats were business class, the take-off was perfect, and Hallie relaxed into her seat, prepared to be thoroughly indulged, only to discover that any woman sitting next to Nick was more likely to be thoroughly ignored. That or she was currently invisible to the women of the world as they dimpled, sighed, primped and preened for him.

The flight attendants settled once the flight was underway and went about their business with efficient professionalism, but the encouraging smiles of the female passengers continued. One innovative young lady even managed to trip and fall gracefully into Nick's lap amidst a flurry of breathless apology and a great deal of full body contact.

'Do women always fall over their feet trying to get your attention?' she asked once the woman had gone.

'Actually, she fell over *my* feet,' said Nick. 'They were sticking out into the aisle. It was *my* fault she landed in my lap.'

'And her breasts in your face? That was your fault too?'

Nick shrugged, trying to look a picture of innocence and failing miserably. 'She was trying to get up,' he said in her defence. 'These things happen.'

'So I see.'

He was used to it, Hallie decided. He was just plain used to women falling all over him. 'You know, you'd save yourself a lot of unwanted attention if you wore a wedding ring,' she said. She was wearing one, along with the terribly traditional diamond engagement ring. As far as the world was concerned she was well and truly taken. Nick's hands, however, were ring-free.

'I wasn't wearing one last time I visited,' he countered. 'It'd seem a bit strange if I turned up wearing one now.'

'No it wouldn't, considering what happened.' She was beginning to sense some reluctance here. 'Say we really were married, would you wear a ring then?'

'You'd have to insist.' He slid her a sideways glance. 'You would too, wouldn't you?'

'Absolutely.' She held her left hand up between them, angling her fingers so that the diamond sparkled in the light. 'Some people actually respect the sanctity of marriage and *don't* hit on a person wearing a wedding ring.'

'Funny,' he said dryly. 'You don't look that naïve'

'Hah. It just so happens I don't think I'm *being* naïve. But I do concede that if you never wear one we'll never know.'

The clumsy young thing was back, all purring solicitousness as she asked Nick if she'd hurt him, if he was feeling all right, and was there anything, absolutely *anything*, she could do for him.

Honestly!

'Oh, I think we've got it covered.' Hallie smiled, sharp as a blade, as her hand- the one with those shiny rings on it – came to rest high on Nick's trouser clad thigh. Nothing subtle about that particular manoeuvre; she was claiming ownership and the other woman knew it. 'On second thoughts, darling, you feel a bit cold,' she said to Nick as she squeezed gently and slid her hand a fraction higher up his thigh. Muscles jumped beneath her palm even as the rest of him went absolutely still. 'Would you like a blanket for your lap? There's one in the webbing in front of you.'

With an annoyed pout and a narrow-eyed glare for Hallie, the other woman made herself scarce. Not that Nick noticed. His *wife* had his attention now. His complete and utter attention.

'What are you doing?' he rasped.

'Practising.'

'For what? The mile-high club?'

Hallie's smile widened. Really, his imagination was so delightfully easy to manipulate. 'I'm practising my possessive moves for when I meet Jasmine.'

'Well, would you mind practising with your hand somewhere else? I'm not made of stone.'

This was debatable. Right this minute, Nicholas Cooper's thigh was hard as a rock. 'Sorry, my mistake. I thought we agreed on physical contact in public places,' she said as she withdrew her hand, reached for the blanket and draped it across his knees. She shouldn't bait him; she knew it. But she couldn't resist. 'This is a public place,' she said sweetly. 'And we did have an audience.'

'You know you're right. You're absolutely right,' he said. He flicked off the overhead light, brought her hand back to his thigh and drew the blanket over his lap with a smile that was pure challenge. 'Feel free to continue.'

Okay, so there was a slight chance she'd been asking for it. Now *he* was asking for it and she was tempted, very tempted, to deliver. But if she did, things would get out of hand. Or out of trousers and into hand, so to speak, and heaven only knew what would happen after that. Come to think of it, she had a pretty good idea what would happen after that…

And what if they were caught?

They'd be thrown off the plane in disgrace. A big red 'deviant' stamp would appear in her passport and then Interpol would sign her up for sexual misconduct reform school and Tris would find out and, oh, the horror…

Nick wasn't the only one with a vivid imagination.

Feigning nonchalance, Hallie withdrew her hand from his thigh and reached for her glass of water. She was flustered; she was aroused; she was totally out of her league.

She was enjoying every minute of it. 'Actually, I've changed my mind,' she said.

'Good call.' He exhaled deeply.

'After all, it wouldn't do to forget that this is strictly a business arrangement.'

'Exactly.'

Exactly. The sinking feeling in the pit of her stomach was *not* disappointment. Nick was her employer, nothing more, and only for one week. After that it was contract fulfilled and goodbye. Surely she could resist his considerable charms for one lousy week.

All she needed was a more professional approach.

'So how do you want to approach this business

of being married?' she said crisply. 'Are we aiming for warm and fuzzy or a fiery attraction of opposites?'

'Think of yourself as a cross between a personal assistant and a German Shepherd,' he said. 'Supportive, loyal, and when necessary, extremely protective.'

A German Shepherd? Ugh. This new approach worked fast. 'Anything else?'

'Are you sure you couldn't manage a simper?'

'Positive.'

Nick sighed. 'Just be yourself then. That'll work too.'

'Oh.' And after a moment's reflection, 'That was a nice thing to say.'

'You realize that was almost a simper?'

'It was not.'

Nick's answering smile was suspiciously gleeful as he flicked on his overhead light, reached for the in-flight paper and snapped it open, effectively ending the discussion.

Hallie glared at the back page of the paper. It was shaking ever so slightly. He was laughing at her, dammit. 'That was *not* a simper.'

'If you say so, dearest.'

A fiery marriage, she decided. A constant battle of words and of wits and it was a damn good thing this marriage was only going to last a week.

Any longer and she'd probably kill him.

Twelve hours and several time zones later, they touched down at Chek Lap Kok International Airport, collected their luggage, and met up with the Teys' driver, who went by the name of Kai. They followed the silent Jet Li lookalike through the streamlined arrivals terminal, out through the huge automatic opening glass doors, and they were in Hong Kong.

'Phew.' Wide-eyed at the sleek steel-and-glass building they'd just emerged from, Hallie paused to gather her composure. 'It's cooler than I thought it would be.'

'It's winter,' countered Nick. 'If you want hot and humid, we'll have to come back in September.'

'Ah.'

They followed the Teys' driver towards an illegally parked Mercedes and Hallie began to watch their guide with increasing interest. Maybe it was the easy, graceful way he moved or the way he seemed to know what was happening around them without ever seeming to notice. Maybe it was the way he loaded their suitcases into the trunk as if they were empty, which was definitely not the case. Maybe it was simply that he was gorgeous, with a quiet intensity about him that drew the eye, but…no. That wasn't it either. He reminded her of someone.

He reminded her of Tris.

'*This* is the Teys' driver?' she whispered to Nick 'I'm guessing that's not all he is.'

'No,' agreed Kai in a soft, cultured voice as he shut the trunk and opened the car door for her. 'I also cook.'

'Nice.' Hallie smiled at the man. 'But you can't fool me. You're security.' High-end protection with supernatural hearing and a penchant for kitchen knives. Lucky for Nick she'd had years of experience when it came to outwitting suspicious, eagle-eyed men whose mission in life was to serve and protect. At least this one wasn't related to her. 'Pleased to meet you.'

'And you, Mrs Cooper.'

Mrs Cooper. Oh, hell. This was it.

For the next five days she was Mrs Nicholas Cooper.

The drive to the Tey residence was a silent one. The driver drove, Nick brooded, and Hallie grew wide-eyed again as they entered the neon-lit tunnel that would take them beneath Victoria Harbour and across to Hong Kong Island. Awe at the tun-

nel added to her anxiety about meeting the Teys
and set her stomach to churning. Funny, but she'd
never actually thought posing as Nick's wife was
going to be hard.

Until now.

Finally, they shot out of the tunnel into real light
again, skirted Hong Kong Island's central business
district, and started weaving their way up a long,
steep slope; towering apartment blocks giving way
to luxury villas that grew bigger and grander the
higher they climbed.

'How do I look?' she asked as the Mercedes
pulled into a paved driveway and swept through no
nonsense wrought iron security gates that closed
behind them.

'Beautiful.' Nick took her hand in his and, with
a reassuring smile, brushed her knuckles with his
lips. 'You look beautiful.'

'Not helping,' she warned, rapidly withdrawing
her fingers from his grasp.

'Beddable,' he said next, which earned him a
glare.

They were as ready as they were going to get.

Nineteen-year-old Jasmine Tey stood at her bedroom window and waited for her father's guests
to arrive with a mixture of anticipation and ter-

ror. Nicholas and his wife would arrive within the hour, their room was ready, refreshments were ready and Kai had gone to collect them from the airport. Everything was as it should be except for the butterflies in her stomach that would not be still and the suffocating fear that within this next hour Kai and her father were going to find out about her late night visit to Nicholas's room, and once that information came out…

If that information got out…

Because Jasmine's current mission in life was to *prevent* that information from coming to light. She had to get Nick off somewhere by himself and apologise and beg his pardon for her earlier behaviour. Somehow, she had to swear him to silence on the matter and she had to do it fast.

Because Kai and her father; they could never know.

Jasmine turned away from the window at the sound of her father's footsteps, slid damp palms down the front of her pretty silk sundress and offered up a smile.

'Everything ready for our guests' arrival?' he asked from the doorway.

'Yes, Father.'

Her father's eyes were smiling and wise. They'd always been wise. They'd always looked on her with love and delight and Jasmine never wanted that to change.

'I wonder what his wife will be like,' he said.

'Me too.'

'He didn't mention her last time he was here,' her father said next.

Jasmine offered up a composed smile – a smile that pretended indifference when it came to Nicholas and his rarely mentioned wife. No secret shame here, nothing to worry about at all. 'He did to me.'

Nicholas's wife was a vibrant, bright-eyed woman not that much older than Jasmine. She had a wide warm smile, golden-brown eyes and the most amazing dark red hair… Jasmine tried not to stare at her hair and did a poor job of it as her father moved in to welcome Nick and they shook hands and clasped shoulders and then Nick turned to his wife and put a gentle hand to the small of her back.

'I'd like you to meet my wife, Hallie Bennett-Cooper,' said Nick and Jasmine stood back, making herself as small as possible, and let the introductions continue until her father beckoned her forward.

'My daughter, Jasmine,' said her father and she put on her best social smile for Nick and

Hallie Bennett-Cooper both. Nick's eyes were still smiley; he was still very handsome.

Best of all, he didn't look angry or wary and when he opened his mouth the words that came out were, 'Lovely to see you again, Jasmine' and not 'don't enter my room uninvited this time.'

Not that he would have said that. Not in front of people, surely. Nicholas Cooper was an English gentleman. Wasn't he?

'Welcome,' she offered, and dragged her gaze away from Nick and turned her attention to his wife – hoping upon hope that Hallie Bennett-Cooper would attribute Jasmine's lack of speech to English-as-a-second-language problem rather than an acute attack of embarrassment and guilt.

Hallie's gaze met hers and Jasmine coloured, because awareness was there in the other woman's eyes. Nicholas's wife *knew*. He'd told her, and any minute now Hallie was going to make mention of it.

Sickness rose up in Jasmine like the tide.

Don't, she wanted to beg. Please don't say anything. Can't we just pretend it never happened? I didn't know. I *didn't* know he already had a wife.

Hallie Bennett-Cooper's smile was surprisingly gentle. 'Nick neglected to mention how beautiful you were,' she murmured, and leaned forward to brush her cheek gently against Jasmine's before pulling back and narrowing her eyes. 'Or how young. Men. Show me one who can give you all the necessary details.'

'Kai can,' said Jasmine, before her brain could catch up with her mouth.

'Okay, I'll give you that one,' murmured Hallie. 'But I stand by the statement that my husband's powers of observation need work. I swear; he and I are going to have words.'

'I'm quaking,' said Nick dryly.

Jasmine had no idea what they were talking about, not that it mattered. First and foremost, it beat talking about that night. 'Please,' she said, remembering her role and trying not to let anxiety render her useless. 'Would you care to come inside?'

Jasmine Tey was *nothing* like the brazen teenage seductress Hallie had imagined. Never mind the exquisite jewel-coloured sundress she wore. Never mind the waist-length black hair held away from her face with a bamboo clasp in a style both youthful and inspired because it drew attention to both face and hair and both were stunning. Hallie didn't even mind the wide, shy eyes Jasmine turned on Nick – Hallie was fast coming to the conclusion that most women *did* have big eyes for Nick… No, what bothered Hallie most was that Jasmine Tey seemed to have not one scrap of confidence in her own appeal and no idea whatsoever of the guilt and mortification that was currently stamped on her face for anyone with eyes to see.

Whatever Jasmine had done the last time Nick was here, boy did she regret it.

'I—I trust your flight went well?' asked Jasmine as Hallie tucked her hand through the crook of Jasmine's elbow and turned the younger girl towards the villa and away from driver Kai's all-seeing eyes.

'It was good,' said Hallie. 'Well, apart from this one woman who fell into Nick's lap on purpose. And it wasn't me.' Hallie rolled her eyes. 'She simpered. She swooned. You can imagine.'

A tiny smile tilted Jasmine's lips. It seemed she could.

'I don't blame him,' Hallie continued, warming to her theme. 'He can't help the effect he has on us. Of course, he doesn't have to enjoy it quite as much as he does.'

'But darling—'

'Don't you darling me, Nicholas Cooper!' He'd wanted possessive, requested jealousy. Hallie stopped and turned around to see if he was following. He was, and so was John Tey. Driver Kai stood by the car, watching impassively. She contemplated a head toss and decided against it. Too dramatic – this was a *very* restrained household, no need to overplay it. Jealous words would more than suffice. 'I've had quite enough of women falling over you for one day!'

'You could always try trusting me.' Nick's voice was dry, very dry, as he reached where she stood, bent his head and touched his lips to hers in the merest whisper of a kiss.

They were in a public place. They were making a point for Jasmine's benefit. Role playing, that was all. But the quiet intensity in his gaze made her heart race and her body want more. Had she really been married to this man she'd want him in her bedroom now. So he could show her with his body and with his eyes just how much he loved her. Not the pretty little flirt on the flight today, not any one of the women who'd tried to engage his interest, but *her*. She was hot, she was sticky, she was well and truly aroused, and dammit she was blushing, her worldliness stripped from her too easily.

She let go of Jasmine's arm, hoping that the reassuring smile she sent the younger woman would suffice. 'Um, I don't suppose there's somewhere I can freshen up?' she asked.

'Of course,' said Jasmine. 'Come, I'll show you to your suite. I also have refreshments prepared for you if you'd care to join us on the terrace a little later. I wasn't sure how hungry you'd be so there's a bit of everything.'

'That sounds lovely.'

More reassurance, because Jasmine Tey still looked like she desperately needed it.

Nick's wide palm rested on the small of her back as they followed Jasmine to their suite, the warmth of his touch searing into her through the thin silk of her top. By the time they reached the room, his touch was a feather-light caress between her shoulder blades and her body was awash in sensation. 'Right, then. Thank you,' she said to Jasmine. 'We'll meet you on the terrace in, um—'

'Half an hour,' murmured Nick in *that* voice, and quietly shut the door.

'Phew.' Hallie blew out a breath and headed for the window, more to put some distance between herself and Nick than to admire the view. It was a magnificent view though, now that she looked at it. The Teys' three-car garage and manicured terraced gardens were spread out directly below them and beyond their walls stood more luxury housing that only the extremely wealthy could afford. Down slope, the villas and the apartment blocks gradually morphed into the towering skyscrapers and neon madness of Hong Kong Island's central business district. Beyond that lay the glittering waters of Victoria Harbour and beyond <u>that</u>, more skyscrapers; the skyscrapers of Kowloon. 'Wow,' she said softly.

'Breathtaking, isn't it,' said Nick, crossing the room to stand beside her. 'How do you think it went with Jasmine?'

'She got the point.'

'You don't think it was too subtle?' he asked.

'We women are subtle creatures.'

Nick didn't seem entirely convinced. 'I think we need more.'

'More what? More jealousy? Look, I'm trying to be supportive here but in my professional opinion Jasmine's not going to come anywhere near you ever again. She's an innocent girl, Nick. You never mentioned that. And you should have. I was all set to play the over-possessive fruitcake. I don't *need* to play the over-possessive fruitcake. I doubt I even need to be here.'

'You're wrong. I know Jasmine's an innocent, Hallie. That doesn't make her without wiles. You do need to be here. And there definitely needs to be more touching.'

'Touching?'

He slid an arm around her waist and drew her gently towards him. 'Like this.'

This was enough to set every bone in her body to melting. Hallie put her hands to his chest, striving for some distance, even as the lower half of her body betrayed her and settled snugly against him. 'Kai's watching us,' she muttered. He was opening the driver's side door of the Mercedes; maybe he was off to put the car away. But he was looking up at them.

'I know.' Nick was hardening against her as they spoke and making no secret of his affliction as his hands slid from her waist to the base of her spine and pressed her even closer.

'Kinky,' she said lightly.

'It may not be the audience.' His lips were curved in a familiar half-smile. 'It could be you.'

Hallie slid her hands to his shoulders, delighting in the feel of him, in the rich musky scent of his skin. 'You mean you don't know?'

'Nope. And there's not enough blood left in my brain to figure it out.'

'Maybe it's both,' she said breathlessly.

'Now you're trying to confuse me.'

'Actually, I'm trying to distract you.'

'Try harder,' he said, and set his lips to her neck, sending a jolt of pleasure straight through her. Role playing, that was all, but she tilted her head to allow him better access, gasping when the heat of his lips was joined by a whisper of tongue as he teased and tasted his way along her neck.

This was madness, she thought, as she buried her hands in his hair and demanded more. Utter madness, as Nick cupped her buttocks and surged against her as his lips rushed over her shoulder, her collarbone, the swell of her breast and it was all she could do not to whimper when his mouth found the peak of her breast through the thin layers of silk. All she could do not to scream when his teeth and tongue came into play.

'Nick.' He'd found the clasp on her trousers, his fingers at her waist setting off feathery tremors of sensation. 'Nick! He's gone.'

'Who's gone?' His eyes were black, his breathing was ragged, but comprehension dawned. 'Oh, yeah. Him.' His hands stilled, and his big body shuddered as he struggled for control. 'Just give me a minute here.'

No problem. She could do with a minute or two herself. Not to mention a few more metres of unoccupied personal space.

He let her go, let her put some distance between them, but her skin was on fire from his touch and her breasts ached for the feel of his hands and his lips on them again. Half blind with unfulfilled need, she staggered towards the centre of the room. And stopped.

The floor was the palest marble streaked with grey. The furniture was intricately carved cherry wood inlaid with mother-of-pearl. The furnishings were red. Not dull red, not blood red, but a bright primary-colour-wheel red. The floor rug, the curtains, the bed… yes indeed, the bed was undeniably red, with enough cushions and pillows piled against the headboard to furnish a small orphanage.

'I thought you said there was a sofa as well,' she said at last.

'There was,' said Nick, frowning. 'It used to be over by the far wall.'

Well, there certainly wasn't one there now. Nothing in this room but a bed. A big red bed.

'The Chinese consider red a fortuitous colour,' said Nick. 'It's supposed to bring good luck.'

'Good,' she muttered. Cause they were definitely going to need it if they were going to be sharing that bed. 'Mind if I take first shower?'

'Go ahead.' Nick gestured towards a door to her right.

The bathroom was marble too, all marble, with gold taps, red towels and the biggest glass walled shower cubicle she'd ever seen. *Two* shower heads in that there cubicle. Two of them, side by side, commanding her attention the way the bed had in the other room.

'Or we could shower together and save time,' he said from the doorway.

Did he honestly think that getting wet and naked with him was going to save time? She slid him a glance; he was leaning against the doorframe, his smile crooked and his eyes dark.

No, he didn't think that either.

CHAPTER FIVE

'WHAT DID HE DO to you?' The question came at Jasmine softly, sneaking beneath her defences and opening her up, laying her bare. Kai had always been able to do that, even with a glance, and when he used words it was worse.

'What do you mean?' Jasmine turned her attention from the perfectly prepared trays of finger-food on the kitchen bench and glanced towards Kai, knowing full well that her heart would trip when she made eye contact, because it had done for years.

'Nicholas Cooper.' Kai's narrowed black gaze told her he wouldn't be dissuaded. 'Last time he was here you couldn't get enough of him. This time I see fear in your eyes when you look at him. So what did he do?'

'Nothing.' Truth and only truth, 'He did nothing.'

'Then why the fear?'

'There is no fear.' Nick hadn't said anything and neither had his wife. His wife had actively tried to set Jasmine's mind at ease with her teasing about the effect Nicholas had on the fairer sex. No one had mentioned anything about Jasmine's shameful lapse of judgement. Maybe they never would. That was the ideal Jasmine clung to now. 'I like his wife.'

Kai just leaned against the kitchen counter beside her. Close enough that she could smell the clean citrus and ginger scent of him, close enough to marvel at how long his eyelashes were, and how beautifully shaped were his lips.

Yes, Nicholas Cooper was handsome and she'd been momentarily dazzled by him, but *this* man was the one who had fuelled a thousand teenage fantasies, was still fuelling them, and Jasmine had a sneaking suspicion that Kai knew it.

Awkward.

'That hair,' Jasmine murmured by way of distraction. 'Such a beautiful red.'

'Yes,' murmured Kai with the kick of a smile. Superstition would have it that Hallie Bennett-Cooper had supernatural powers on account of her hair colour. Jasmine didn't believe it, but still…

Hallie Bennett-Cooper had something.

'If he hurt you I need to know,' said Kai, never one to be guided in a different direction for long.

'He hasn't hurt me.' Just saying the words made Jasmine realise the truth of them. 'I acted the fool last time Nicholas Cooper was here. Nicholas listened to me and I liked that. He laughed with me and I liked that too. He's very handsome. A little bit undisciplined.' Jasmine smiled ruefully. 'He was new. Interesting.' Diversion and defiance and so very, very different to Kai. 'I misread friendliness for flirting and easy charm for encouragement and now I'm embarrassed when I look at him because I know he never meant to mislead me.'

Give Kai a taste of the truth in the hope that he would be satisfied.

And when those penetrating black eyes of his doubted her, give him some more.

'I'm nineteen years old, I live with my father and I never go anywhere without you. I make mistakes. I don't know love.' She barely knew kisses. 'Allow me that.'

Kai shifted his gaze from her to the floor. His

profile was as beautiful as the rest of him, his cheekbones cut with a master's blade.

Finally he nodded, still not looking at her. Explanation accepted.

'You want those trays out on the terrace?' he asked.

'Not yet. I thought to wait another ten minutes or so – Nicholas and his wife may wish to shower and change clothes first.'

Kai ran a hand through his short cropped black hair, too short to make a mess of it but an uncommon enough gesture that Jasmine stared all the same.

'I'll talk to your father again about allowing you more freedom,' he offered. 'More contact with people of a similar age.'

'You should save yourself the trouble,' she said. 'I know how that conversation goes and so do you.' She felt the hitch in her breath and prayed that Kai couldn't hear it. 'My father says no.'

Nick knew women. Knew the feel of them in his arms and in his bed. More than that, he liked women and they could generally be counted on to like him right back. But he'd never met a woman who affected him the way Hallie Bennett did. Hell, when she was in his arms it was all he could do to recall his own name let alone the terms of their agreement.

So she was amusing…women often were.

So she was beautiful… there were plenty of women out there who were that, too.

But since when had he ever wanted to watch a woman's face forever, just so he wouldn't miss whatever she came out with next? Since when had a woman ever distracted him from his work and his goals for the company? Since when had a woman ever had *that* kind of power over him? Since never, that was when. And he didn't like it, not one little bit.

Hallie Bennett was here to *solve* his woman problems, not cause more.

By the time she emerged from the bathroom, sleek and elegant in a moss-green sheath, he was thoroughly riled. It didn't help that he knew he was being unreasonable, that she'd only been doing what they'd agreed on in the first place. It certainly didn't help that she took one look at him and judged his mood in an instant.

'Pick a topic, any topic,' she said airily. 'Religion, politics, whatever you like… I'm sure we can come to a disagreement about something.'

'Sport,' he said abruptly. There wasn't a woman

of his acquaintance who could talk sense when it came to sport.

'Of course, there's only one real sport and that's soccer,' she stated firmly.

'Football,' he corrected.

'Whatever. I favour Brazil, myself.'

'Because they win?'

'Because Australia has no world cup team and Brazil wear green and gold shirts. Green and gold is very Australian.'

'You support Brazil because of the colour of their shirts?' Now they were getting somewhere. 'That's ridiculous.'

'Would you rather I supported them because they're fascinating to watch and they have the best striker in the world?'

'Er, no.' That would defeat the entire purpose of the conversation. 'I'm trying to find something to dislike about you.'

'Ah.' And with a very sweet smile. 'About the shower… I'm afraid I used all the hot water.'

'Hmph.' Even that wasn't a problem, he thought glumly as he gathered up his shaving kit and stalked towards the bathroom. A cold shower was just what he needed.

'Nick,' she said from the other side of the bathroom door, just as he was about to step under the spray. 'I think I'll go down and find Jasmine. That okay with you?'

'Why?'

'Well, for starters you didn't take any clean clothes into that bathroom with you, which means you're going to come out wearing a towel or less, which I'm sure is a very good look for you but frankly, it's going to damage my calm. Secondly, Jasmine Tey is scared stiff of you at the moment and I need to find out why.'

'Couldn't you just ask *me*?'

'Do you know?'

'No.' Nick turned away from the shower, opened the bathroom door a crack and peered out, keeping most of his naked self hidden.

'That's what I thought.' Hallie was pinning her hair up and using the dresser mirror as her guide. Her gaze met his, sweeping quickly downwards, before she remembered herself and refocused on his eyes. 'I'm thinking that if she's surrounded by overprotective alpha males – which she is – the thing she'll be worried about most is *them* finding out.'

'Well, they won't find out from me.'

'But Jasmine doesn't know that. She's a baby, Nick. You need to reassure her that you'll keep your mouth shut.'

'I will keep it shut. I *am* keeping it shut. Incident forgotten. Crisis averted. Wife on board. That would be you.'

Hallie sighed. 'Just…if you get a chance to reassure her that her secret is safe with you, do it.'

'Okay. I will.' Nick turned on the shower taps ever so slightly too hard. 'Nag nag nag.'

'*Hello.*' He could still hear her, even with the door shut and the water running, and the exasperation in her voice made his smile grow wide. 'Wife.'

Nick's shower helped. Helped enough so that when they went downstairs he was back to thinking that having a wife on board was going to solve a multitude of problems. He could do this. They could do this. Besides, it was far too late to back out now.

He found them in a light filled room that opened onto a terrace overlooking the Teys' hillside garden. This much land, this close to Hong Kong was a clear indication of John Tey's astonishing wealth, and the spacious, fortress-like home that sat on the land confirmed it. Nick didn't know why John Tey had invited him to stay in his home while doing business together. John Tey had offices in the city centre and most of the hotels had business facilities for hire. They could have kept their dealings more businesslike and all of this could have been avoided.

Next time, thought Nick grimly. Next time he'd know to do just that. Right now he settled for nodding at the ever present Kai, accepting the long tall glass of lime water from Jasmine with a thank you and what he hoped to hell was a reassuring smile, and heading in Hallie's direction, which was over by the terrace wall with John Tey. No need to launch straight into business here, that was not the John Tey way, so Nick took a back-seat and watched his new 'wife' at work and quite clearly at play.

Within five minutes she'd discovered that their host clipped his own hedges and spent an hour every morning practising Tai Chi. That he owned an extensive art collection and that Jasmine was an accomplished silk painter. Five minutes and Jasmine was giggling, John was smiling, and even the po face Kai had relaxed his guard and it was all Hallie's doing as she charmed them with her warmth, wit and enthusiasm for life. Whatever the moment held, she embraced it; be it a computer game or a kiss, she gave it everything she had.

Damn but the woman could kiss.

'Do you collect antiquities?' John asked her as

she bent to examine a little jade horse set on a marble pedestal.

'My father does. John, this is exquisite. Early Qing dynasty, isn't it? I've never seen one in such good condition.'

Nick blinked at her knowledge of little green horses. John beamed at the compliment.

'Kai will drive you to some of our smaller private galleries in the morning if you wish. There you will find many beautiful pieces. Perhaps even a memento of your stay with us.'

'Perhaps.' Hallie smiled easily, her glance encompassing them both. 'I don't want to disrupt any plans you have in place but I'd love to see a little more of the city. And the lion dancing… Maybe buy some oranges…'

Jasmine was nodding her head in vigorous agreement. John's gaze was wry as it rested on his daughter.

'My daughter has also suggested she show you these things. Would tomorrow be suitable?' And to Jasmine, 'You will let Kai know when you wish to leave.'

'But Father, surely we can go alone.'

'No.' It was the first time Nick had ever seen him refuse his daughter anything.

'But Father—'

John Tey held up his hand and there was instant silence from Jasmine.

'Kai will accompany you.'

Jasmine bent her head in acquiescence. 'Yes, Father.'

'So it is settled.' John was back to playing the charming host. 'Come, Nick. You must try the spring rolls. Jasmine makes them herself.'

As far as Hallie was concerned the evening passed pleasantly and far too quickly, the problem being that as soon as they retired for the evening, she and Nick would have to confront that big red bed. The sofa was gone, that much was certain, and the floor was made of marble. *She* certainly wasn't going to sleep on a marble floor, nor did she expect Nick to. No, they were going to have to share the bed and somehow she was going to have to keep her hands to herself.

So she was slightly nervous as they headed for the guest suite, slightly bug-eyed as he followed her into their room, loosening his tie as he closed the door before automatically proceeding to the buttons of his shirt. Habit, that was all, there was nothing sexual about it. But she couldn't let him continue.

'Bathroom,' she said sternly, pointing the way.

'Right.' Nick scooped up his toiletries *and* his pyjamas and headed for the bathroom without another word.

One week. Be professional. She could do this.

Hallie's gaze slid to the bed.

How on earth was she going to do this?

By the time he'd finished in the bathroom and Hallie had had her turn and slipped into her Mickey Mouse singlet and boxers-for-girls she had it figured. Fortunately, Nick wasn't in bed yet. He was standing at the window, a dark silhouette against the night sky and if she thought he looked good in a suit, it was nothing compared to what he looked like in tight black boxers.

'I'll take the floor,' he said.

'You can't take the floor. The floor is too hard. Anyway, I have a plan.' Hallie strode over to the bed and began stacking cushions straight down the middle of it.

'*This* is your plan?' he asked, somewhat sceptically.

'*This*,' she said, busily stacking cushions, 'is the Great Wall of China. You are the Mongol horde and I am the Emperor's finest troops.'

He looked like he wanted to laugh, caught her glare, and must have decided against it.

'Well, that hardly seems fair,' he said finally.

'Why can't I be the Emperor's finest and *you* be the barbarians?'

'Fine. Just stay on your side of the wall, okay?'

'I will defend this wall with my very life.'

'Whatever.' That'd teach her to mix metaphors with a computer games master. She slipped beneath the covers and lay down. Moments later Nick approached the bed and the mattress dipped as he lay down. Her plan was working. And then Nick's head and torso appeared above the cushions, his elbow skewing them haphazardly.

'The Emperor's troops are allowed on the wall, right? I feel like I should be patrolling it.'

'Trust me, you don't have to patrol the wall. There is nothing happening on your northern border tonight. Get some sleep.'

He disappeared behind the wall of pillows only to return again almost immediately.

'No raiding party?'

'No. There is nothing on your side of the wall that the barbarians want.' This was a lie. She knew for a fact that there were enormous treasures to be found just a cushion's length away.

'Here's the problem,' said Nick. 'I've never slept in the same bed with a woman and not *slept* with her if you get my meaning. I feel like I should be doing something.'

'Go to sleep. Think of the wall.' She, however, would be spending the rest of the night fantasizing about what it was he thought he should be doing.

'Have *you* ever slept with a man and not slept with him?' he asked.

'Yes.' Did sharing tent space on a camping trip with a nine-year-old brother count? 'It's not hard.'

'Wrong,' he said. 'It's extremely hard. A raiding party would know this already.'

Hallie's stomach clenched and her toes curled as she tried not to picture in vivid detail exactly which part of Nick was hard. 'Sending a raiding party over that wall would be suicide,' she countered.

'What if I invited you over for peace negotiations?'

'Hah! I'm not falling for that old trap.'

'I can't believe you ever thought this plan was going to work,' he said as the bottom-most pillow tumbled from the bed.

'Fine then. I'll sleep on the floor.'

'You can't sleep on the floor. The floor is too hard.'

'Then go to sleep before I strangle you,' she yelled. And after a moment's reflection, 'You're deliberately inciting the Mongol horde, aren't you?'

'Is it working?'

'No.' She punched the pillow at her head until it was shaped to her liking and deliberately turned her back to him. 'The Mongol horde is wise to your tricks.'

She heard his low sexy chuckle followed by the rustle of sheets.

'Goodnight, Mrs Cooper.'

And much, much later, when the regular, even rhythm of his breathing told her he'd fallen asleep, 'Goodnight, Nicholas.'

CHAPTER SIX

NICK WOKE BEFORE THE dawn with a sleeping Hallie snuggled tightly into his side. Her head was on his shoulder, her arm was resting on his chest, her legs were entwined with his, and there wasn't a pillow in sight. What's more, he noted with no little satisfaction, she was on his side of the bed, *his*, which meant that, technically, *she* was the one doing all the invading. Her body was relaxed, her breathing slow and even. The Mongol horde was vulnerable. Question was; what was he going to do about it?

A gentleman would slide on out of bed without waking her and head for the shower. A rogue would wake her with kisses, drive her to distraction with pleasure and *carry* her to the shower. Tough choice.

He was still debating tactics when he felt her stir.

Her long, smooth legs tangled even more closely with his and her hand traced a leisurely path from his chest to his stomach, sending a shiver of pleasure straight through him. Even in sleep she knew just what to do to get his undivided attention. And then she stopped.

Nick felt her body stiffen, heard her sharply indrawn breath. She was awake.

'Morning,' he said huskily, although at this hour, with silvery darkness still enveloping them, that was debatable. She jerked up on one elbow, looked around wildly, and her knee connected with his crotch. 'Oomf!' His eyes crossed. His breath left his body. So much for his wakeup-sex fantasy.

'Sorry,' she muttered, removing her knee and patting him better abstractedly. 'What happened to the pillows?'

'Try the floor,' he wheezed as the patting continued. Was this heaven or hell? He couldn't decide. He levered himself up on his elbow and looked over the side of the bed. 'Yep. There they are.'

'Oh.' She stared at him and all of a sudden the hand on his crotch stilled. Nick watched her eyes grow round and her cheeks grow rosy with no little satisfaction.

'I, ah…I, ah…okay,' she said weakly. The colour in her cheeks had spread to her chest, her nipples had pebbled against the thin cotton of her singlet. Her eyes were downcast, hiding her expression. But it was her hand that held his attention. Because it hadn't moved.

'Possession,' he murmured, 'is nine-tenths of the law.'

He was still playing the gentleman, heaven help him he was, but a man could only take so much. She was driving him mad. He couldn't see her eyes, couldn't figure what she wanted. He, however, was absolutely certain about what *he* wanted. He put his hand beneath her chin – that determined little chin – and brought her gaze up to meet his. Her eyes widened, there was uncertainty in her eyes and curiosity too; he was used to both from the women who shared his bed, but it was desire he looked for. Desire he found.

His gaze fastened on her mouth as he drew her closer, close enough to bend his head and set his lips to hers, every whisper of a touch, every leisurely rub maddeningly erotic and not nearly enough. He wanted more, demanded it with a nip to her bottom lip so she'd open for him and damn near lost control when she did. He couldn't get enough of her taste and her texture, couldn't get enough of that soft, lush mouth against his own. He broke the kiss with a groan, craving more, much more, and needing to know he could take it. They were breaking all the rules here – he needed to know she was with him. 'Is this what you want from me, Hallie?'

'I'm not sure. I think so,' she whispered, and Nick groaned.

'"I think so" is not good enough,' he muttered, even as he slid his hands around her waist and urged her slim body closer, a shiver of response rippling through him as her legs tangled with his and her breasts pressed against his chest. 'You have to say yes.'

Hallie closed those glorious golden eyes, took her lower lip between her teeth and moved tentatively against him. 'Persuade me.'

Lord but she was sweet as her hands slid to his shoulders as she rolled with him to the middle of the bed. She wanted him above her but she did not get her way in that. He wasn't a small man. Better for Hallie to come at him from above – if that was her intent. It did seem to be her intent, if her incoherent little mutterings were any indication. Those tiny gasps of hers that lit his blood and made thinking a challenge.

She was beautifully wanton as she lifted her

arms above her head, helping him to remove her top, and then her hands were on him again as she wrapped her arms around his neck and bent down to deliver another of those soul-stealing kisses. He felt her shudder, felt himself arch up into her, her urgency igniting his own.

He wanted to make sure she was prepared for him - he *always* made sure a woman was ready for him - but with Hallie what he wanted and what he needed were two completely different things. And he needed to be inside her, buried in her up to the hilt; dammit, she drove him to madness. His hands were fast and urgent as he slid her tight little boxers from her body, and then shed his own, his need for her clawing at him as he spread her thighs wide and positioned himself between them. She was so wet and warm and tight.

And she froze.

No! His soundless roar of protest came from somewhere deep and primitive within. No! He wouldn't let her stop now. Couldn't. But he stilled, that much he could do, because they were forgetting things here. Preliminaries. Safety. 'We can go slow,' he muttered, knowing even before he heard himself speak that his voice would be harsh and strained.

She pushed herself into a sitting position, her

face flushed and her breath coming fast. 'I don't think I can do this.'

'Really slow,' he said. And turned his considerable will towards proving that he could.

Gentle, as he cupped her hips and positioned them so that she dragged against him. Slow, as he rocked back and forth, watching, always watching, to see that what he was doing pleased her. And heaven help them both, she was easy to please.

'Nick, I- Oh…'

He licked at her nipple, flicked his tongue back and forth across that hard little bud. So easy to please, as he grazed her with his teeth and soothed her with his tongue before taking her breast more fully into his mouth and suckling hard. She arched back at that, whimpering her approval before demanding he pay attention to her other breast. He could do that. Did exactly that as his hands skittered down her spine and then she was wresting that breast from him and devouring his lips with her own, each nip, each slide of that clever, honeyed mouth dragging him deeper.

'Work with me here,' he muttered, 'I'm pretty sure I can go slower. You just have to stop kissing me like that.'

'Oh, my God!' she said.

He nipped at her jaw, the slender curve of her

neck, the sweep of her shoulder and everywhere he touched she responded with a shudder, a purr, a gasp. He was dizzy with the feel of her, wild with need for her. He slid his fingers between her legs, found her soft and damp as he parted her protective folds to expose her tiny bud and position himself against her more fully. Against but not in, always rocking, always intensifying the sweet slide of skin against skin until her breath came in short, sharp gasps and her eyes turned molten. Her fingers dug into his shoulders, her movements grew more frantic. He sucked in his breath as she trailed her hands down his chest to his nipples and stroked them to hardness, carefully passive, and aching with the control it took to stay that way as she moved her hands lower, positioned herself above him and guided him in, a fraction at a time.

That's when he felt it. A barrier in his way.

No! Surely not. It couldn't possibly be what he thought it was. Could it? Her eyelashes were shielding her eyes, her brow was furrowed as she focused intently on the task at hand and, dammit, she was chewing on her bottom lip. Oh, no. Please no. 'You're not a virgin, are you?' he asked with an impending sense of doom.

'Does it matter?' she said, still trying- unsuccessfully- to accommodate him.

What did she mean, 'Does it matter?'

'Of course it matters!' he roared. 'Oh hell. You *are* a virgin!'

'Well, technically, yes,' she admitted. 'But I'm not *that* inexperienced. I've had sexual relations before.'

'Don't you dare bring politics into this conversation,' he snapped, snatching his hands from her body and pressing them against the bed as he struggled for control. 'You! A virgin! What next?'

Her eyes narrowed, her chin came up. He loved that look. His *body* loved that look. His body, he thought with increasing alarm, was almost past the point of stopping.

'Get off,' he ordered.

'You've got to be kidding me.' She bit her bottom lip again, pressed down hard, and suddenly, suddenly, he was in.

Her eyes watered, her breath seemed to catch in her throat.

Oh, God! His control was moments away from shattering. She was so hot, so tight, so *wet*. 'Don't panic!' he muttered. 'We can fix this.'

How on earth were they going to fix this?

Hallie started to giggle.

'Don't laugh,' he ordered. 'Don't move!' If she moved, he was history.

She moved, and so did he, rolling with her, rolling her onto her back and moving over her, into her, his movements carefully restrained as he tried, God help him, to be gentle with her.

She looked up at him then, her eyes dark and slumberous and her lips curved, and he felt her melt into him, felt her body grow accustomed to him, as his strokes grew longer until at last he was sheathed inside her completely. He managed a smile, shuddering with the effort it took to rein himself in. 'You okay?' he muttered.

'Absolutely.'

And then she was threading her hands through his hair and dragging his lips down to hers and he was surging into her, his control a thing of the past. Trying to be gentle with her and not at all sure he was succeeding as he rode out his need for her, his fascination with her, each stroke destroying him, what was left of him, and all around them was the rich scent of sex and the slide of sweat-slicked bodies. His need for her was outrageous, his satisfaction darkly overwhelming as she gave herself over to him, came for him, convulsing around him with a soft, sexy cry that screamed through his senses.

Now. As she cried out again, wrapped her legs around him and urged him deeper.

Now.

Later, much later, he carried her to the bathroom, turned the shower on hot and hard and stood her under the spray, one arm wrapped around her waist to support her. Gentleman or rogue – he figured he had his answer. Figured he was going to have to live with it. 'Can you stand?' he asked gruffly.

'Of course I can stand.' She pushed his arm away and took a couple of wobbly steps towards the soap. 'Walking's the challenge.'

'Here…' He adjusted the showerheads so that the water cascaded over them both and handed her the soap. He'd never in his wildest dreams imagined that sassy Hallie Bennett was a virgin. She was twenty-four. What woman in this day and age reached her mid-twenties still a virgin? And why? 'I, ah, hope you weren't saving yourself for your future husband,' he said awkwardly.

'I wasn't.' Hallie's lips twitched as she started soaping herself down. 'Don't panic, Nick. I was a virgin, yes, but I was ready for that to change. I'm not out to trap you.'

That was a relief. Until a new and wholly unwelcome thought occurred to him. Whether she was out to trap him or not, they'd just had unprotected sex. He'd never been so careless with a woman before. Ever! What if she fell pregnant and had a child? His child. There was no way any child of his was going to grow up without a father and, as far as Nick was concerned, that meant marriage. His blood turned to ice, his breath caught in his throat. What had he done?

'Are you okay?' she asked him. 'You don't look so good.'

'I, ah, guess it's unlikely you were protected against pregnancy, what with you being a virgin and all.' He was being wildly optimistic, he knew he was, but he clung to that slim thread of hope the way a shipwrecked sailor clung to a life raft.

'Actually, I *am* protected,' she said. 'That's something we don't have to worry about.'

The breath left his body in a whoosh. Regular breathing resumed.

'Call it a complete stab in the dark,' said Hallie dryly, 'but I'm guessing marriage and children aren't on your to-do list.'

'I, uh…' He was still recovering, still trying to regroup. 'No, they're on the list,' he said at last. 'They're just not at the *top* of the list at this point in time.'

'Ah.' She smiled. 'Good to know.' And from beneath lowered lashes, 'For what it's worth, I think you're an incredible lover. I'm glad you were my first.' Then she lifted her face to the water and put her hands to her hair in a move so innately sensual he felt the force of it like a punch to his stomach.

Definitely not part of the plan, he thought as he dragged her up against him with a muffled curse. And took her again.

Nick soaped up beneath the spray as Hallie stepped from the shower and wrapped herself in a towel. She slid him a dreamy smile, followed up with a stern warning for him to keep his distance. Not a problem, he thought wryly, because, frankly, he was spent.

Lovemaking had always been a pleasurable pastime for Nick. Sometimes it was slow and lazy, sometimes quick and playful. This time had been different. This time his climax had ripped through him like a tornado, leaving him dazed and shaken. And worried.

So what if she was a generous lover?

So what if towards the end there he'd hardly known who or where he was, only who he was with? It wasn't as if he'd found The One. Hell, he was only thirty; he was far too young for that. He had years and years left before *that* happened.

Yeah, whispered his brain. Years and years of

mediocre sex that will never *ever* measure up to what you've just experienced with one Hallie Bennett.

'No,' he said fiercely.

Oh yeah, throbbed his heart. Years and years spent searching for another Titian-haired, golden-eyed witch whose smile warms you through and whose kisses make your soul tremble.

'No!' Louder this time. This was not happening. Regardless of her sweetness, her savvy and her thorough understanding of football, Hallie Bennett was definitely *not* The One.

He wouldn't let her be.

Hallie was lying on her stomach on the freshly made bed, leafing through the travel guide to Hong Kong he'd given her, when Nick finally emerged from the bathroom. Her trouser-clad legs were bent at the knees, her dainty little feet- clad in strappy little sandals- were crossed at the ankles. Her arms were bent at the elbows, her collared shirt showed a modest amount of cleavage. She looked casual, comfortable and perfectly at ease. Perfectly approachable, which was good because he was about to re-establish the boundaries of their relationship.

Just as soon as he put some clothes on.

She looked up at him and smiled as he crossed to the wardrobe and there was lazy satisfaction in that smile, a woman's awareness. His doing, his alone, for there'd been no one else before him and damned if he didn't relish the notion.

No way. No. This was *not* happening.

He turned his back on her and dressed fast, deliberately avoiding her gaze as he headed for the sideboard and his business papers.

'I've been thinking,' he said gruffly.

'It shows.'

He shot her a glance, darkly amused. 'I've been thinking we should stick to the plan from now on.'

'Fine.'

'I mean, the whole point of bringing you along was so that this kind of complication *wouldn't* crop up.'

'I know.'

'We got a bit carried away, that was all.'

She smiled at that and he had the uncomfortable feeling that she'd anticipated each and every one of his defences.

'I promise it won't happen again,' she said, and it was all he could do to keep his jaw from hitting the ground. 'That's what you want to hear, isn't it?'

Well, yes. It was just that he wasn't expecting to hear it quite so readily. Where was the dismay? The protest at having to give up such incredible lovemaking? The businessman in him was relieved. The lover was insulted. The lover, he thought darkly, was the one who'd got him into this mess in the first place. 'I think we need a new rule,' he said firmly. 'No more sex.' And then as she sat upright, slid on over to the edge of the bed and winced in doing so, 'How are you feeling?'

'Tender,' she confessed, blushing to the roots of her hair. 'I don't think I'm going to have any problem complying with your new rule.'

Great. Just great. Now he had guilt. This, he remembered grimly, was one of the reasons he'd never taken a virgin to his bed. He didn't know what to do. How to help. 'Maybe you should take it easy today, postpone your sightseeing trip. I'm sure Jasmine wouldn't mind.'

'I'd mind,' said Hallie. 'I want to see the galleries.'

So much for trying to get her to rest. What was it with women and shopping? Which reminded him. He sifted through his computer case for his spare cash; found it at the very bottom of the case, beneath the computer. 'Here,' he said, holding it out towards her. 'Take it. You might see something you want to buy at the shops today.'

Hallie stared at the thick wad of money, stared

at him. 'I thought we agreed you'd pay me at the end of the week.'

Nick nodded. 'And I will. This is just shopping money.'

'Shopping money.' She said it slowly, looking at the money as if it were poison. Looking at him like he was a snake. 'Keep it,' she said, with a bite in her voice that was new to him.

'Look, you're going to the galleries,' he said, thoroughly baffled by her reaction. 'I'm assuming that whatever they sell there won't come cheap and, if I know Jasmine, she'll consider your outing a failure unless you find something you can't resist. I certainly don't expect you to use your own money for that kind of thing. Put it in your handbag just in case.'

'No!' She sounded fierce, looked fragile. 'I know you're paying me to pretend to be your wife, and I know I let you buy me clothes for the trip, but you can keep your *shopping* money. I won't take it.'

'Why not?' The way he saw it, it was all part of the same deal.

She looked away. 'Because it'd make me feel like even more of a whore,' she said finally.

Nick blinked. Then he scowled. 'Don't be ridiculous!' Okay, so his timing could have been better. He shouldn't have offered her money so soon after sex. But she'd seemed just fine about the sex, he thought morosely. Not to mention the ceasing of it. They'd finished that discussion, hadn't they? And moved on. 'This money's got nothing to do with the sex!' he snapped. 'Don't you dare think I'm trying to pay you for sex!'

She looked slightly mollified. A little uncertain. But her chin was high. 'I'm still not taking it.'

Then they were at an impasse. Because Nick was equally determined that she would. 'What if I commissioned you to buy me a gallery piece while you were out shopping today?' he said. 'What if I secured your professional services as an antiques expert, so to speak? Would that be acceptable?'

'I'm listening,' she said warily.

'Buy me something.' He tossed the money down on the bed beside her.

'With this much money I could probably buy you Hong Kong Harbour,' she said in a small voice, staring down at the notes scattered across the bedspread. 'What do you want?'

'You're the expert. You choose.'

'Yes, but a buyer usually has *some* idea what their client is after.'

Buyer and client now, were they? He should have been pleased that she was going to take the money. He should have been happy she'd finally come to her senses and recognised it as a necessary part of the charade rather than some kind of post-coital payoff, but he didn't feel pleased. He felt… hollow. 'Buy me a vase,' he said. It was the first thing that came to mind.

'Fine. A vase it is.'

He watched her shove the notes into a zippered section of her handbag, smile a bright false smile, and head for the door. Something was bothering him. Something big.

'You didn't really think I'd treat you like a whore, did you?' he asked quietly.

She didn't answer.

CHAPTER SEVEN

THERE WAS SOMETHING TO be said for being chauffeur driven around Hong Kong in a Mercedes, decided Hallie some two hours later as Kai expertly negotiated the traffic with the ease of long familiarity. Jasmine sat beside her in the back seat, cheerfully pointing out places of interest; from museums to major corporations, the Bird Garden to the Goldfish Market. Any other day and Hallie would be embracing the opportunity to shop for antiques with a knowledgeable guide and a chauffeur to boot, but not today. Today her mind was on Nick and his lovemaking. More specifically, on what had happened afterwards.

Good Lord, what a mess.

She'd been expecting Nick to pull back after their lovemaking. She'd started preparing for it the minute she'd stepped from the shower, and she'd been doing all right as they'd re-established the rules of their relationship. She'd been doing pretty well considering that this had been her first morning-after ever. Very well considering her feelings for Nick weren't nearly as casual as she'd made them out to be.

And then he'd acted all concerned for her well-being and she'd let her guard down and allowed herself to believe, just for a moment, that she meant something to him. That he'd found their lovemaking as incredible as she had. And then he'd offered her the shopping money, and boy, hadn't she taken *that* the wrong way. Hallie leaned her head against the windowpane, closed her eyes, and tried to wish it all away. The lovemaking, the misunderstanding, the money...

The sooner she got rid of the money weighing down her soul and her handbag the better.

'Hallie, are you well?'

Hallie straightened up, opened her eyes, and smiled at the younger girl, who was looking across at her in concern. 'I'm fine. Just a little tired.'

'Did you not sleep well? Was the bed uncomfortable?'

'No, no. The bed was very comfortable.' Sharing it was the problem. 'It's probably jetlag kicking in. I'll be okay. Really.' With a determined breath she focused on the younger girl and their outing. 'So tell me… Where's your favourite place in the whole city?' she asked.

'The Lucky Plaza food hall,' said Jasmine promptly. 'They have the finest selection of food in the city. You can try a little of everything! I usually do.'

'We could go there for lunch,' said Hallie.

Jasmine looked uncertain.

'Your father would not approve of your choice of eating venue,' said Kai in his quiet, implacable way.

'I'll ask him,' said Jasmine lifting her chin in a defiant gesture that was vaguely familiar. A quick conversation on her mobile and it was done. 'He said yes,' she told Kai sweetly.

Hallie watched with interest as Kai's gaze clashed with Jasmine's in the rear-view mirror, his stony, hers limpid. It was like water meeting rock; the rock endured but the water was fluid and tricky, not to mention flawlessly beautiful and sur-prisingly strong-willed. Jasmine held Kai's gaze in silence until finally he turned his attention to the road. The smile Jasmine slid Hallie was impish. Hallie returned it in full.

'So when would you like to eat?' asked the younger girl. 'One o clock?'

***

Lucky Plaza was a well-maintained seventies shopping complex. Inside was clean and nondescript with a worn look that spoke of many feet. The shops were jammed full of goods for sale – with barely any space for browsing. 'You ask for what you want,' explained Jasmine. 'And they find it.' Orderly chaos, thought Hallie and thought about the shoe shop she'd left behind. At least the retailers here were busy.

The shop signage was fascinating – not that Hallie could read it. And then they reached the food hall and Hallie discovered that here was where the people of Asia came together to celebrate food.

'See? I knew you would like it,' said Jasmine, accurately judging her fascination. And to Kai, 'And she hasn't even tried the food yet.'

He steered them towards an empty table in a corner and sat them down unceremoniously, his gaze not on Jasmine but on two dark-suited Asian gentlemen standing by a nondescript staircase some twenty metres away. 'Stay here,' he told Jasmine.

'Go.' Jasmine waved him away. 'We shall make our food selections while we wait for you.'

Hallie watched as Kai strode towards the staircase, according the staircase sentries the barest of nods before taking the stairs. 'So what's with the sentries?' she asked. 'Where's Kai going?'

'To pay our respects,' said Jasmine. 'One does not enter another's territory without observing the formalities.'

'What territory? You mean Triad territory?'

'Oh no,' said Jasmine hastily. 'Kai would never allow us to go *there*. Lucky Plaza is owned by another of Hong Kong's criminal organisations. They are…less than the Triads but still worthy of respect. You can see why I had to ask my father if it was appropriate to bring you here.'

Yes, well, she did *now*. So much for thinking Kai's objection to the lunch venue was a simple power play. Jasmine guided them towards an empty table. The table top was clean but small. Space really was at a premium here but the scents wafting from the various kitchens were divine. 'How long has Kai been your bodyguard?' she asked.

'Eight years.' Jasmine looked pensive. 'My mother… she died when I was eleven and she didn't die well. Kai joined us shortly after that.' Jasmine took a deep breath. 'My father is a very rich man. My mother was kidnapped and held to ransom. It happens.'

'What happened?' Too blunt a question for a revelation like this one, not corporate wife tactful at all, but Hallie couldn't help it.

'The ransom was paid,' said Jasmine quietly. 'They killed her anyway.'

'Oh, Jasmine. I'm so, so sorry.'

'Me too,' said Jasmine with a resigned shrug. 'My father has never forgiven himself for not taking better care of my mother; for not offering better protection. That's why Kai goes where I go. That's why I've never gone to school – why teachers and tutors and friends all come to me. That's just the way it is.'

'Did you ever find out who was behind the kidnapping?'

'Of course.'

'And?'

'Justice was served. Lessons were learned. It would take a very foolish kidnapper to come after me.'

'Yet Kai still goes where you go?'

'Apparently the world is full of fools.' Jasmine smiled slightly. 'Would you like me to order for you?'

'Please,' agreed Hallie. 'I want to taste all your favourites.' But she couldn't stop thinking about Jasmine Tey's mother and the impact her death had

had on Jasmine's life. How lonely she must have been. How well and truly trapped.

'My mother wasn't kidnapped,' Hallie offered tentatively. 'She died of cancer when I was a child. It was a slow and ugly death. She fought so hard, I can remember that much.'

Jasmine's eyes showed an understanding way beyond her years.

'She left behind my father, four older brothers and me. My father was shattered. He retreated into his work. My brothers took on the task of raising me. It was…interesting. Funny as all go get sometimes. And sometimes not. I'm twenty-four years old and they're *still* protective.'

'But surely now that you're married, your brothers have pulled back to allow your husband to assume the role of protector?' said Jasmine.

Oh yeah. That.

Truth was, Hallie had absolutely no idea if her brothers would change their ways if she really were married. It would depend on the husband. On their liking and respect for said husband. And, yes, Nick could match them for size, but they wouldn't be testing him for size, they'd be testing his resolve, and Hallie knew from experience just how that was likely to end. No potential suitor upon meeting all four of her brothers

en masse had ever been brave enough to stick
around.

'He looks to be a wonderful husband,' said
Jasmine with a wistful sigh.

'He is,' Hallie said. Or he would be, once he
finally got it in his head to settle down. 'He gives
me the freedom to make my own mistakes.' Like
making sure that it had been *her* decision to make
love to him that morning. 'He has this easygoing
way about him, a certain reckless charm.' Oh, he
definitely had that going for him. 'But when you
get down to it, he's a lot like my brothers. He
likes his own way.' The 'shopping' money in her
handbag was a perfect example. 'Thing is, I like
Nick's way too. It doesn't feel like a cage. It just
feels…right.'

'I feel trapped,' said Jasmine pensively. 'Sometimes all I can think about is finding a way out.
When Nick first came to visit I saw him as an
opportunity for escape. Of course he's handsome
and kind as well; a woman could do worse than to
be married to such a man… And you must understand, I didn't know about you.' Jasmine looked
away, her face reddening. 'I tried to seduce him,'
she said in a small voice. 'You should have seen
your husband's face. The dismay…'

'Oh, Jasmine…' Maybe Nick had called it

correctly when he'd gone in search of a pretend wife for a week. 'Surely you don't have to marry in order to gain a little freedom? There has to be another way. You just have to find it.'

'I'm trying.'

'You could study abroad,' offered Hallie. 'Travel. Take Kai with you if you have to.'

'Kai's part of the problem,' said Jasmine. 'He'd drive me crazy. I'd drive him crazy. He doesn't even like being around me any more. It's like…he just doesn't want to be there.'

'Maybe he needs to move on.'

'I don't know why he hasn't,' Jasmine confided in a small voice. 'He's not happy doing what he's doing, no matter how often my father tries to involve him in business.'

'Maybe he needs a woman,' said Hallie. 'Maybe he *has* one and things aren't working out.'

'No,' said Jasmine with a firm shake of her head. 'I would know if there was a woman. Kai hasn't had a woman in his life for years.'

No women at all? 'He's not…?'

'No!' said Jasmine indignantly. 'Definitely not! He's just…discerning.'

'I guess he can afford to be,' said Hallie, watching the younger girl closely. 'He's very hand-

some, don't you think? Almost as handsome as
Nick.'

Jasmine's lips tightened. 'I guess,' she said, off-
hand.

'And he does the strong, silent thing very well.'

'If you like that kind of thing.'

'Many women do,' she assured the younger
girl and smiled outright when Jasmine's eyes
narrowed. Jasmine seemed to be harbouring a few
protective instincts of her own when it came to
Kai.

'How old is he?' Hallie asked next.

'Twenty-six.'

And how old was he when he came to you?'

'Eighteen.'

Hallie blinked. 'That's young, for bodyguard
work. Although I do concede that he has all the
moves.'

'He always has,' said Jasmine.

'I also noticed that your father treats him like a
son.'

'Yes. He always has.'

Now there was a wayward thought. 'But he's *not*
your father's son, right? By blood, I mean.'

'Of course not!' Jasmine looked offended by the
very thought. 'If Kai were blood my father would
claim him. Family is *everything* to my father, and

as for Kai—' Jasmine shook her head vehemently. 'It's not that. Whatever lies between Kai and my father, it's not *that*.'

'I'm sorry,' said Hallie gently. 'It was a foolish idea and disrespectful as well. Please accept my apology.'

'Accepted,' said Jasmine, but her disquiet stayed in place. 'I think perhaps that you're simply very frank. But we are both being frank, it seems. And I don't want that to stop.' The younger woman smiled awkwardly. 'I don't have very many female friends I can talk to.'

It sounded to Hallie as if Jasmine didn't have anyone much to talk to at all, apart from Kai and her elderly father.

'So what *kind* of things drive Kai crazy?' she asked. 'Maybe we can fix him.'

'He used to let me cook with him all the time. Now it's as if he can't wait for me to get out of the kitchen,' offered Jasmine glumly. 'We used to practise Wing Chun together – Kai was my first teacher, my *only* teacher until I was sixteen. That's when Kai persuaded my father to let me join a proper Wing Chun school. You have no idea how much I wanted that. Kai was my hero for getting my father to agree.' Jasmine's eyes dimmed.

'And then Kai stopped teaching me, he stopped

training me, he stopped sparring with me. I know he still trains. He trains before dawn every day. Just not with me. We used to be able to talk together. Laugh together – he has the sweetest smile, you haven't seen it yet. He doesn't use it any more. Not around me.'

Maybe Hallie was on the wrong track again, like with the half-brother thing. But she'd mentioned that as a possibility so she may as well mention this and Jasmine could make up her own mind. Sometimes an outside eye was clearer than an inner one.

'So for years you and Kai were close.'

Jasmine nodded.

'And then as you grew older he started pulling away. And now he's edgy around you.'

Jasmine nodded again.

'Now I'm really inclined to think he's having woman problems,' Hallie said lightly. 'Maybe he's pining for an *unavailable* woman.'

'There *is* no *woman*!' said Jasmine hotly.

'There's you,' said Hallie. 'Maybe Kai has feelings for you and doesn't know what to do with them. It's possible.'

Jasmine blinked. Then she went white.

'Or not!' said Hallie hurriedly, cursing her wayward mouth. 'That might not be it at all. It was just a thought. I've only been here two days. What do I know?'

'I never—' said Jasmine with a tiny shake of her head. 'It *can't* be that. I'd know. I mean, Meng Kai cares for me, yes. But not like *that*.'

'Let's finish this conversation some other time,' said Hallie swiftly, her gaze meeting Kai's as he reappeared at the bottom of the stairs and started towards them with that silent, ground-eating stride. 'Because here he comes.'

Jasmine nodded and deliberately didn't look at him as he drew closer.

He was a warrior, this one, a warrior steeped in the old ways; Hallie knew the breed. Honour-bound to protect his charge; he would be equally determined to resist any feelings for Jasmine that he deemed inappropriate.

Not that he had the slightest chance of doing that indefinitely, thought Hallie, as Kai's hooded gaze connected with Jasmine's newly aware one. Particularly if Jasmine decided she had feelings for him.

Water always prevailed in the end, no matter how hard the rock. Everyone knew that.

Lunch was a feast of flavours and hugely entertaining. The food hall was large, the crowd was raucous, and Hallie loved it. Almost as much as she enjoyed the silent byplay between Kai and Jasmine. Kai seemed to sense Jasmine's disquiet and watched her closely. Jasmine watched *him* when he wasn't watching her.

When Hallie could eat no more, when she was full to bursting and couldn't contemplate another mouthful, they cleared their table and headed up the escalator to browse the shops on the next level. Collectors' shops, Jasmine told her distractedly before excusing herself and hurrying down a side corridor towards the bathrooms.

Kai watched her go, his gaze never leaving her retreating form. Moments later he was striding after her, catching her by the arm and swinging her round to face him just as she reached the bathroom door in an unmistakable display of baffled masculinity.

Hallie grinned and left them to it, more than happy to browse this shopping level at her leisure. It was quieter on this shopping level. There weren't nearly as many people and there was a great deal more space available for walking and looking. The goods on display here looked vastly more expensive.

Hallie wandered towards an odd little corner shop while she waited. It was hard to tell what it sold, the red velvet curtains in the display windows weren't giving away any clues. And then she saw it. A solitary Chinese funeral vase sitting on a pedestal. It was old, so very old, and almost luminous in its fragile beauty. It was absolutely breathtaking.

The stark black sign-work on the entry door was in Cantonese. Hallie had no idea what it said. But a glance through the door showed more funeral vases inside, some on pedestals, some behind glass, and she simply couldn't resist a closer look.

The mood inside the shop was a sombre reflection of the stock, the salesman young and immaculately presented in a tailored grey suit. He looked up, surprise and wariness crossing his face as she came further into the shop. Maybe he didn't speak English and was worried about how to approach her, thought Hallie. Or maybe he'd forgotten how to speak at all; that was a possibility too given the number of customers he probably saw in a day. She sent him a reassuring smile and turned to the vases on display. Many of them were old. They were all beautiful. But none were lovelier than the one in the window.

'Excuse me,' she said to the young salesman, who still hadn't spoken but was watching her closely nonetheless, 'but do you speak English?'

'Some,' he said with a slight smile.

Some was good. Some was definitely better than none, which was the exact extent of her Cantonese. 'May I have a closer look at the vase in the window?'

'Madam probably wishes to buy a different kind of vase,' said the young man with surprising firmness. 'There are many other vases for sale on the next shopping level.'

'I'll keep that in mind,' she said. 'Right now I'm more interested in *these* vases.'

'Madam *does* realise that these vases are not for flowers.'

'I know. They're funeral vases.'

'Indeed so. They house the ashes of our beloved deceased.'

Yes, they did. And the one in the front window was perfect for a certain pretend husband whose post-coital sensitivity was non-existent. Nick wanted a vase. Hallie wanted his money gone. Definitely a win-win situation. 'Would I be able to take a closer look at the one in the window?'

'It's very expensive, madam.'

'I suspected as much,' she said smoothly. Not exactly salesman of the year, this one. She waited. So did he.

Finally he moved to the window, retrieved the

vase and placed it carefully on the counter in front of her. She wanted her magnifying glass, contented herself with examining the vase inside and out. Definitely a collector's item.

'No refunds,' he said. 'Madam has to be very sure.'

'I'm sure.' She'd found what she was looking for, the tiny mark of a renowned dynasty craftsman. She wondered if the salesman knew what he had. 'How much?'

He named a price that made her gasp. He knew.

But the value was still there. The vase was in immaculate condition. It was even functional. Besides, it appealed to her sense of humour. She looked up at the salesman and gave him a wicked smile. 'It's for my husband. He deserves it.'

This time the salesman smiled back. 'And your husband's name?' He whipped a palm pilot from his pocket, far more co-operative now that he had the sale.

She gave him Nick's name, the Teys' address, and all the cash Nick had given her that morning and then some.

'Do you have a picture of your husband?'

It was a strange question, thought Hallie. And no, she didn't.

'No matter, we will take care of it.' The salesman handed her the receipt. 'When would you like the vase delivered?'

'Today?' Hallie figured they probably didn't pack dynasty vases to go.

'Not possible, madam.' The salesman was shaking his head regretfully.

'Well, I definitely need it before the end of the week. Can you do that?' she asked him anxiously.

'Certainly,' said the salesman. 'That we can do. We are not slow like some.' His smile was charmingly crooked. 'We are professionals.'

Jasmine worried over Hallie's words on the way home from their shopping trip, testing them for validity and trying to prevent the tiny sliver of hope in her stomach from growing into something more. Kai was her protector. Once upon a time he'd been her confidant. For many years he'd been one of her only companions and of a certainty he was beautiful. Of course she had a crush on him.

That didn't mean her feelings were reciprocated.

Don't turn those long, inscrutable looks he gives you into anything. Don't tremble at his touch – just *don't*. A mantra Jasmine had been whispering to herself for years.

So Jasmine was preoccupied when they returned home and when Hallie confided jetlag and sleepiness, she was slow to suggest that Hallie retreat to the guestroom and rest.

But Nicholas's wife was funny and not shy about saying what she wanted, and she did it in a nice way, nothing awkward about it. Just, 'I'm thinking of having a mid-afternoon nap; will that fit in with your plans?'

And it did.

'If I'm not back downstairs in an hour or two will you *please* come and wake me,' Hallie continued. 'I do *not* want to be wide awake all night tonight. That would be bad.'

'I'll wake you,' said Jasmine. 'Two hours at most.'

So much could happen in two hours when a person had a plan.

Fifteen minutes later, Jasmine had changed into fitted black trousers and a white short-sleeved T-shirt. She tied her hair back into a long, slender ponytail – her Wing Chun instructor labelled long hair a liability, but Jasmine wasn't about to cut it off to satisfy him and she didn't necessarily want to defeat anyone today. She simply wanted to test Hallie's theory when it came to what might be bothering Kai.

The garden was where she wanted to be. Private and arranged into three descending terraces, each terrace acted as a room. The first terrace had a long, low bench, a waterfall and a koi pond. The second terrace favoured azalea bushes and sculpted forms, an orderly arrangement with everything in its place. The third terrace was farthest from the house and boasted a meticulously clipped grassy area and a tall cassia tree that shed dappled shade and painted the world a vibrant yellow-green. It was here that Jasmine, Kai and even her father practised Tai Chi and Wing Chun. Here with the house at their back and the city spread out before them in the distance. An unforgettable view, most visitors said. Jasmine saw it every day. There were advantages to being her father's daughter – luxury and privilege, no need to ever worry about money. But it came at the cost of freedom, and the older she got the more confining the walls of her world became. There was her father and there was Kai – the two constants in her life. Everyone else was just passing through.

That Kai might have hidden feelings for her…if he did…

There was nothing simple about that scenario. If he did it was going to rock the foundations of Jasmine's world.

She started with the simpler forms; empty hands

and an overflowing mind. Within minutes her mind had turned to reliving years-old conversations she'd had with Kai; running them through a new filter now and coming up with maybes and possibly and Jasmine you're dreaming. Again.

Her body flowed automatically from one remembered pattern to the next, and that was something to be proud of even if her mind refused to quiet.

Kai found her, twenty minutes later. He always found her; that was his job.

He stayed by the garden steps, hands in his trouser pockets and leaned back against the grey stone wall. He looked relaxed. Curious but not captivated as he tracked her body's movements. Jasmine held his gaze and completed her second form.

'Practice with me,' she said. 'Sticky hands.' A method for developing awareness of muscle movement and predicting what moves an opponent might make next.

'No.'

'You're so busy?' It wasn't as if his dark, loose-fitting trousers and simple short- sleeved shirt would restrict his movements. 'Master Wong says I'm much improved.'

She'd missed those training sessions with Kai

so much. She'd loved being able to focus wholly on him, and there'd been the added bonus of touch and Jasmine always had been starved for that.

Control was key. Control of her breathing when finally Kai moved forward to stand in front of her and finally raised his forearms to hers. They started out slowly, fluid, in the way of dreams, and she took the role of aggressor and he blocked her, move for move, slow and easy as she made sure of her balance and her centre line. Two years it had taken her to get comfortable in the role of aggressor. Jasmine wondered how long it would take her to become comfortable in the aggressor's role when it came to the wooing of men.

Though perhaps it wasn't like that.

Their arms moved faster, action and reaction and a slow blooming heat because the touch of hand against hand, against forearm or wrist, and wrist was still skin on skin contact and a kiss with a fist was still a kiss. Jasmine picked up the pace and still she couldn't slip past Kai's defences and land a body strike; he blocked her every step of the way.

'I'm working on a new theory for why you've been so irritable lately,' she told him, but if she thought talking would weaken his defences she was wrong.

'Is that so?'

The form had been abandoned; they were sparring in earnest now. Kai giving ground and moving them out into the sunlight. Defending, because that's what he did. Jasmine pushing him because sometimes that was what she did, getting up in his space because that was the way of Wing Chun, getting up into his head and forcing the mistake.

'Unrequited love,' she said.

Kai said nothing.

'Or longing.'

'Whose?'

'Yours.'

A swift dance of hands now, and twin lines of displeasure between Kai's brows. 'You're not concentrating,' he said.

And he was avoiding the question. 'Do you want a woman you cannot have, Meng Kai? Is that what's been bothering you?'

She wasn't ready for Kai's attack. Nothing *but* attack, snake-fast and relentless; whisper-soft touches to face and to neck. Punishment for pushing him, for forcing upon him questions that he did not care to answer.

And then he had hold of her wrists and the sparring was over and Kai was breathing hard and so was she, and there was touch – one long, hot line from shoulder to knee and Jasmine couldn't take her eyes off the rapid beating of the pulse at Kai's throat. Her breath squeezed harsh and laboured along her too tight throat and her lips had gone dry. Instinct, to wet them with her tongue, pure instinct, and finally she dragged her gaze from that telltale throb at his throat and raised her eyes to his.

He did want her. She could see it in his eyes; fierce and heated desire in amongst all that finely contained fury.

Kai's fingers squeezed tighter around her wrists, tight for the space of a heartbeat, and then he let go of her altogether and slowly stepped away.

'You need to get out more,' he said, and the lash of his words fell hard for all that he'd spoken so softly. 'It's time you *made* your father let you go.' He took another step back. 'It's wrong to shelter you.'

She was only half listening to him. The rest of her was lost in newfound revelations. 'You want me.'

'No.'

Jasmine's gaze tracked to the pulse point at his throat once more. 'Yes.'

'You're wrong.' His voice sounded huskier than usual. 'Jasmine, listen to me. Please. There's *so* much more to life than what you see before you. I promise you… Once you see what's out there… Once you come into your own…' He shook his head. 'You'll barely remember me.'

CHAPTER EIGHT

NICK RETURNED TO HIS room just on five-thirty that afternoon to find Hallie fast asleep on the bed, clothes on, shoes off, and pillows everywhere. You could tell a lot about a person by the way they slept, thought Nick. Those who slept curled and guarded were careful, guarded people. Those who slept tidily and peacefully could generally be counted on to be the same awake. It was the sprawlers you had to worry about, and Hallie Bennett was most definitely a sprawler. A Titian-haired dryad, who even in her sleep had the ability to charm him with her vulnerability even as she overwhelmed him with her fearlessness. It was a wicked combination. Apply it to lovemaking and it was deadly. No wonder a man couldn't think straight afterwards. No wonder he'd botched his retreat and thrown money at her not two minutes later. He'd hurt her. He knew he had. And deeply regretted doing so.

Turning away, he loosened his tie and the top button of his shirt, saw the jug of water on the sideboard and poured himself a glass. He didn't need this. Didn't need Hallie dominating his thoughts in the middle of complex negotiations so that instead of thinking profit margins he was thinking of ways to apologise and put the warmth back in her eyes and in her smile when she looked at him.

Not that he'd come up with a solution that didn't leave *him* exposed and vulnerable, which meant that he hadn't come up with a solution at all.

'Hey,' said a sleepy voice from the bed. 'How's business?'

Nick turned to face her warily. 'Fast.' He was expecting coolness from her, didn't find it, so he told her more. 'John wants negotiations settled by the end of the week. Apparently if they drag on too long it could signal the start of an inauspicious union and we wouldn't want that.'

'Absolutely not.' Hallie smiled and sat up on the edge of the bed looking tousled and inviting. 'Can it be done?'

'John has a team working on it. From his perspective it is. From my side of things there's just me and an inch of fine print in two languages to wade through, and that's *after* we finalise the conditions.' She looked concerned, then thoughtful. He hadn't meant to tell her that much, didn't know why he had other than that she was a good listener when she wanted to be. 'It's doable,' he said with a shrug. 'How was your day?'

'Fun,' she said with a smile. 'I got your vase. It's being delivered. We also went sightseeing and did a great deal of eating. Oh, and I have something to tell you about Jasmine, too. She only tried to seduce you because she saw you as an escape route from her father's over-protectiveness. I don't think we have to worry about her broken heart.'

Great, just great, all this subterfuge for nothing. Women! Nick scowled. Here he'd been trying to protect Jasmine from heartbreak and she'd been trying to *use* him.

'What?' said Hallie. 'I thought you'd be pleased.'

'I am.' He was. But between Hallie's blithe acceptance of his no more sex rule and Jasmine's ulterior motive for trying to seduce him, he was beginning to feel thoroughly under- appreciated. 'John's invited us out to dinner this evening,' he said by way of changing the subject before his ego was battered beyond repair.

'What time?'

'Seven.'

She glanced at the clock on the sideboard. 'Excellent. Enough time for me to wake up slowly. A person could really get used to this afternoon dozing caper.' She snagged a pillow and lay back down haphazardly. Her eyes drifted closed.

Nick couldn't move, wouldn't, for fear his feet would take him towards the bed and all this morning's rulemaking would be for nothing. 'How are you feeling?' he asked huskily and cursed himself the moment the words left his lips. He knew what that question was about, knew exactly where it was heading. He wanted to know if she was physically able to take him again.

She came up onto one elbow in a single fluid movement and fixed him with those glorious golden eyes. 'Are we talking mentally or physically?'

'Both.'

But Nick's dark, searing gaze slid from her face to her breasts and Hallie just knew what lay behind his question. 'You *want* me,' she breathed. 'You want to make love to me again!'

'No I don't.'

Oh yes he did. And the knowledge that he did was downright empowering. She smiled slowly, arched back so that the thin silk of her shirt stretched taut across her breasts and had the satisfaction of seeing him pale.

'Stop that,' he ordered.

Hallie smiled. 'You're absolutely right. Mustn't forget the rules.' She slid from the bed and sashayed towards the window with newfound confidence. 'You think anyone behind those windows over there in the distance would have a pair of binoculars?' she said. 'Because I thought I saw a glint of sunlight off something.'

'I didn't see anything,' he said.

That's because he'd been too busy watching her. 'Could have been a telescope, I guess. Or a camera.' She turned slowly, every move a subtle challenge. 'That's the trouble with a city this size. There's always someone watching.'

'We do *not* have an audience,' he said firmly.

'That you know of,' she corrected with a wicked grin. 'Better close the curtains just in case. Because if there was someone over there watching, they'd have an awfully good view of the bed.' Nick glanced at the bed at her words and Hallie thought she heard him mutter something beneath his breath. It didn't sound like a curse. Maybe he was praying.

'I'm going to shower before dinner,' he said doggedly. 'And I'm taking my clothes in with me.'

What, no parading that glorious body of his around in a towel?

Spoilsport.

'Go.' Hallie waved him away. 'I've already showered. All I have to do is change clothes and I'm ready for dinner. I'll do it while you're in the bathroom. And I'll cut you a break and head down and find Jasmine after that. Wouldn't want you breaking any more rules.'

Hallie tried hard not to smirk as he collected up fresh clothes and disappeared into the bathroom, closing the door behind him with far more force than was strictly necessary.

He wanted her. Nick Cooper, womaniser extraordinaire, wanted *her*, no matter what he'd said this morning. And heaven help them both, she wanted him.

With distance came rational thought. Hallie stood on the terrace and looked out over the immaculately groomed gardens then up at the clouds gathering in the sky and thought about the situation sensibly. The heady recklessness that had come with the knowledge that Nick wanted her had settled and reality had swooped down on her like a cloak. Nick didn't *want* to want her. He couldn't afford the distraction, he'd told her that from the start. Hence their deal, their rules, and the ten thousand pounds he was paying her when the week was up. He was counting on her to stick to her side of the bargain.

Don't get too close to him. Far better if she kept to the plan and played her role and never forgot that it *was* just a role. Come the end of the week she'd never see these people again. Not John Tey or Jasmine or beautiful, enigmatic Kai. She needed to keep a greater distance between herself and them too, only that was easier said than done for it wasn't Hallie's way to be shy or standoffish. She made friends easily. She'd enjoyed her shopping trip and lunch date with Jasmine. Their conversation had gone beyond that of polite strangers what with all their talk of mothers and brothers and Kai. Hallie felt a certain kinship with Jasmine already.

And bless her sweet and innocent heart, Hallie suspected that Jasmine Tey was in desperate need of a friend. She could see Jasmine from the corner of her eye, hovering uncertainly by the terrace door. Probably wondering what Hallie was doing moping around all by herself.

'Hey,' she said by way of greeting, and that was enough to get Jasmine moving forward to join her. 'This view is magic.'

'Yes.' Jasmine spared a glance for the view in question. 'So people say.'

'So what did you do this afternoon?' Not a corporate wife question, and Hallie half wished she could take it back and replace it with something else, but they'd exhausted the view conversation and she really didn't know what corporate wives usually talked about. Maybe her next comment could be about shoes.

'I spent some time in the garden,' said Jasmine. 'I did some Wing Chun.'

Hallie nodded and figured that of a certainty they could talk about martial arts without danger of the conversation becoming too personal. 'That's the one that was developed by a woman, isn't it? The one that's all about the very soft hands?'

'Yes. You know it?'

'Only in passing.'

'Legend has it that Wing Chun was a young village girl who caught the attention of a local warlord. He tried to force her compliance, and at the suggestion of an old village nun, Wing Chun challenged him to a fight. If Wing Chun lost, she would marry him. If she won, he would withdraw his suit. He was the best fighter in the region. She had one year to prepare.'

'And she won?'

'But of course.' Jasmine's smile made her look even younger than she was. 'The old village nun turned out to be one of the five elders of the Shaolin temple, and she trained Wing Chun in a such a way that a small woman had a chance against a much larger, more powerful rival. The system became known as Wing Chun.'

'I like that legend,' said Hallie. 'I'll have to ask Jake if he knows it.'

'Jake?' Jasmine shot her a questioning glance.

'He's my karate brother. He runs a karate school in Singapore. Kyokushinkai is the style he favours.'

'Very hard hitting,' said Jasmine. 'Very aggressive.'

'That's the one. Probably why he chose it.'

'Your brother is aggressive?'

'No.' An instinctive answer rather than an honest one. 'Okay, yes. Some would say yes. He has a world championship title. You don't get that by holding back.' Hallie smiled wryly. 'I remember when the pressures of raising four younger siblings got too much for him he either used to go and beat on an inanimate object until he was exhausted or go and find my middle brother and spar with him. Luke's the only one who can stand his ground when Jake stops holding back. He's the only one Jake trusts enough to let loose on.'

'So if brother Jake is a world champion and brother Luke is the only one who can match him…what does that make Luke?'

'Smug,' said Hallie with a grin and watched as Kai came out of the garage carrying a black sports holdall in one hand and two martial arts long sticks in another. 'What about Kai and martial arts? Is he any good?'

'Yes. Not that I really know how skilled he truly is. As with your brother, Kai holds back.'

'He needs a brother.'

'He has a mother on the mainland and two married sisters.' Jasmine hesitated. 'I asked Kai if he had feelings for me.'

Hallie spluttered and turned it into a cough. Jasmine saw through her efforts anyway.

'You don't think that was wise?'

'Depends what you want the outcome to be,' said Hallie. 'Did he respond?'

'He told me to get out and see the world.'

'Oh.' Hallie was beginning to understand just what she might have set in motion by pointing out to Jasmine that her handsome young bodyguard might just have unexplored feelings for her. Because even if he *did* have feelings for his young charge, there were complications aplenty when it came to acting on those feelings. Status differences and the issue of wealth. Differences in age and experience. And then there was Kai not wanting to take advantage of his existing relationship as protector to a young woman who'd barely begun to experience all that life had to offer. 'Jasmine, have you ever had a boyfriend?'

Jasmine lowered her gaze, delicate colour stained her cheeks and Hallie had her answer.

'Have you ever had a male friend?'

'Distant cousins,' said Jasmine. 'And Kai.'

'Female friends?'

'My calligraphy teacher when I was younger.'

'School friends?'

'My schooling took place at home, for the most part.' Jasmine bit her lip but her gaze was steady. 'I know you think I'm too sheltered. Kai thinks it too.' Jasmine reached around the back of her head to pull her ponytail over her shoulder. Even then her hair still fell to her waist. He thinks that the only reason I have feelings for him is because there's no one else in my world to have feelings *for* and I have to bestow them on someone.'

Hallie said nothing. The fact that Jasmine had been so readily swept away by Nick last time he was here suggested exactly that. Which made

Kai's suggestion that Jasmine step out and see the world kind of inspired.

'You should do it,' said Hallie. 'Go travel the world. Study. Learn. Open yourself to new people and experiences.'

'I could visit you and Nicholas in London.' Jasmine looked hopeful and Hallie's breath got stuck halfway down her throat.

'You could,' she croaked. How on earth were they going to make *that* work without Jasmine unearthing their subterfuge? 'Australia's a good place to visit too. My family home is in Sydney.' Maybe if she offered that, and then Nick could be away on business somewhere and Hallie would be on home turf and capable of offering Bennett hospitality to Jasmine rather than Cooper hospitality. Maybe *that* was an option. 'My family home is modest, but given that nobody lives there any more it doesn't have to be very big, and it *is* very central. I know Sydney far better than I know London.'

'But Nicholas is a Londoner, is he not?'

'Yes.' Damned if Hallie knew for sure. 'And London *is* very beautiful and loaded with history. Nick's mother's an architect. She's the one who can *really* show you round.'

Hallie hated this. The encouraging Jasmine to see more of the world with one breath and not being able to say come and visit me with the next. The wanting to reach out to the younger girl and not being able to.

'*Would* Kai have to accompany you?' Hallie asked hesitantly. 'Just how strong *is* the threat of you being kidnapped or… whatever? Is there still a known threat or is it mainly because of what happened to your mother?'

'It's a good question, isn't it?' said Jasmine. 'Maybe I should ask my father.'

Hallie sighed. 'I'm really not a good influence on you, am I? I make suggestions when I don't know any of the background details and I ask the wrong questions. I'm making a mess of this, Jasmine. Whenever we talk, I feel like I'm meddling in something I really shouldn't be touching at all. You shouldn't take too much notice of me.' It seemed like the best advice Hallie had given all day. 'You just shouldn't.'

Jasmine turned to look at the view, her forearms resting lightly on the terrace railing. 'Then who should I listen to?'

'Lots of people, Kai and your father included. Get as many opinions as you possibly can. And then make up your own mind.' Hallie turned to face the view too, bumping shoulders with the younger girl, a throwback gesture to the bumps her brothers had so often inflicted on her in lieu of hugs.

'Maybe I could go to Singapore for a while and learn Kyokushinkai from your brother,' said Jasmine with a tiny smile.

'And if you do that, do me a favour and don't mention my name to either Jake *or* Kai. I happen to like breathing.'

'Your brother would not have me for a student?'

'Let's just say you'd probably awaken memories that he's spent the last ten years trying to forget. Him and Kai, though, they'd probably get on just fine.'

'Hallie, what am I going to do about Kai? Because I think you were right. I think he might have feelings for me. And I have always had them for him.'

Hallie sighed and looked to the skyline for answers. 'Kai's in a difficult position; you know this already. He's loyal to your father. He has a duty to protect you. He's unlikely to confess to having feelings for you, even if it's true. I think honour would prevent it, don't you?'

'I do *now*,' said Jasmine glumly.

'On the positive side, he's given you some advice. He wants you to assert your independence and get out into the world and experience every facet of it. Only then will he be able to take your feelings for him seriously; if indeed your feelings for him remain strong.'

'He seems to think they won't.'

'Well, it's always nice to prove your doubters wrong.' Hallie grinned; she couldn't help it. 'Look at that world down there, Jasmine – just waiting to be tasted. I for one think Kai's advice is brilliant.'

Eventually Jasmine excused herself in order to go and get ready for dinner. With Jasmine gone, Kai gone off somewhere in the car, Nick in the shower and John Tey nowhere to be seen, Hallie took a stroll through the gardens. This wife for a week caper wasn't at all what she'd expected. How *did* Nick plan to manage any ongoing relationship with the Teys that did not involve her? Did he plan to bring her in every time he needed her? It seemed unlikely, not to mention fraught with difficulties. Maybe he had a quickie divorce planned. Which probably wasn't going to do much for his reputation as a stable man to do business with.

Hallie finished her tour of the garden just as Nick stepped out from inside. He headed her way, freshly showered, close shaven, and thoroughly eye-catching in dark trousers and yet another one of those crisp white shirts he wore without a tie. How a woman was supposed to keep her resolve around such a man was anyone's guess.

Hallie made sure her smile was warm but not provocative, her body language welcoming but not enticing as he joined her.

'I've had a rethink about the whole *wanting* dilemma,' she said casually, as if they were talking about nothing more important than the weather. 'I'm thinking denial is our best option.'

'I'm way ahead of you,' he said.

'I mean it's only for a few more days; I'm sure it's possible. That way you get to concentrate on your work and I get the money to finish my diploma.'

'Exactly. Thanks, Hallie,' he said with a relieved smile.

'Don't smile,' she warned him. 'My resolve is not altogether reliable. I'm also thinking I should be more supportive. More corporate wife and a whole lot less of me. Trust me, you'll thank me. What can I do?'

'Just do what you've been doing. Help keep the conversation easy, find common ground with Jasmine.'

'Oh, there's plenty of that,' she said dryly. 'And

I don't mean you. Have you any idea how *sheltered* she's been from real life? She's like a desert waiting for water. And she wants to come and visit us in London.'

Nick blinked. 'So… What did you say?'

'I said a very vague yes. You *do* have a plan in place when it comes to ongoing relations with these people, don't you? Because I'm starting to feel really slimy.'

'I have a plan,' said Nick. 'And it's a good one.'

Hallie shot him a look she'd learned from Tris, the one with the dagger-sharp tips. 'Or we could come clean about our relationship before we leave here.'

'Before or after I sign a binding business contract?' Nick sounded weary.

'Pretty sure I'm thinking before.'

Nick rubbed his hand up and over his face, over his hair. Definitely a weary man. One who probably had more use for sleep right now than he did a night out on the town with his hosts.

'Leave it with me,' he said. 'I know it's wrong, Hallie. I'll fix it. Soon. Just… give me a little more time.'

To what end? she wanted to ask him, but she wasn't his conscience and it didn't seem right to berate him now, when she was the one who had made this charade possible in the first place.

'So what's the purpose of this dinner?' she asked instead. 'Will you and John be discussing business?'

'From what I can gather, no. I have no plans to. I think this dinner is meant to be purely social. You, me, John, Jasmine and Kai. John says the restaurant we're going to doesn't look like much but it has the best Chilli Crab in Hong Kong. I hope you like it hot and messy.'

She did. Hallie felt her mouth begin to water, even as she looked down at her black trousers and pink shirt. The trousers were fine. The shirt was a problem. Chilli crab juice splattered over pink silk was not a good look. 'Maybe I should change my shirt. I have a patterned one that'd work.'

'Not the swirls.'

'You remembered!'

'Hard to forget.'

'I'll be five minutes.'

'I'll be waiting,' he said and smiled as she slipped away.

Something about tonight's expedition wasn't going to plan, thought Hallie as Kai returned from his sparring session and drew John's attention with a swift glance towards John's office. John nodded and excused them and together they went to attend to whatever business might have come up. Hallie glanced questioningly at Jasmine, who watched them go with wary eyes. Everyone but Kai was ready to go out to dinner.

'Twenty minutes,' said John when he rejoined them, with Kai now nowhere to be seen. 'Something came up, but we'll be ready to leave in twenty minutes.'

Hard not to be a little jumpy when half of Hallie's mind was turned towards wondering whether the 'something that had come up' might be that she and Nick weren't married and that she was here under false pretences. Another part of her overactive brain was wondering whether Kai was in there giving his notice because of the way Jasmine had confronted him earlier today. Hallie wasn't exactly blameless when it came to that scenario either.

Meanwhile, John remained the genial host, and there were pre-dinner drinks to continue with and then there was Kai's eventual appearance, and wasn't that worth waiting for, because Kai wore black trousers, a superbly cut Chinese-collared blazer and a black round-necked T-shirt under that. Moments later, Kai's phone beeped and he half turned away to look at it. Hallie studied the lines of his body in profile, tilting her head to afford her a better view.

'Are you checking out Kai?' Nick murmured. 'Because, you know, husband right here.'

Hallie smirked and slid her hand to Nick's neck and planted a kiss on his cheek. 'I was trying to see if Kai was carrying concealed. I think he is.'

'And you know this how?'

'Tris carries concealed a lot. I like to guess where.'

'Can't wait to meet him,' said Nick wryly. 'Really.'

Hallie watched as Kai pocketed his phone and nodded at John. Moments later their host pronounced them ready to leave for the restaurant.

A limousine sat waiting for them in the driveway, complete with driver. A man Hallie had never seen before stood just outside the Teys' front door. Two other men stood in the shadows of the garden, their faces hidden from view.

'Security,' said John as if it was all perfectly normal.

Maybe it was.

But Jasmine had only ever mentioned Kai when they'd talked about security. At no time had she mentioned that her father had an entire security *team* at his disposal.

'I've arranged for us to travel to the restaurant by ferry,' said John. 'It's worth it.'

'I am *so* ready,' said Hallie, and maybe her face had lit up as if it was Christmas, or maybe it was just that people needed a distraction, but John Tey was beaming at her, and Nick was smiling, Jasmine was moving forward towards the car and the tension was broken.

Kai was coming with them. The rest of the security team was staying behind. If Jasmine could live like this day-in day-out then Hallie could of a certainty do it for a week.

The limousine took them to a nearby ferry terminal and sat there purring silently as they made their way to the ferry. As soon as they were on, the engine fired up and the ferry pulled away from the dock. John steered them towards the bow of the boat. Jasmine lingered behind to speak with Kai, and Kai indulged her, his head bent towards hers, and they made a pretty picture, thought Hallie before glancing away and turning her attention to the view.

Jasmine joined her moments later, her shoulder brushing Hallie's as she slipped into position beside her at the railing. 'Kai says someone was watching the house earlier this afternoon, hence the extra security. He also said to tell you that, yes, he's carrying.'

'And a mind-reader too.' Hallie was impressed. 'Good to know.'

'He wanted to know why you were so observant. I told him about your brothers.'

'Yep. It's all their fault.'

Jasmine giggled, drawing her father's attention. John Tey looked pleased, indulgent, and of a certainty he enjoyed being out on the water. It showed in the pride with which he pointed out various landmarks. Jasmine teased her father about his enthusiasm, but Hallie readily fell in thrall, right along with her host. Hong Kong Central on one shore and Kowloon on the other, each of them trying to outshine the other with their neon-draped skyscrapers and their laser displays that lit up the night. The harbour itself was vibrant with activity; the playful breeze and the gentle slap-slap of waves against the boat a sensual delight; but it was the skyline that truly dazzled her, the thousands upon millions of lights that turned the busy harbour into fairyland.

'You've made John's night,' said Nick. 'Just watching your face was enough.'

'Nick, it's so beautiful.'

'Yes, it is,' he said quietly. But he wasn't looking at the lights of Hong Kong. He was looking at her.

Disconcerted, Hallie clasped her arms around her waist and looked away.

'Cold?'

'No.'

But he pulled her closer anyway, so that his warmth was at her back and his arms were around her waist, and she let him because they had an audience.

Because it felt right.

The restaurant was nothing more than a daytime pavement converted by plastic tables and chairs into a night time eating area. Large bins of live crabs, their pincers tightly tied, lined one side of the makeshift square, bamboo growing in tubs lined another. The shop front made the third side of the square. The fourth side was the gutter. It was badly lit, full of people, had no tablecloths whatsoever and, more importantly, loads of paper napkins.

A ragged waiter hurried over to greet them and escorted them to a vacant table, only to discover the tabletop sticky with beer. He skirted around it with an apologetic smile and showed them to an adjacent table. Bottled water arrived not thirty seconds later, along with cups for everyone. Chopsticks and crab claw crushers appeared in front of each person. There was no menu. The restaurant served crab; that was all it served.

'Cooked any way you like,' the waiter assured them.

They ordered a chilli crab platter along with beer and white wine, and Hallie sat back to wait while her stomach growled and her mouth watered with every fragrant, steaming platter that emerged from the shop front doorway.

'You're drooling,' said Nick. 'A good husband would point this out to his wife.'

'I am not drooling,' she said indignantly. 'I'm embracing the atmosphere.' As for him being a good husband... Ha! She wasn't even going to *start* thinking along those lines. As soon as this week was over she'd probably never see him again. She would do much better to think about *that*.

Another waiter emerged from the doorway, steaming crab platter in hand, and wove his way towards them, turning at the last minute to deliver the tray to the people who'd arrived just after them and been seated at the sticky table. 'Damn,' she muttered. 'So close and yet so far.'

'You're really not a half measures kind of girl, are you?' Nick was looking at her with a sort of wry resignation.

'Er, no. Is that a problem?'

'Not exactly.'

Hallie watched the activity at the next table as the waiter deftly served the topmost whole crab to a dark-haired European man and then distributed various bits and pieces of crab to his Asian companions.

'The first serving always goes to the honoured guest,' said Jasmine, noticing her preoccupation. 'It is the best.'

Hallie nodded. The Chinese were one of the most widespread and successful cultures on earth and force had nothing to do with it. Why use force when flattery and business acumen worked better? Only this time the flattery didn't seem to be working well at all. The dark-haired European was making strange choking noises and his face was turning an unnatural shade of purple. His hands were clutching at this throat; his eyes were glassy with tears.

'Just how hot *is* the chilli crab?' she whispered to Jasmine.

'Not that hot,' whispered Jasmine as the man toppled to the floor, foaming at the mouth, his chair sliding out from beneath him to ram into a half full tub of crabs and knocking it over.

The rest was chaos.

Diners fled. Crabs scuttled beneath nearby tables, some with their pincers tied, some with them snapping. Nick was over by the fallen man and Kai with him. John Tey was barking what sounded like directions into his mobile phone and the crabs…the crabs were on the run.

'Feet up,' said John and neither Hallie nor Jasmine wasted any time arguing that it wasn't very ladylike. Jasmine leaned over and dangled her chopsticks in front of a crab and, when it bit, deftly lifted it up and shot it back into the tub.

'Don't do it again,' ordered her father.

Jasmine just smiled.

The kitchen staff descended; the apron-clad cook protesting loudly that this wasn't his doing while nimble-fingered kitchen hands scooped escapee crabs into buckets.

By the time the paramedics arrived, the crowd around the fallen man was six deep. Hallie stood well out of the way as he was stretchered into an ambulance that zoomed off with its sirens wailing. He hadn't looked well. Truth be told, he'd looked practically dead.

'Probably just a reaction to seafood or something,' muttered Jasmine, worrying at her lower lip.

'Yeah,' said Hallie, reaching for Jasmine's hand and watching in silence as Kai casually liberated a piece of crab from the victim's plate, wrapped it in a napkin and pocketed it. He did the same for a crab piece from another plate. 'Reckon he's going to get them tested?'

'I think so,' said Jasmine, her attention all for Kai as he rejoined them.

'What?' he asked, eyeing Jasmine warily.

'Go wash your hands.'

CHAPTER NINE

NICK SHOULD HAVE KNOWN by now that when Hallie Bennett was added to the mix, events took distinctly erratic turns. No one was interested in continuing with crab for dinner. Kai rang for a car and a limo turned up, seemingly out of nowhere, to take them back to the house. Not Hallie's fault, the dinner debacle. Not anyone's fault, but the ease with which Hallie breezed into the next plan spoke of a flexibility that fascinated him.

Hallie Bennett did good chaos.

And she was very observant.

'Do we need to stop by a supermarket on the way home?' he heard Hallie whisper to Jasmine as the limo wove through the streets of downtown Hong Kong.

'I have noodles,' whispered Jasmine. 'I can't feed guests *noodles*.'

'Of course you can,' countered Hallie. 'Nick loves noodles. May I help you prepare them?'

'My father will have a fit if you do,' said Jasmine.

'Leave him to me,' he heard her say, and John heard her say, and Hallie knew it and smiled while Kai hid his smile behind his fist as he looked out of the window.

'Jasmine's going to give me a cooking lesson,' she told John cheerfully when they reached the house and he tried to usher them into the formal sitting room. 'She's going to show me how to cook stir-fry noodles. They're one of Nick's favourite dishes.'

Which was how they all came to be in the kitchen, every last one of them, with John fixing them drinks, Jasmine raiding the fridge for ingredients, and Kai setting a wok to heating and a huge pot of water to boiling on a gourmet gas stove.

'What are you up to now?' Nick asked her, pulling her aside when she would have headed over to help Jasmine.

'John's really embarrassed about the restaurant incident,' she whispered. 'I'm trying to avert disaster.'

'By eating in the man's kitchen? He's old

school, Hallie. He probably thinks this *is* a disaster.'

'We're going to have a simple meal in simple surroundings and we're all going to enjoy it,' said Hallie firmly. And when he still looked uncertain, 'John won't relax until you do. Trust me, it'll be fun.'

She was right, decided Nick a few minutes later. The informality of the kitchen and the routine task of preparing food went a long way towards dispelling the sombre mood that had descended after they'd left the restaurant. It wasn't quite the way he envisioned a 'real' corporate wife would have handled the situation but there was no denying that it worked. He watched Hallie quiz Kai about the type of oil he used and the paste he added, watched Kai chop ginger into slivers, his blade little more than a blur of speed. Watched Jasmine show similar skill with the cutting of bamboo shoots, and winced when Hallie immediately wanted to know how to speed-chop too. He watched, with fatalistic resignation, as Jasmine handed her the knife and Hallie took her turn at the cutting board, albeit under Kai's careful tutelage.

'So is this a traditional noodle recipe?' she wanted to know.

'Not quite,' said Jasmine, covering her grin with

a sip of white wine. 'This is a whatever we can find in the fridge recipe. We make it a lot.'

Kai shot her an admonishing frown.

'Well, we do,' said Jasmine.

'So will I,' declared Hallie.

Kai just shook his head.

'Your wife is a lovely woman,' said John from beside him. He too was watching the byplay. 'I'm glad she could accompany you this time.'

'So am I.' Now was the time to tell John Tey the truth. Parts of the truth, at any rate. Now, while Hallie, Jasmine and Kai were busy by the cook top and he and John were over by the kitchen table.

*John, she's not really my wife w*as all he had to say. No need to bring Jasmine into it at all. *John, she's not yet my wife, she's just Hallie and I needed her with me*.

That ought to cover it.

'John—'

'My daughter is often reserved around new acquaintances but not with your wife,' observed John. 'She has the knack of making others feel comfortable. She makes them smile from within. It is a rare gift.'

Yes, it was. Nick just wished he was immune to it, that was all. Because he wasn't. 'John—'

'Nick, I can't remember if you like bamboo

shoots or not,' said Hallie. 'Say you do, because I *really* like cutting them up.'

'Love 'em,' said Nick. 'John—'

'Bamboo shoots bring good fibre,' said Jasmine.

'So true,' said Hallie. 'And who doesn't need that. I'll cut up some more.'

Maybe now was not the time for true confessions, thought Nick. That cook top – not to mention the variety show assembled around it – was way too close for privacy.

'You were saying?' said John.

'Never mind,' he said wryly. 'Nothing that can't wait. Good wine.'

In what seemed like a remarkably short time, the vegetables were frying in the wok and noodles were bubbling away in a steaming pot of water. Hallie looked towards him, saw him watching her, and sent him a conspiratorial grin that warmed him through, before heading over to join them.

'Jasmine tells me you're fascinated by the Chinese Lion Dancing,' said John.

'Yes, we saw some boys practising their routines in the streets today. I made Jasmine stay and watch until they'd finished. They were so young, the boys beneath the lion's head. And so skilful!'

'Lion dancing is often an honoured family tradition. The boys are taught by their father or their grandfather from a very young age,' said John. 'The current national champions are performing at the Four Winds Ball on Friday evening. I've taken the liberty of acquiring tickets for us all if you're interested in attending.'

'I'm in,' said Hallie immediately, and with a somewhat belated glance in Nick's direction. 'Provided it suits everyone else?'

Nick nodded. It would take a stronger man than him to disappoint her.

'The ball is quite a spectacle,' said Jasmine as she set a heaped bowl of stir-fry in front of him, another in front of her father. 'There are fireworks at midnight and paper lanterns and decorations everywhere. Did you bring a gown?' she asked Hallie.

Hallie nodded. 'One. But it's kind of plain. Nick chose it and his mother agreed with him.' She sighed heavily. 'I was outnumbered.'

Plain my ass, thought Nick. There was nothing plain about the way the floor-length gold sheath had clung to every delectable curve. Nothing ordinary about the way it made her skin glow and her eyes turn to amber.

'We could shop for another one tomorrow,' suggested Jasmine.

'No.' Hallie waved the suggestion aside. 'I was

only teasing Nick. I love the gown. I'd have chosen it myself had I been given the chance. It may be plain but the cut is superb.'

'You could accessorize,' he said, remembering the jewellery he'd borrowed from Henry for just such an occasion. 'You could wear your necklace.'

'I have a necklace?' asked Hallie. 'Why did I not know this?'

'It's a surprise.'

'So you chose it without me?'

'With Henry's help.'

'I could have helped,' she said. 'I would have loved to help.'

'I think you'll like it.'

Hallie sighed. 'I dare say I will but that's not the point, is it. The point is I didn't get to help you choose it.'

Oh, yeah. Modern woman. Freedom. Equality. Respect. 'That was before I knew you liked to be in on the whole decision making process,' he said by way of defence. 'I wanted to surprise you.'

'I think surprise gifts are wonderful,' said Jasmine. 'They're so romantic. What did Nick give you for Valentine's Day?'

'A bright and shining future,' said Hallie. 'And a book about Hong Kong.'

'No flowers?' asked Jasmine.

'No.' Hallie shook her head sadly. 'He missed the boat there.'

'Maybe next year,' said Nick smoothly.

'I don't know how you keep up,' murmured Kai as he set another three bowls of noodles on the table and took a seat beside him.

'She sleeps a lot,' Nick countered dryly. 'That helps.'

Hallie was looking forward to getting some well-earned sleep. What she wasn't looking forward to was that pesky little time before she went to sleep. That five-metre walk from bathroom to bed, with her in her sleepwear and Nick over by the window all brooding and sexy. She made it to the bed by refusing to let her memories of this morning's lovemaking get the better of her. Did it by counting pillows. Denial was a hell of a lot easier when you didn't know what you were missing, thought Hallie glumly.

'I still have some work to do before tomorrow,' said Nick. 'It may be a while before I come to bed. I'll try not to disturb you.'

She risked a glance and immediately wished she hadn't as those knowing dark eyes met hers. 'It's okay,' she said, wiping damp palms down the sides of her boxers for girls. 'I have a plan.'

'You do?' His lips tilted. 'I can't wait to hear it.'

Actually it was more theory than plan. 'I think I need to sleep on the other side of the bed tonight.'

'You mean *my* side,' said Nick. 'And that would be because…?'

'It's obvious, isn't it? Last night I was trying to get to that side of the bed in my sleep so I figure if I start there tonight I'll stay there.'

'That's it? That's your plan?'

She nodded.

'No pillows?'

She shook her head. Fat lot of good the pillows had done. 'I'm keeping it simple.'

'Let me get this straight. You want to sleep on my side of the bed tonight because that's what's going to stop you from wrapping yourself around me and—'

'Yes,' she interrupted hastily. 'That ought to do it.'

'What if it doesn't?' he asked silkily.

Good point. 'Well, maybe one person could sleep on top of the sheets and the other between them.' Yes, that could work. She hurried on. 'I'll sleep between the sheets and you can sleep on top of them. You slept without a sheet over you most of last night.'

'That's because I couldn't find it, not because I didn't want it.'

Oh. 'A gentleman would offer the sheets to the lady,' she said finally.

'Whatever happened to equality?' Nick's smile was pure rogue.

Hallie sighed heavily. It wasn't always easy, practising what you preached. 'Or we could toss a coin.'

Nick dug in his wallet for a coin and sent it spinning towards her. 'Tails and I get to sleep between the sheets,' he said.

It was tails.

'Fine.' Hallie lifted her chin. 'I'll stay on top of the sheets.'

Nick's smile deepened.

She lay down on the bed with her back to him and tried to block him out, tried to get her weary body to relax and sink into sleep but it wouldn't comply. It was no good. She needed something over her. The red satin bedspread that she'd shoved to the bottom of the bed was her only option. She sat up, fully aware of Nick's amused eyes on her, drew the coverlet over her and lay back down. There. Much better.

Ten minutes later she sighed heavily and shoved the cover aside. She was too hot beneath it. She sneaked another look at Nick. He wasn't working; rather, he was watching her. Laughing at her, to be more precise.

'Change of plans?' he enquired.

'Yes. Separation by sheet has been abandoned.' She crawled between the sheets defiantly, wrenching the top one into place so it covered her from chin to toe.

'I don't suppose you have a new plan?' he asked her.

'Er, no.' Nothing sprang to mind.

'We could always sleep top to tail,' he suggested. 'I could have my head up this end and you could have yours up there. That way if we moved towards one another through the night we'd end up next to feet.'

'No!' she said hastily. 'Absolutely not!' That would be bad, really bad and it had nothing to do with feet. Because if he pulled the sheet *up* and she followed it *down* as she was wont to do, they'd end up next to something altogether different to feet and dear Lord, she was getting all hot and bothered just *thinking* about what a man of Nick's obvious sexual experience might think to do in such a situation. Never mind keeping her own rampant curiosity under control.

She was still tender, still a little sore from this

morning's lovemaking. What if Nick took it into his head to, you know, soothe her? She'd be lost. Possibly begging. Hell, she was close to begging already and she was only thinking about it. 'No top to tail.' She tried to make her voice sound firm, had the sneaking suspicion she'd just done a halfway decent Marilyn Monroe impersonation.

'Why not?' he said.

'Because I'm a lot shorter than you, that's why, and I might, ah, move *down* the bed somewhat. Especially if you're pulling the sheets that way. I might not end up next to feet at all.'

'You're right.' His eyes darkened. 'Top to tail is definitely out.' He didn't look amused any more, he looked… dangerous. 'I guess willpower will have to do.' He came over to her then, came right over to the bed and tucked the sheet firmly around her. 'Get some sleep,' he ordered, and leaned forward just enough to set his lips to hers for a kiss that would have been chaste but for the tip of his tongue that went skittering across her upper lip.

It was enough. More than enough, given where her thoughts had been to have her gasping in help-less delight and clenching the sheets to keep her hands from reaching for him. But her body arched towards him anyway, ached for him and Nick knew it did, dammit. And groaned for the both of them.

'Stop it,' he muttered. 'Stop me. We are *not* doing this. I have too much work to do.'

'Then go do it,' she whispered, closing her eyes tightly as if maybe, somehow, if she didn't see him he'd be easier to resist.

It was a long time before she fell asleep.

Even longer before Nick finally went to bed.

Hallie woke the following morning snuggled into Nick's side with her head on his shoulder and a hand at his waist. She lay perfectly still, her brain trying to figure the best way to extricate herself from his embrace while her body wondered why she would ever want to, her body being more than happy to stay right where it was, but that wasn't the point. The point was that she and Nick had decided lovemaking was out and it was going to take a joint effort to stick to that agreement. If either of them weakened they were both lost; it was as simple as that.

Hallie held her breath as she eased her hand from his waist and started to inch away from him, watching his face for any signs of waking, but he was sound asleep. There were shadows under his eyes that made him look vulnerable, shadows along his jaw that made him look dangerous. And a strength in his face that called to her even as she railed against it. What was it about this man that made him so hard to resist?

Because it wasn't his face and it wasn't his body, although both were gorgeous. No, it was something far more intrinsic than that, something that called to her very soul. And made it tremble. She backed up some more, felt the edge of the bed with her toes. Almost there. One foot on the floor and now the other as she eased her body from the mattress and stood up. Mission completed.

But she'd taken the sheet with her, which left her with a new problem. To cover Nick up again or not to cover. He didn't look cold. No goosebumps on that gloriously sculpted chest. Uh oh. She made the mistake of letting her gaze travel down his body and swallowed hard at the substantial bulge beneath his boxers. Never mind if he was cold or not, she needed him covered up. She gathered up the sheet and was just about to float it over his body when some sixth sense made her glance up at his face.

He was awake, watching her through slitted eyes, with a smile on his face and an invitation in his eyes that was practically irresistible. 'Going somewhere?' he said.

Hallie dropped the sheet and took a hasty step backwards, almost falling over her feet in the process. 'I, ah, yes. I thought I'd get up early and go down and see if Jasmine needs a hand with the breakfast preparations.'

Nick's smile deepened. 'Good of you,' he said.

'Yes, well, things to do.' Hallie smiled brightly as her heart pounded and her skin tingled at the sound of his sleepy, sexy rumble and with one last wayward glance for the dazzling display of blatant masculinity spread out in front of her she fled to the bathroom before temptation and Nicholas Cooper's smile got the better of her.

Jasmine hadn't really expected that last night's fun in the kitchen would make Kai less reserved around her this morning, so it came as no surprise when Kai refused her help with breakfast preparations and handed her a cup of piping-hot tea instead. She leaned against the counter and blew on the tea gently as she watched him ignore her. No conversation to be had here unless she initiated it, so that was what she did.

'Is the extra security still necessary?' she asked.

'For now.' This time Kai did look at her. 'Something feels off.'

'But you don't know what?'

'Not yet.'

'So where does the extra security fit in with your advice for me to get out and see the world?'

'I'm working on it,' was all Kai said.

And eventually Jasmine took her cup of tea to the library, which had for most of her life doubled as her school room. Curiosity led her to the computer, where she typed in the name Jake Bennett Martial Arts Singapore. Several links popped up. One for a karate school. Two were video clip links. Jasmine chose the videos, and was halfway through watching the first one when Kai came in and set a small plate of fruit at her elbow, before shifting behind her for a better view of the screen.

She liked him behind her; he made her feel safe.

He also made her blood quicken and her breath hitch, but those were responses he didn't want to know about.

'One of them is Hallie's brother,' she murmured.

'Which one?'

'I don't know yet.' They were both westerners. 'But he wins it.'

The competitors looked evenly matched, for a time. And then one of them blocked what would have been a crippling blow and it was as if he suddenly stopped holding back. 'That one,' said Jasmine.

Ten seconds later it was all over.

'This is the man who raised Hallie and her other three brothers,' murmured Jasmine. 'No wonder she's fearless.'

'Does Hallie fight too?'

'I didn't ask.' Jasmine pressed the replay link. 'Could you take him?'

Kai watched the fight from start to finish. 'No. I lack the rage.'

'Isn't rage a weakness?'

'Not for him. It's too much a part of him.'

'All this you can tell from one fight?'

Kai's lips tilted ever so slightly. 'It's just an opinion.'

'Will you lend me another opinion, Meng Kai?' Jasmine turned in the computer chair to look up at him and got caught in his eyes and couldn't look away. Neither, it seemed, could he.

'Ask.'

'I've been thinking about what I might want from this life. Where I might go. What I could do. I'm thinking of going to university in Singapore. Or even Shanghai.'

'To study what?'

'Life,' said Jasmine. 'And a communications degree.'

'Have you spoken to your father?'

'Not yet. I need to know if you think I'll need a bodyguard in this new life of mine before I approach him.'

'Your father will want to set you up securely, yes.'

'That goes without saying. What do *you* think I need security wise? Please, Kai. I need honesty from you on this, not just what you think my father will say. You've been part of my family for close to ten years now. You know things I don't. Have I ever been in real danger?'

'After your mother first died, yes. Lately, no. Your father has made it his mission to forge alliances that strengthen your safety and his.'

'Meaning?'

'Meaning no criminal organisation known to me would touch you for fear of the retribution that would follow.'

'Criminal organisations fear my *father*?'

'They do now. Money is always power. Your father has a great deal of money. And as I said, alliances have been forged.'

'With *criminal* organisations?'

'With other powerful business dynasties, yes.'

'Why did I not know this?'

'You've never asked.'

Jasmine's world was cracking wide open and

she didn't like the colour of what she found inside. She was still sitting looking up at him and it made her feel like a child. She stood up. Kai stepped back. Satisfaction flickered deep inside. Maybe he should be scared of her, of the truths she could drag out into the light. Wisdom suggested that maybe she should be scared too, but Jasmine didn't back down. She was so tired of being protected from the truth. 'So why do we have you?'

'Your father lost something very valuable. He demanded something of equal value in return from those who were ultimately responsible for your mother's death. A firstborn son – given freely. One charged with protecting his daughter.'

'*You?*'

Of all the reasons she'd ever contemplated when it came to Kai's continued presence in her life, this hadn't been one of them.

'Me,' offered Kai quietly.

'Your *father* was responsible for my mother's death?'

'In my father's defence, he was dealing with a takeover bid at the time. He did not authorise your mother's kidnapping. The perpetrators were family nonetheless. In order to avoid wholesale slaughter of our family, reparation was made.'

'You,' she said again.

Kai shrugged. 'In *your* father's defence, he has treated me like a son. Had I wanted to study, I could have studied. I'm privy to all your father's business dealings. I represent him in some of them. They're all legal, by the way. Should I want out of my family's business, your father has given me a way out.'

'And do you want out of your family business?' she asked faintly.

Kai's lips twisted briefly. 'I am still my father's loyal son.'

'Kai, I don't even know what that *means*.'

'It means I do as I'm bid.'

And presumably had no say in the matter. 'Does this…arrangement have an expiry date?'

'Your father may choose to release me. He hasn't yet.'

'My father will release you,' she said fiercely. 'I'll *make* him release you.'

'Leave it.'

'How can I *leave it* if you're here against your will because of some crazy deal made by two stubborn old men? If you wanted me to leave it, why even *tell* me?'

'You asked if I thought you needed a bodyguard once you leave your father's house. Recent events notwithstanding, I don't think you do. Between your father's reach and mine, you could study in either Singapore or Shanghai and still be fully protected. You don't need me at your back – not in person. You never have.'

'So I'm free.'

'As free as you want to be.'

'And you're not.'

Kai said nothing.

'Can't you see how wrong this is? What they've done to you?'

The ghost of a smile flashed across his features. 'Better this than dead. And there would have been a *lot* of dead. In serving your family I also serve my own. Reparation has been made. It continues to be made.'

'My father is a monster.' Jasmine felt hollow. 'And so's yours.'

'When you are older you will understand.'

'What? That it's perfectly all right for an innocent man to pay for another's mistakes?'

'That honour has been served.' Kai's tone was implacable. 'Let it go, Jasmine. You're not a part of this. Keep it that way.'

Not a part of this? 'How can you say I'm not a part of this, Kai? I've been a party to this for almost ten years.' She wanted to push at him and beat on him, cling to him and take him with her into the pit of despair that opened beneath her feet. 'How can I not be a part of this when they gave me you?'

Jasmine would have gone to confront her father right then and there but for the hand Kai wrapped around her upper arm. He stepped in close and there was no wrenching away. Jasmine knew from yesterday's sparring exercise exactly how that would turn out.

'Settle,' he whispered, with his lips to her ear. 'Don't challenge your father over this. He has too much to lose. He won't back down. He can't.'

'He will. Let you go or lose me; those are my terms.'

'Only a child would judge things so simply. Are you still a child, Jasmine? Or would you rather I saw you as an adult?'

She turned her head and caught his swift expulsion of breath and wanted to chase it right back to his mouth, so firm and fine and close. 'I hate you.'

'No, you don't,' he muttered, and then with a stifled curse, he touched his lips to hers, soft and fleeting, and the desire that raced through her – hot on the heels of fury – now wasn't that a fine sensation.

She might have gasped. He might have hesitated before transferring his lips to the curve of her lower lip and then gently, ever so delicately, wetting it with his tongue.

Kai's kisses weren't as good as his kisses in her dreams – they were better. Jasmine tilted her head slightly and positioned her lips more fully against his and his taste, when finally his tongue curled around hers, was sharply perfect.

Mine. That thought sang through her, dark and disturbing.

More. She wanted it, put her hand over his heart in search of it as his hand came up to cup her jaw and tilt her head for better access.

More bruising now, his mouth against hers, and she wanted that force, returned it, tasting deep inside his mouth and then she closed her eyes and sucked gently on his tongue and his heart kicked at that so she did it some more.

When he wrenched away from her she let him go, eyes half closed and her heart thundering in her chest as if she'd climbed a thousand stairs.

'How can you still want me?' he asked harshly, as if he'd run those thousand steps right along with her. 'Knowing who I am?'

'How will I ever *not* want you?' she accused right back at him. 'Knowing what you are.'

CHAPTER TEN

HALLIE EYED JASMINE'S FACE and mouth curiously when Jasmine entered the breakfast room but opted to comment on the delights of chilled red dragon fruit rather than Jasmine's dishevelled appearance, and for that Jasmine was grateful.

'Like kiwi fruit only better,' said Hallie, before scraping the last of the flesh from the fruit and swallowing it with a satisfied sigh. 'Do you have any plans for today?'

'Apparently I'm supposed to settle.' Kai's words, not hers.

'Settle for what?'

'Exactly.' Why had Kai kissed her exactly? To confirm what he already knew? That she was half-way to being in love with him? To remind her that she was no longer a child? Or maybe he'd thought that a kiss between them wouldn't work the way it had.

Rapture or despair? Because both were right there, waiting for her to choose.

She couldn't help the choked laughter that bubbled from her lips. Grow up, Kai had as good as told her. Grow up and step into the real world.

'Jas?' said Hallie quietly. 'Everything okay?'

Her mother used to call her that. Hallie didn't know. Couldn't know.

'Jasmine?'

'Jasmine is better,' said Jasmine faintly. 'My mother used to call me the other.'

'Jasmine it is.' Hallie Bennett-Cooper understood. 'How can I help?'

'Just talk.'

'About what?'

'University. Living abroad. Brothers. Marriage. Anything.'

And, obliging guest that she was, Hallie did, while Jasmine turned her attention towards the little things that made up her days. The clearing away of food, the replacing of spent incense sticks, taking receipt of the dry cleaning that was delivered to the door, welcoming the gardener who came twice. Mid-morning saw her and Hallie back in the library, Hallie browsing through a collection of books on Chinese art while Jasmine arranged two upcoming social events for her father.

'Gaps,' said Hallie suddenly.

'Gaps?'

'I'm watching you run your father's household, taking on some of the duties that your mother would have performed, and it reminded me of the gaps that have to be filled when a family member isn't there any more. In our family, Jake tried to fill them all.'

'You didn't take on any household duties in your family?' asked Jasmine curiously.

'No. I was the youngest. And then Jake got married and his wife tried to mother us and take on the household duties and, boy, did *that* not work out. And then Ji left and it still took me years to realise that the best part of Jake had gone with her. Jake stayed with us because we had no one else, and we let him because we were too young and too blind to realise what it cost him.'

'Why are you telling me this?'

'You told me to talk. I have been but I'm all out of small talk. I'm up to the spilling of confidences. Other people's confidences, at any rate. Would you rather I stopped?'

'No!' Jasmine shook her head as if embarrassed.

'No, I like hearing it. I like the comparison. I would hear more of the nature of gaps.'

'You know how sometimes you just want to go back in time and redo something, only this time you'd do it all differently?' said Hallie. 'Whenever I think of Jake's ex I want to go back and do it all differently.'

'You should write to her. Tell her your regrets.'

'No. It's too little too late. Besides, I don't even have an address for her.'

Hallie deserved the look Jasmine sent her.

'Would you help me look for one?' asked Hallie suddenly. 'As in now? Today? Because I've tried to find Ji online before but she's Chinese and I come unstuck with the language.'

'Of course.' It would help take Jasmine's mind off other things. 'What's her name?'

'Jianne Xang. Bennett,' Hallie added as an afterthought.

Twenty minutes later they had an address and Jasmine wrote it out carefully on a thick vellum envelope and then Hallie dictated her childhood address and Jasmine wrote that one on the back before handing the envelope to her with a flourish.

'I feel like a child again,' said Hallie shakily. 'About to beg forgiveness.'

'I felt like that yesterday,' said Jasmine. 'Today I'm a disillusioned old woman.'

'What happened to glories of young woman-hood?'

'I appear to have skipped them.'

'That's too bad.' Hallie held up the envelope. 'I'm going to put this upstairs. Come with me and tell me if the gown I plan to wear tonight is appropriate. I'm pretty sure the young woman in you will know.'

The young woman in her did know. The gown was glorious and Hallie was going to look stunning in it.

And then they rustled through Jasmine's closet and she didn't have a thing to wear.

She didn't want to look fresh and pure and youthful. She needed a colour that would hold up against Hallie's gold and a cut that would showcase what womanly curves she'd managed to acquire.

'How much time do we have before your father and Nick get home?' asked Hallie after rifling through Jasmine's closet as well and coming up empty.

'I'm not sure. I believe it depends on how long the lawyers take. Today everyone is in the same room. Nick and his representatives, my father and his. Together they will work through the contract, making changes along the way.'

'Sounds very collaborative. Is that how it's always done?'

'This close to closure, yes.'

Jasmine waited for Hallie to pump her for more information, but Hallie just nodded and for that Jasmine was grateful. She'd have liked Hallie a lot less had she begun to pump Jasmine for information regarding her father's business.

'Do we have a driver who is *not* Kai who could take us gown shopping?' asked Hallie and Jasmine smiled. This almost felt like friendship. And she badly needed a friend right now.

'We still have the extra security,' said Jasmine. 'Why don't we ask?'

The clothing store Jasmine took them to didn't do price tags. They did private viewings, three sales assistants for every customer and one customer at a time, and they did accessories and shoes and if it wasn't for Jasmine's innate poise and comfort in such a place, Hallie would have been out of there within thirty seconds of walking through the door.

Shopping with Clea had been upmarket but fun.

Shopping in hushed and deferential silence was

no fun at all, especially when there seemed to be a look but don't touch policy in place and hardly any clothes on display.

'Are you sure we'll find what we're looking for here?' Hallie eyed the red beaded confection wrapped around a dressmaker's dummy with scepticism. Clea would have loved it. Hallie loved the colour. But it was an older woman's choice. They all were. 'Music would be good,' she murmured and one of the saleswomen nodded and shortly thereafter, soft music began to play, the remaining sales staff asked Jasmine what she was after and gown after gown started appearing from behind closed doors.

Jasmine smiled. 'Better?'

'Much,' murmured Hallie. 'I'm all for broadening my horizons, and this… this definitely qualifies. 'Let's find you the perfect gown.'

The sales staff tried – they did try – but so many of the gowns they brought out for Jasmine to see were simply too loud, too sophisticated or too much of a fashion statement.

'Not flattering,' she said of a black sheath with a low-cut neckline, for Jasmine simply didn't have the curves or the confidence to pull off such a combination. 'No,' she said to the next one, and no again to the one after that.

'No,' said Hallie with a shake of her head for a strapless red gown with gold embroidered accents on the bodice.

'This is very nice,' protested Jasmine.

'It is. But I've seen what else is in your cupboard and this is too much of a departure from it. Trust me; this is a mistake I've already made. I wasn't allowed to *wear* half the clothes I bought home from my first solo shopping trip.'

Two of the three sales assistants glared at her. Hallie addressed her next words to the third woman. 'This dress is beautiful, yes, and it does look flattering on, but more than anything else, we need something stunning, simple and *subtle*. Miss Tey is a widower's daughter. Let's not give her father reason to send the dress back.'

The next dress they brought out was a full-length midnight-blue gown with a sweetly demure neckline and next to no back. It fitted Jasmine to perfection.

'Hair up,' directed Hallie with a hand gesture that signified as much. Within moments, the sales staff had Jasmine's long hair wound around into a roll and secured with chopstick-like hairpins with pearls dangling from the ends. Everyone but Jasmine stood back and nodded. Jasmine looked at herself in the full length mirror and frowned.

'It's so plain.'

'Understated,' said Hallie firmly. 'Not plain. Turn to the side and look,' said Hallie. 'Better?'

Jasmine turned. 'Yes.'

'Now from the back.'

Jasmine turned again and looked over her shoulder at the mirror and gasped.

'Bingo,' said Hallie.

This was the one.

They returned to the Tey residence just after two. No sign of anyone else yet. Time enough for Hallie relax and watch the sheen of misery fall back over Jasmine's eyes.

'I thought I chased that away,' she murmured around a steaming cup of green tea.

'Chased what away?'

'The sadness.'

'You did, for a while.' Jasmine's lips curved into a regretful smile. 'And I am grateful.'

'Want to tell me what's troubling you?'

'I can't,' said Jasmine.

'Any plans for Kai at the ball?'

'Not yet.' Jasmine chewed on her lower lip. 'Hallie, what would you do if you found out that someone in your family had been lying to you by omission? Keeping ugly truths from you? What if they turned out to be…less honourable than you believed them to be?'

'People often lie,' said Hallie carefully. 'Sometimes they do it to protect another person's feelings; sometimes it just seems like a good idea at the time.'

Never again was Hallie going to pretend to be someone's wife for a week. Not even if they offered her planet earth as compensation.

'I don't mean the little things,' said Jasmine. 'What if it's a lie that changes the fabric of your world?'

'Then I guess after I'd stopped beating on them that I'd have to ask them why they did it.'

'And if you didn't like the answer?'

'Guess I'd have to beat them up some more.'

'Could you ever turn away from them? From Nick?'

'No.' Hallie thought about it a moment more. 'No. My family may not be perfect but neither am I. They're mine. I'm theirs. I wouldn't turn away.'

'Okay,' said Jasmine raggedly. 'Okay.'

The defeat in the younger girl's voice set the hair on Hallie's arms standing on end. 'Jasmine?'

Hallie waited until Jasmine had lifted her gaze from the intricately patterned carpet that graced the floor between them.

'You know how I said yesterday that you should make up your own mind rather than listen to some clueless stranger's advice, particularly when that clueless stranger has no real grasp of the bigger picture?'

'I remember.'

'That advice still stands.'

***

CHAPTER ELEVEN

NICK, JOHN AND KAI returned just on two-thirty that afternoon. 'We're almost there,' said Nick when Hallie dragged him into the garden to get the low-down on what had transpired throughout the day. 'The lawyers are going through finalising the contracts tomorrow. All we have to do then is sign them.'

'And you're happy with the deal?' she asked him.

'It's a little less than I was hoping for in some respects, a little more in others. I think John feels the same way.' Nick shot her a weary smile. 'I have a new appreciation for haggling as an art form but in the end we got there. It's a fair deal. We both stand to make a lot of money.'

'What about coming clean?'

'Soon.'

'When? Because I'm here all day with Jasmine, Nick. And I really like her and if ever there was a person who needed a friend…'

'Softie,' said Nick. 'If it's any defence for the mess I got myself into last time I was here, I thought that too.'

Hallie ran her palm along a fragrant, waxy-leaf hedge. 'I like everyone here, Nick. I like John Tey and Kai, and in spite of the fact that you were the one who got me into this mess, I also like you. I'm in *like* and the being married to you lie is doing my head in.'

'You planning to bail on me, Hallie?' He looked good standing half in shadow and half framed by light.

'No. But I'm struggling. Dirty conscience and all. Not that I'm harping.'

'You are so harping.'

'Wife,' said Hallie by way of explanation. 'Surely there are perks?'

'What did you do today?' Nick asked next.

'We bought a ball gown for Jasmine.'

'Should I be afraid?'

'No, you're not paying for it, luckily. Kai's the one who should be afraid.'

'Why Kai?'

'Because Jasmine cares for him and she wants

his attention and she's a very beautiful and thoughtful girl.'

'He's her bodyguard.'

'Bonus points for him.'

'Is this your doing?' Nick asked suspiciously.

'You give me far too much credit.'

'I'm really not sure what to give you.'

'Reassurance that everything is going to turn out just fine would be good. Because I need it.' She really did. 'Too Cinderella?'

'Have you ever considered a future in computer game development?' Nick asked with a wry grin as he drew her into his arms and let her rest there. 'Because, seriously. Xia's not nearly as interesting as you.'

'Xia's your fighter girl, right? The one with the—'

'That's the one,' said Nick. 'She could use your input.'

'Geek.'

'Guilty,' he said. 'When was I not?'

'Oh, when you were charming and funny and convinced me that pretending to be your wife was a good idea. And there was *nothing* geeky about your performance the other morning in bed.'

'Geeks are very thorough,' he said with an engaging grin. 'That performance was pure geek.'

'And what was *my* performance?'

'Memorable,' he said with a sigh. 'You want to know what I was thinking about during a heated discussion of clause thirty-six paragraph two today?'

'Virgins?'

'You. Who is now *not* a virgin. Because of me.'

'Are you still on that guilt trip?'

'Yes.'

'It was a gift given freely, Nick. Let it go. And *don't* try and give me more money.'

'Got it. I am *still* sorry for that confusion. I will be forever haunted by that confusion.'

'Truly, Nick. We're good.' But Nick still looked conflicted, and his eyes looked tired. 'Why don't you go upstairs and rest for a while? Take a nap.'

'I would but the bed upstairs holds a few too many memories of you in it. I won't rest if I go up there and I sure as hell won't sleep.'

'Are you flirting with me?'

'Nope.' He eyed her darkly and then looked away, looked out on that glorious view, and ran a hand through his hair. 'And even if I am, I'm not.' He took a deep breath. 'Feel like coming into the city with me? Just you and me? Take a break from being here?'

'Absolutely,' said Hallie. 'We can relax for a

while. Be tourists instead of fake man and wife. I can be me. You can be you. Press the pause button and get away from the game for a while. I do hope Xia and Shang have a pause button, by the way. Preferably connected to the online ordering options for the nearest food delivery service. I'm thinking that feature would win you many friends. Am I talking geeky enough for you?'

'Keep talking,' he murmured with a curve to his lips that Hallie found arresting. 'It's not geek-speak exactly, but I like it.'

Twenty minutes later they were standing on a chaotic sidewalk in downtown Hong Kong, Kai having dropped them off and Nick having assured him that they'd catch a taxi back. He was tired, he was irritable, and denying his fierce sexual attraction to Hallie really wasn't working for him, but there was no denying that the suggestion they take a break was a good one.

'Where to first?' he asked, because in this he could indulge her. Whatever Hallie wanted to do this afternoon, he was of a mind to make it happen.

'I have no fixed plans,' she said, standing stock still on the busy Hong Kong sidewalk and staring up at the neon signs that flashed all around them.

'Except if I see something we can get for Jasmine as a thank you for having us gift – at which point the plan is to get you to buy it for her.'

'Do you have anything particular in mind?'

'I'm sure I'll know it when I see it,' she said blithely.

Nick groaned. This was bad. This was going to take forever.

'I am open to suggestions,' she added.

There was a God.

'Perfume,' he said firmly, not two minutes later as they stood at a department store perfume counter. 'We'll get her some perfume.'

'Predictable,' said Hallie with a sigh.

'Reliable,' he corrected, and, staring at the dazzling selection of perfumes on offer, 'You choose.'

'I'll have to smell them first and find the one that fits Jasmine best. Of course, I already know what half of them smell like so it shouldn't take too long.'

Maybe perfume hadn't been such a fast and easy solution to the gift-buying problem after all, thought Nick gloomily as Hallie picked up a nearby tester bottle and sniffed.

'This one's too overpowering. Jasmine's far more delicate than that,' she said with a grimace, hastily returning the bottle to the counter and pick-

ing up another. 'And this one's too old-fashioned.'
She moved along the counter to the next cluster
of little glass bottles, plucked one from the middle
and handed it to him. 'Try this one.'

He took it, sniffed it. 'Nice.' But Hallie rejected
it.

'It is nice, but it's all top note, there's no depth.
It's too chaste. Jasmine's a woman not a girl.'

'Maybe she could wear it in one of her more
girlish moments,' he suggested, and stifled a sigh
at Hallie's measured, 'No'. This was going to take
forever.

The next one was nice too. Hell, they were all
nice but according to Hallie they just weren't right.
And then Hallie pointed towards a small vial high
on a shelf and the salesgirl obligingly got it down
for her. She lifted the stopper, took a deep sniff of
the perfume and sighed happily. 'This is it,' she
said. 'This is Jasmine.'

Nick took it and smelled it. Nice. Why it was
Jasmine and the others weren't was beyond him
but if Hallie was satisfied, so was he. 'I see what
you mean,' he said, with a nod for good measure.

'Liar!' Her laughter was warm and spontaneous,
a reflection of the woman. 'Tell me why I chose
it.'

'Er, whim?' Her eyes narrowed and her chin came up. He still loved that look.

'I've just given you some huge hints on how to buy perfume for a woman. Huge! You could have at least paid attention.'

'I did pay attention.'

'Alrighty then.' Her hands went to her hips. 'Choose one for me.'

Nick stared at Hallie, stared at the perfumes, all two hundred odd bottles of the stuff, and nearly broke out in a cold sweat. 'I could use a hint,' he said.

Hallie moved down the counter again, to yet another cluster of bottles, her hand hovering over one particular bottle before finally picking it up. 'Here. This is one my mother used to wear; it brings back some wonderful memories of her. It's warm, elegant, beautiful. I love it, but I don't wear it.'

'You call that a hint?'

'Big one.' Her voice was grave but her eyes were laughing.

Nick sighed heavily, took the perfume her mother used to wear out of her hand and sniffed. He knew that smell, loved it of old for Clea wore it too. It wasn't Hallie, she was right. But it was close.

He attacked the problem systematically; working his way through the entire cluster of perfumes in front of him and rejecting all but three bottles. He took his time with these, undecided, before making his final choice and handing it to her. 'This one.'

'Are you sure?' she teased. 'How do you know? Because I swear your nose went on strike ten bottles ago.'

'Smell it,' he urged.

She took a deep sniff. It had some of the same ingredients as her mother's perfume, the same warmth in the base, but it was different too. More exotic and youthful. More vibrant.

'Well?' he asked gruffly.

'I like it.'

'How much do you like it?'

'A lot.'

The approval in Hallie's smile made Nick's heart stutter. 'Promise me you'll wear it for me to the ball.'

'You are bad news,' she said as a shop assistant hovered in the background. Hallie held up the chosen perfumes for both her and Jasmine and the assistant ducked behind the counter to get them. 'Smooth as silk one minute and sweet as Friday's child the next.'

'It's a gift.'

'It's a weapon. Your mother should have warned me. Now I'm going to choose a fragrance for you.'

'Don't!' he said hurriedly. 'What if we clash? Besides, I already have perfume back at the Teys'. He had antiperspirant deodorant in his toiletries bag. Close enough. 'Walk with me through the alleyways for half an hour. That's all I want. Let me show you the Hong Kong I like best.'

She could do that.

Hallie loved doing just that, because it was here that she found what had been missing in the spotless airport and glittering department stores; here she found the hawker stalls and the food carts; the scent of yesteryear and the bustle of an exotic, vibrant culture.

This was the Hong Kong Nick liked best? She should have guessed. Nick would always seek out the real, it was part of his charm.

What kind of woman would he choose when he finally *did* take a wife? Hallie wondered. Would she laugh with him and delight in the boy beneath the man? Would she be worldly and elegant? An asset to his business interests? Would he choose a *real* corporate wife? Hallie was so preoccupied with her thoughts she almost fell over Nick as he knelt down to examine a tiny street urchin's meagre fake watch selection that had been lined up with military precision on a dirty scrap of towel.

'Cartier,' he said, grinning up at her. 'Bargain. You want one?'

Dammit, she knew this would happen. She was falling for him, heart over fist. 'That one,' she said, pointing towards a plain-faced gold watch in the middle of the row. 'Does it work?'

'The hands are moving. That's always a good sign,' he said as he handed over enough money to buy ten fake watches and waved away the change. 'Where to now?' he said, handing her the watch.

'There's a rollercoaster,' she said, and watched Nick's smile break out. 'At Ocean Park. I read about it in your guidebook.'

'Too far away for today. But I could definitely make it happen before we go.'

'In that case, how about we find a bar with a view and just sit and watch the world turn for a while? I've already shopped today. I'm all shopped out.'

'I know of a bar or two with a view,' he said.

'I do love a knowledgeable man.'

'Are you flirting again?'

'Not at all. I'm speaking. There's a difference.'

'You may have to point it out,' he murmured, his attention fixed on the cars whooshing past them at speed. 'Because my body's having trouble picking the difference.'

'Can your brain pick the difference?'

'My brain's enchanted either way. I think it's karma coming back to bite me for thinking this plan was ever likely to work in the first place.'

They were standing beside a busy road and a free taxi was heading their way in the centre lane. Nick saw it about the same time as she did and stepped to the side of the pavement and raised his hand. The taxi swerved abruptly and shoehorned itself into the side lane to the accompaniment of blaring horns and rude gestures.

'I think he's seen us,' said Nick.

'Yeah, but do we want to get in a car with him?' she muttered. The taxi wasn't slowing down. If anything, it was speeding up. 'He's not stopping,' she said and stepped back from the kerb just as someone stumbled into Nick from behind, pushing him onto the road.

'Nick!'

It all happened in a screaming blur. She lunged for his shirt, caught the very edge of it and heaved him backwards with all her strength as the taxi sped past, mere millimetres from the gutter. There was nothing to break her fall as they tumbled back in a heap, her elbow connecting painfully with the cement, her head hitting it moments later, followed by Nick's big body pushing every last ounce of breath from hers as he landed on top of her. Then he was on his hands and knees beside her and she was seeing double, triple even. Either that or the entire population of Hong Kong was staring down at her.

'Hallie. Hallie! Can you hear me?'

Nick's face loomed above her, a familiar face against a sea of oriental ones and she clung to it as a shipwrecked sailor clung to a beacon. 'He wasn't going to stop,' she whispered.

'No. He wasn't.' Nick looked almost as shaken as she felt as his hands carefully brushed a stray strand of hair from her eyes. 'How do you feel? Where do you hurt?'

'I scraped my elbow,' she said. 'I hit my head.'

'How many fingers am I holding up?'

'None. Your hands are in my hair.'

'Right,' said Nick. 'How many now?'

'Two.' Her head was starting to clear, her vision was returning. She tried to sit up, and was immediately assisted in this by a hundred helpful hands that didn't stop at sitting but lifted her gently to her feet. 'Thank you,' she said, and 'Thank you again,' as someone handed her her handbag and the bag with the perfumes in it. There was an animated discussion going on somewhere in the crowd, lots of shouting and hand waving. Finally a business suited Chinese man approached them both.

'You were pushed,' he told Nick. 'This man says he saw it.' He pointed to a wizened little man at the back of the crowd. 'He says it was a man wearing a red cap, zip jacket and jeans. A young man.'

Nick nodded, thanked both men.

'I thought I saw someone push you too,' said Hallie. 'But I didn't see a face.' She'd been too busy trying to grab him.

'C'mon.' He was leading her towards a quiet doorway of a shop that had already closed for the evening. 'I think we should get you to the hospital. Get you checked out.'

'No Nick! That'll take hours! I fell over and you landed on top of me, that's all. I grew up playing football with my brothers, I'm used to it.' Okay, so she was exaggerating. Just a little. He didn't look like he was buying it anyway. He lifted her arm for a closer look at her elbow, she turned her arm so she could see it herself. It was a nasty graze. Damn. Hallie scowled. 'This is so not going to go with my gown.'

'Be serious,' he said gruffly. 'You could have concussion.' He threaded his hands through her hair and tilted her head forward, examining her skull with gentle fingers.

'Ow!' She winced when he hit the spot that had connected with the concrete.

'It's swelling,' he told her. 'You're going to have an egg.'

'Not if I get some ice on it.' Which could happen at any nearby bar, no need for a view. 'Really, Nick. I feel okay. Let's just… sit somewhere for a while. If I start to feel woozy you'll be the first to know.'

His eyes were dark and searching as his hands moved from her hair to frame her face. 'You scared me,' he said simply. And lowered his lips to hers.

He was very gentle, very careful, and Hallie trembled at the tenderness she found in his embrace. She closed her eyes, lifted her hands to his shoulders, and opened her mouth to him, revelling in his warmth and the dark delicious taste of him. He took his time, such an agonisingly long time he took before his tongue touched hers and duelled. There was no rush, no haste and he built that kiss so slowly and surely that stars exploded in her head for the second time that afternoon. *Here* was what she'd been waiting for all her life. Passion laced with sweetness. Strength tempered by caring and she wound her arms around his neck and drank in that sweetness and that strength with no thought for anything but the aching need to have it.

It was Nick who broke the kiss, his breathing ragged as he rested his forehead against hers. 'We have an audience,' he muttered. 'And we're in a public place. The way I figure it, we're still within the rules here.'

'Lucky us,' she whispered. It didn't feel like they were still working within the rules. It felt like they were breaking every last one of them.

He stepped back, seemingly reluctant to let her go. 'Let's find somewhere to sit. And in five minutes' time exactly, according to your new watch, you're going to let me know if you want to see a doctor?'

It was a question, couched inside an order, and drove home the point that for all the similarities between Nick and her brothers, in this he was quite, quite different. Seeing a doctor was her call, her choice to make and she was grateful for it. 'Deal,' she murmured, and tucked her arm around his waist, and if it was more so that she could remain close to him than for balance, well, what was one more deception amongst the many?

Nothing like a close encounter with true disaster to put things into perspective.

CHAPTER TWELVE

NICK HAD NEVER BEEN more relieved to walk through John Tey's front door. Hallie had been silent for most of the taxi trip back to the villa, and that alone had been enough to send Nick's anxiety skyrocketing. When she'd tipped her head back and closed her eyes he'd nearly had a fit. 'Hallie,' he'd said urgently. 'Hallie!'

She'd opened her eyes, shot him a sideways glance and that increasingly enchanting grin and said, 'Stop it. I'm fine. You need to trust me on this.'

Which was a hell of a lot harder in practice than in theory.

'What happened?' cried Jasmine as she swept them through to the nearest sitting room and urged Hallie into the nearest chair. 'Stay there,' she ordered and disappeared at a run. When she returned she had Kai and a first aid kit with her and Nick almost sighed his relief as Jasmine fished cloth and antiseptic from the kit and set to work on Hallie's elbow. She'd scared him half to death when he'd seen her lying there on the pavement looking so small and broken and only half conscious, and her decision not to consult a doctor didn't sit well with him. 'She hit her head as well,' he told Jasmine.

Jasmine's gaze flew to Hallie's eyes. 'We need a torch,' she said firmly. 'We need to check her pupils for dilation.'

'I'm not concussed,' protested Hallie. 'I'm fine.'

'Don't argue,' he said. 'Just let her check.' And with a wry smile, 'For my sake if not for yours.'

'You *are* as bad as my brothers,' she grumbled.

'Yeah, but my delivery's far better.'

'What happened?' Kai asked him.

'I was trying to hail a taxi and stood a little too close to the kerb. Hallie pulled me back and we fell.'

'You were pushed,' said Hallie, and to Kai, 'Someone pushed him off the kerb and into the path of an oncoming taxi. I only saw a big jacket and a cap but there was an old man there who saw his face. He said it was a young man and that he did it deliberately.'

'You were pushed?' asked Kai.

'Someone stumbled into me,' he countered. 'I don't know that it was deliberate.'

Hallie stared at him defiantly. 'If it was an accident, why didn't he stick around to make sure you were alright?'

'Maybe he was too scared to.'

'Did you get the old man's name?' asked Kai.

'I didn't think it was necessary,' said Nick. 'Why?'

'I checked on the sick diner from the restaurant. He's in a coma. The doctors suspect some kind of poison. I took the crab meat to a private lab for testing but so far the tests have been inconclusive. If it does contain poison it's a rare one.' Kai paused. 'There is another disturbing fact about last night's incident,' he said quietly. 'The platter was not meant for that particular party. It was meant for us. And if it is as I suspect and only the topmost portion of crab was poisoned, that means it was meant for you.'

'What? You're saying someone's trying to kill me?' Whatever direction he'd thought Kai's conversation was going to go, this wasn't it. 'Are you serious?'

'I'm always serious,' said Kai.

Nick had taken the news that someone could be trying to kill him surprisingly well, thought Hallie as she watched him pace their guest room later that evening. They'd stayed in for dinner. Kai and John had both been on the phone to the authorities.

'Do you have any idea who would want to kill you?' she said.

'No.'

'Maybe it's someone who doesn't want you going into partnership with John. Maybe they've invented a game just like yours and will lose everything if they don't stop your product from hitting the market.'

'Hallie…' he began warningly.

'Or a resentful distributor who failed to get your business,' she said. 'How many did you reject before you decided to go with the Tey Corporation?'

Nick rolled his eyes. 'A few, but I really don't think—'

'Or a woman scorned. There's a thought. I bet there are plenty of those.'

'I do not scorn,' he snapped. 'I just…'

'Leave?'

'Yeah, and since we're on the subject, I'm terminating your contract. I'm sending you home.'

'Oh?' She was prepared to be calm, at least for now. 'And why is that?'

'I don't want you involved in this. I want you back home and safely out of the way.'

Now he was definitely starting to sound like her brothers. And she'd had such high hopes for him too. 'What happened to *we're in this together as equals*?'

'It stopped when I found out someone was trying to kill me. You didn't sign on for this, Hallie. I don't want you involved.'

'I want to stay and help,' she said stubbornly.

'No,' he said, equally stubborn. 'You can't help with this.'

'I did today.'

'And look what it got you! A busted elbow and a concussion headache!'

'I do not have a concussion headache,' she said indignantly. 'It's just a normal one.'

'Look…' His expression softened. 'You saved my life today; don't think I don't appreciate it but I don't want you getting hurt again. Not because of me.'

'Fine,' she said, waving him towards the telephone. 'Book the plane seat.'

Five minutes later he slammed the phone down in frustration. 'You knew there wouldn't be any seats available,' he said accusingly.

'Of course I knew. It's Chinese New Year. Everyone's travelling to visit their families. I'm betting you couldn't get plane tickets back to the UK any earlier than the ones we've already got.' Nick's scowl told her she was right. 'Cheer up, Nick. It's not that bad. You're the one they want dead, not me. And they only *might* want you dead. We're not exactly sure about that yet. I'm probably not in any danger at all.'

'But you *might* be. Hallie, be serious.'

'I am serious,' she said. 'This turned serious the minute you almost got jostled beneath a taxi. I'm all for letting Kai and the authorities deal with this and getting it sorted. I can lie low until it's time to go home. I can go somewhere far, far away from you if you really think that's going to get me out of danger. I just happen to think that me staying here – in John's already well-guarded fortress – is as good a suggestion as any.'

She stood and headed towards him. 'I swear, you're forever wanting to get rid of me.'

'Not true,' he said as she began to run her hands over his body as if checking him out for bruises or swelling. 'What are you doing?'

'I'm making sure you're not hurt. Don't think I didn't notice how you made sure that the focus this evening was on me. I know that trick. Now strip.'

'Excuse me?'

'I want to see the bruises. Or lack of them. And then I want you in the shower.'

'Bennett, I'm pretty sure you could have me anywhere, but that's not the point.'

'Don't make me undress you, Cooper. Because I probably can. Why is your shirt still on?'

Nick unbuttoned it and shrugged it off with an impatient sigh. 'Do you see a bruise or a scratch?' he asked.

'No.' She saw lean, rangy muscle and smooth, supple skin, and her throat went suddenly dry because, dear heaven, she wanted to run her hands all over him again and she'd used up her excuse.

'That's because I fell on *you*,' he said darkly. 'Now take *your* shirt off.'

'Nick, I *told* you I'm fine.'

'You wanted equality, Hallie. I'm very obliging. Shirt off.'

Grumbling, Hallie removed her shirt, careful not to wince. Nick looked at her and his mouth drew into a tight forbidding line. Not really the reaction she was looking for, given her wispy ivory lace bra. Admiration would have been better. She looked down and saw the broad reddish bruise painted across her hip. It was still going strong when it disappeared beneath the waistband of her trousers. 'It's not so bad,' she offered. 'It's not even purple. And I have very fair skin – you have to factor that in. It goes with the hair. I can run into a pillow and get a bruise like this.'

'Liar.'

'Practice makes perfect.' Hallie let her gaze rove over Nick's broad shoulders and flat waist and hitched an eyebrow in the direction of his trousers. 'I still want to check out the rest of you. Take them off.'

'You do know I'm going to demand equality.'

She knew. Hallie yawned and then stretched her arms in the air for good measure. Now *there* was Nick's appreciation for all that expensive ivory lace.

He shucked his trousers fast. There wasn't a mark on him.

Little bit of swelling, though.

Hallie turned her back on him as she lowered her own trousers, looking back over her shoulder to check just how bad the bruise on her hip was. Not that bad, although the dark fury in Nick's eyes suggested otherwise. 'I'm not fragile.' Words to live by. Her brothers had conceded the point eventually. Hopefully the very clever Nicholas Cooper would figure it out faster. 'That's not a mistake you want to make.'

He stepped up behind her and touched gentle fingers to the marks on her skin. 'God, Hallie—'

'A back rub, for example. That is definitely something you could do for me.' Hallie finished shucking her shoes and trousers and crawled onto that very fine red bed. 'I might even sleep.'

She looked back at Nick, who had his eyes closed and his hands in his hair. Could be he was praying.

Hallie was careful where she placed her grazed arm as she lay face down on the bed. Careful not to signal victory as Nick prowled up over her and eased his knees either side of her hips, settling down lightly on top of her, most of his weight on his knees as he placed those big hands of his on her waist.

'No oil,' he murmured huskily.

Plenty of heat, though. 'Dry is fine.'

He started slow, warm hands and strong thumbs stroking up towards her neck, no fumbling when it came to her bra, he just unhooked it and pushed it aside and continued on his merry way.

Touch had always been welcome in Hallie's

world. She'd always demanded a great deal of it. Touch meant care and love and connection.

Nick's touch left her hungry for so much more.

She shifted restlessly and Nick's hands stopped working their magic. 'Don't fidget,' he said.

'It's my bra. It's digging into my—'

'And don't talk,' he added hurriedly. 'For some reason the world around me gets so much more complicated when you talk.'

'I can see why you like computer characters so much,' she murmured, rising up on her good elbow and getting rid of her bra altogether before settling back down on the bed, arms up and her hands beneath her head on the pillow. Nick's hands ran up and over her shoulders and halfway to her elbows before slowly reversing and then starting all over again. Hallie groaned.

'No groaning,' ordered Nick.

'Your computer characters groan,' she offered lazily. 'I've heard them.'

'My computer characters don't groan, they grunt. There's a difference.'

'When Xia went down in battle she definitely groaned. I distinctly remember applauding the subtext at the time.' Nick's thumbs found a knot in her shoulder and dug deep. 'Mmm.'

'No sex noises at *all*.'

'Absolutely not,' she murmured, her eyes drifting closed. 'For that there would have to be sex. Mmmmm.'

Nick's fingers skated lightly over her hip and lingered on the bruise; he shifted his weight and suddenly Hallie felt lips where his fingers had been and that was definitely whimper worthy. 'What are you doing?'

'Kissing it better.' His words were little more than a gravelly growl.

'Is it working?'

'It is for me,' he said darkly, right before his lips trailed down to her panties. Those hands of his were on her upper thighs now, coaxing her buttocks off the bed and her thighs a little wider. 'You can make sex noises now,' he told her and set his tongue to tasting flesh, but he didn't stop there. He dragged his mouth over the silk of her panties, nibbled at the elastic, and with every sweep of his thumbs along her inner thighs he elicited a whimper, a curse or a moan.

'You're a noisy lover, Hallie.'

'Oh, *God*. Do that again.' It stood to reason she'd have trouble staying quiet in the bedroom. She'd had to shout to be heard her entire life. Strong hands pushed her knees up under her hips as his mouth closed over the thin wisp of silk covering her centre. Hallie cried out and pushed back against him as his tongue flicked over her, and then she cried out again as orgasm ripped through her, fierce and unexpected. 'Nick!'

It wasn't supposed to happen like this; this fast; she wasn't this wanton, she *wasn't*. It was just… she'd wanted him all day and most of yesterday and there'd been flirting and talking and that stupid fall and then there'd been touching. Hallie closed her eyes and hid her burning cheeks in the pillow.

'Hallie—' Nick's voice sounded strained. 'I— oh, *hell*.'

He reared back up over her and Hallie looked back at Nick, at his stomach muscles all bunched up tight, at his fingers wrapped around his cock, and gasped at the reckless beauty of Nicholas Cooper, eyes glittering and breath hitching as he rode out his pleasure.

'Really not meant to happen,' he gasped when his breath had returned enough for him to talk. 'I just— don't move..'

He was off the bed and headed towards the bathroom before it dawned on Hallie that she wasn't the only one with a restraint problem.

Nick returned with a warm and wet washcloth and wiped her down with a gentle touch. Hallie didn't moan this time. But she wanted to.

'You're going to be the death of me, Hallie,' Nick said gruffly.

'I've heard that line before,' she said. 'And for what it's worth, everyone's still alive.'

'I'll turn the shower on for you.'

'Thank you.'

There hadn't been any kissing, she thought belatedly. There was an order to these things, and she wasn't a stickler for rules, necessarily, but steps had been left out and she felt the emptier for them. She watched in the mirror as Nick rinsed out the cloth. Maybe he sensed her watching, maybe the water was too hot or too cold, but his shoulders tensed and his gaze lifted to meet hers in the mirror. 'What?'

'There should have been kissing.'

'There was kissing.'

'The *other* kind of kissing. I think we skipped a step.'

'Trust me, we skipped several.' Nick turned to look at her, still mostly naked and so was she. To his credit he kept his eyes on her face. 'And I broke the rules with you. Again. So much for not getting involved,' he muttered, almost beneath his breath. 'Why I *ever* thought I could get away with not getting caught up in you… It's not as if I don't have experience when it comes to wayward women. I have more than sufficient. I should have taken one look at you and ran. And if you *ever* have unprotected sex with a stranger again I am going to lock you up in a tower and swallow the key.'

'You're not a stranger,' she said. 'I know your mother. *And* you put a clean bill of health certificate in the fact file you sent me. Which I appreciated, by the way. You, on the other hand, neglected to ask me for one, which to my way of thinking makes *you* the one in need of a tower, a lock and a key, not me. You're reckless.'

Nick opened his mouth to protest and must have thought the better of it and ran a hand roughly over his face instead. 'I *know* I have a brain,' he murmured. 'It's in here somewhere.'

'About the kissing…' she began tentatively and got an incredulous look for her trouble. 'Kissing implies a certain involvement in one another's physical and mental wellbeing, right? And seeing as we appear to be somewhat invested in one another's welfare… I'm thinking why *not* allow more kissing in private if that's what we want? And hugging, and regular everyday holding. Because I'm feeling a little fragile. It's not as if one little hug is going to *hurt*.'

Nick reached out and drew her into his arms and,

with sexual appetites momentarily sated, Hallie finally got the kiss she'd been missing. The sweet and easy motion of Nick's mouth on hers. The now familiar taste of him to savour on her tongue and the gentle slide of his hands through her hair.

Oh, she liked this step.

'Better?' he murmured against her lips.

'Much.'

So he drew her closer and his mouth stayed slow and gentle as he kissed her some more.

Jasmine didn't know whether waiting to ambush Kai as he left her father's office the following morning and headed for his own living quarters over the garage was a good idea or not. The last time she'd cornered a man he'd taken one horrified look at her and fled. She'd learned from her mistakes, however, and adjustment number one was that this wasn't Kai's room. Adjustment number two was that she had a legitimate reason to want to speak with him – one that didn't necessarily involve begging for his touch.

He'd seen her, sitting in the open area of the lounge room, he had to walk straight past her to get to the front door and it looked as if he was going to do just that – walk right on by with nothing but a flicker of acknowledgement unless she stopped him. 'Kai.'

He stopped. But he didn't come any closer. That deep vein of wariness had been a part of him far too long for her to be surprised by it. 'Have you found out anything about the attempts on Nick's life?'

'No. Your father's contacts are working on it. As are mine.'

'Do your contacts include your father and *his* contacts?'

'When warranted, yes.'

'And is it warranted?'

Kai just looked at her.

'It's part of a larger question,' she said. 'I want to know how much contact you have with your father and the rest of your family.'

'Why?'

'I want to know how much contact I would have with them should I become more closely involved with you.'

'Too much.' Kai regarded her impassively. Only the slight tightening of his jaw suggested that he wasn't in perfect control. 'You wouldn't like the world I've come from, Jasmine. You wouldn't understand it.'

'Maybe not now,' she murmured. 'But in a few years, after I've devoured the world, who knows?'

'I don't *want* you to understand it.'

'That's the trouble with free will, isn't it? People don't always get what they want. I want you to show me your world, Meng Kai. The one you came from. The one you're in no hurry to return to. I want to know what you *really* do for my father – what his plans are for you – but no one's in a hurry to tell me that either. So I guess we all just continue to want what we want and plot to take it when we can.'

Jasmine stood, and finally approached him. 'Your father is the head of a Triad association, isn't he?'

Kai said nothing. It wasn't a no.

Jasmine took a deep breath and continued. 'Triad societies have not always been so closely linked to crime. Their origins are political. Some might say noble.'

'You are so young,' he said.

'You have no tattoos,' she countered.

'I am no foot soldier.'

'Leadership of such organisations is not hereditary,' she continued doggedly. 'You came to us when you were younger than I am now. You are outside the chain of command. Your father let you go. Loyalty to your father is not the same as loyalty to Triad.'

'Are you asking me if I have sworn oath?'

'Have you?' Jasmine knew how important this question was and her body reacted. The kick of blood in her veins and the sudden thundering of her heart, her shortness of breath. Fear held her; fear of what he might say and what it would mean for his future and hers. 'Have you sworn Triad oath?'

'There are thirty-six of them, Jasmine,' offered Kai quietly. 'And, yes.'

'Oh.' Jasmine clasped her arms around her waist in a futile attempt to prevent the sick feeling from spreading. This wasn't the end of her hopes and dreams for a future with Kai. She wouldn't let it be. Maybe, just maybe, the Triad he was involved with would let him walk away. Not that any Triad she knew of had ever made a habit of *that*. 'You said my father had given you a way out. A chance at legitimate business.'

'Your father continues to offer me legitimate business opportunities, Jasmine. He's a stubborn man. My father encourages me to take them. But it is not a way out.'

'Because you are sworn?'

'Yes. You think me a good man and maybe I want to be. But the oaths I took cannot be broken. *Hear* what I'm saying to you. *Think* about what you'd be getting involved with were you to get involved with me and stay away. Go find someone else to be with.'

'I *will* try,' she said, and meant it. 'I'll do this for me and I will do this for you. I'll give it three years. Time enough for a degree. But you have to promise me something first.'

'I am already burdened with oaths,' he countered curtly. 'I need no more. I won't wait for you, Jasmine. I make no promises.'

'I'm not asking you to wait,' she said, and tried to keep her voice even and unbroken. 'But if I do return and come looking for you I would ask that you treat me as a woman a man could come to love rather than a child who does not know her own mind. A child you are sworn to protect. I want those two things gone from our dealings. You owe me that much.'

'I owe you nothing.'

'No? For *years*, Meng Kai, for almost *ten formative years*, my world has been framed by you on one side and my father on the other. That's not normal. Little wonder, you say, that my eyes have been dazzled by you and my heart has reached out to you. Go away, you say. Go away and look elsewhere, but then you feed my hunger, and yours, with a kiss you *know* I won't forget, and with your next breath you push me away again. You owe me,' she said fiercely. 'I may not seem like an adult to you yet, but you owe it to me to see me as an adult upon my return.'

Fear and rage and longing and need – all of them vying for dominance within her. Time to leave before she broke down and wept, but as she turned, Kai's hand shot out to stop her. A hand to her waist and she felt the burn of it through her clothes, heating her skin. How was she supposed to forget this? Forget him?

How?

'Okay.' His voice sounded hoarse and strained. 'Three years, and if you still want to see me, I will do as you ask. I'll show you my world – whatever I've managed to make of it.'

'Swear,' she said.

'I swear.'

This time when she walked away he let her.

Five minutes later, Jasmine stood in front of her father's desk in his expansive home office and tried to convince herself that cutting ties with her father couldn't possibly be any harder than severing her ties with Kai.

Kai had known that a reckoning was coming, though. Kai had actively pushed her away, whereas her father... all he'd ever wanted was to keep her safe and close.

'University?' he echoed blankly, when she told him. 'You've never spoken of furthering your education before.'

'I'm speaking of it now.'

'Now is not a good time. I have little time to spend on you this morning. There will be more time later.'

'It won't take long.' Jasmine was far more used to obedience than she was to being a voice of dissent. And yes, she knew her father's attention was for Nick and the deal in progress. Yes, they had guests who seemed to require additional protection and that was of concern too. But this was important, and her courage was with her *now* and she had no notion of where it might be later.

'Singapore or Shanghai,' she said quietly. 'Either would suit.'

'Why not here?'

'It's a big world. I've been here. I've stayed here, indulged and overprotected. It's time I stepped out on my own; built a life of my own and made you proud.'

Her father watched her warily, tugging the sleeve of his suit down with his fingers. 'I am proud,' he said finally.

'And I am a dutiful daughter. I am. I try to please you and I always will. But you have to let me go. I'm not asking you, Father, I'm telling you. I intend to strike out on my own – with or without your blessing.' Jasmine smiled faintly and let the tip of her anxiety show. 'Of course, I would prefer it to be with your blessing.'

'Let me investigate your options,' he said.

'No.' Just be firm; that was all she needed to be. 'Let me.'

That was all she'd wanted to say. No need to take up more of his time. She headed for the door.

'Jasmine.' Her father stopped her with a word well before she reached it. 'Does this have any-thing to do with Kai asking me to release him from his duties here?'

'He did that?' Hard to think of Kai not being here without getting tearful. 'When?'

'Ten minutes ago,' her father said somewhat dryly.

'What did you say to him?'

'It's complicated.'

'*What did you tell him?*'

'He's told you, hasn't he? Who he is and why he's here. Is that why you want to leave? Because you want nothing to do with him?'

'No! How can you say that? Kai has been nothing but good to me. A friend to me for years. How can you even think that?'

'Good.' Her father nodded, as if to himself. 'Good. I wanted that for you. Nothing good ever comes of hate. Kai's a good boy.'

'If you like him so much, why do you use him as a pawn?' Jasmine asked heatedly. 'How did you answer him, Father? What did you say to the boy you took in payment for my mother's death?'

'I offered him a senior position in one of my companies in Shanghai.'

'He doesn't want a position in one of your companies in Shanghai!'

'So he said.' Her father's face held a sadness Jasmine hadn't seen for years, not since those first few months after her mother's death. 'I thought he could be happy here.'

'You wanted him to turn his back on his family.'

'Not his family. Just the crime.'

'He can't.'

'He can try. A man's fate is not governed by the vows he makes as a child.'

'They'll kill him.'

'I'm working on that.'

'Have you *told* Kai that?'

Her father nodded. 'He seemed…unimpressed. He repeated his request for release from his duties.' Her father looked at her through hooded eyes. 'It's complicated, Jasmine. You don't understand the balances in place.'

'*What did you say?*' She wasn't yelling, but it was close.

'I said no.'

CHAPTER THIRTEEN

NICK WOKE FROM HIS slumber with Hallie pressed hot against his side, her head resting in the crook of his shoulder and her hair spreading a silken cage across his heart. His arm tightened around her and his lips brushed against her head.

He'd known her less than two weeks, made love to her twice—okay, maybe somewhat more than that, but time-wise it hadn't been very long at all.

Too soon to be thinking the thoughts he was thinking.

Way too early to be promising for ever after.

Maybe when they got back to England they could slow this ride down some. He could walk away for a while, regain his equilibrium.

Because he certainly didn't have any balance here.

Hallie stirred and Nick lifted his hand and

stroked his fingers through her hair and tried not to recall that she might be in danger because of him and that if he had any sense he'd call one of her brothers – the cop one – to come and get her.

'Do me a favour today and stay here where people can keep an eye on you,' he murmured when she shifted against him again. He wasn't quite fool enough to take her sleepy yawn for acquiescence. 'Give me your word.'

'Okay.' She still sounded sleepy but she knew what she was saying. 'Although what if something untoward happens here and the general consensus is that it might be more prudent to go somewhere else?'

'Where would you go?'

'Airport,' she said.

'Not the police?'

'Maybe the police. I could ring Tris. And then he'll kill me.'

'Do that,' he said.

'You're awfully cavalier about my demise.'

'Wrong. I'm becoming increasingly fearful when it comes to your demise. You need to give me the phone numbers of some of these brothers you keep warning me about. If something happened to you I wouldn't even know who to call.'

'If I give you their contact details you might take it into your head to call them regardless.'

'That could happen too.'

'Traitor.'

'Perspective is everything. I just want you safe, Hallie. I know I'm not alone in that.'

The hand Hallie had resting on his heart inched its way up and over his shoulder and hooked around his neck. The rest of her gloriously naked body shifted over on top of him and she pressed a moist kiss to the side of his neck before settling her head into the curve of his neck. Nick liked having her this close. Neither his body nor his brain entertained the notion of wanting to get away.

'You do a lot of hugging,' he said.

'I had a deprived childhood,' she explained.

'And here I thought your brothers must have passed you round from arm to arm.'

'Nope. In our family the comforting shoulder nudge is King.'

'What about your father?' She rarely spoke of him and it made Nick curious. 'Doesn't he hug?'

'He… has his work…' Hallie sighed and her breath blew gently across his skin. 'You want the truth?'

Hallie seemed to require an answer from him, or

maybe she just needed more time to form her reply. 'Spill.'

'Truth is he's never been much of a father. Even when my mother was alive he always had academic papers to write or to mark, always a bright new student to supervise or a lecture to prepare. There was never much time for any of us and when my mother died… when he could have and *should* have stepped up as a parent… he retreated even further into his work. Jake was the one who made sure we all got to school on time and got fed and the electricity bills got paid. He was the one present at all my parent-teacher interviews, the one who took us to the doctor's whenever we got sick.'

'I see.'

Nick closed his eyes and traced a lazy path from her buttocks up to the base of her neck and she shivered beneath him.

'Do that again,' she demanded.

'Bossy.' Also gloriously uninhibited, fearless and eager to learn. But he did it again and she melted against him and sighed her satisfaction against his neck.

'What are we going to do about this ball?' she murmured. 'Do you still want to go?'

'Do you?'

'Yes,' she said. 'I want the entire Cinderella at the Hong Kong ball experience. The beautiful gown, the handsome prince – that would be you. I want to primp for the ball with Jasmine, and I want to see Kai's face when he first sees her, and I definitely want to dance with you. I have a feeling dancing could easily equal hugging in the pleasure stakes. You do dance, right?'

'My mother insisted.'

'Your mother is a wise woman.' Hallie shifted restlessly and Nick automatically ran his hand over her again. 'You should probably phone her today and touch base,' she offered. 'And then you should do that again. And I probably shouldn't get too set on going to this ball, because it really all depends on what Kai and John find out about these accidents.'

'We're probably jumping to conclusions about someone trying to kill me,' Nick said sleepily.

'This is true.'

'Kai did say he'd arrange extra security,' Nick said next.

Also true.

'I just can't think of any *reason* for it,' said Nick. 'Taking me out won't stop this deal from going ahead. It won't stop the people I work with from continuing to develop gaming software. And, contrary to popular belief, I can't think of any ex-lovers who might want me dead. There's just no *reason* for this to be about me. There's no evidence of poison in the crab, we don't really know if it was meant for me, and whoever was behind me at the kerb the other day could have simply stumbled and then ran. Maybe Kai's being over-vigilant.'

'Does this mean I *can* go sightseeing again today?'

'Absolutely not,' said Nick. 'I may be sceptical but I'm not crazy.'

Nick had to prod Hallie for her cop brother's phone number later that morning, but she handed it over eventually.

Just in case, she told him firmly. 'Tris knows where I am. I left him a note – although he may not have found it yet because he could still be in Prague.'

'Hallie, does *anyone* in your family know where you are?' asked Nick with a distinct sinking sensation. 'Have you done anything except leave your absent brother a note?'

'Two more days and I'll be back in London. Why bother them?'

Nick figured that for a no. 'Give me Jake's number as well.'

'You really don't want to be calling that number,' she said.

'You're absolutely right. Give it to me anyway.'

'I'm weirdly impressed,' she said, and set her lips to the curve of his jaw.

Nick felt his body stir. Hallie apparently felt it too, and rocked into him, seeking friction and finding it. 'Do that again,' he murmured.

And Hallie obliged.

Half an hour later, Nick sat at the desk in the guestroom and added the cop brother's number to the list of contacts in his phone. Hallie lay dozing on the bed again, it was still early morning, but Nick couldn't get back to sleep. His body was sated but his brain was wide awake. Hallie's revelation that no one in her family knew where she was disturbed him – especially given the oddness of recent events.

Hallie's brothers did need to know where their sister was.

As in now.

It was time to make a few calls.

Nick didn't know whether to be relieved or dismayed when the cop brother's phone rang out without anyone picking up.

He tried the Singapore brother next. The time

zone there was the same as this one. Hopefully brother Jake was an early riser.

Someone picked up.

'Bennett,' said a deep, impatient voice.

'Jake Bennett?' he asked and watched as Hallie's eyes slitted open. Nick nodded at her – yes, he was doing this – and she groaned and buried her face beneath the pillow.

'Yup,' said the voice on the other end of the phone.

Chatty.

'My name's Nick Cooper. Your sister's here with me in Hong Kong for the week and I need to give you some contact details.' No need to mention the finer details. Why worry the man?

'Put her on,' said Jake and Nick held his phone out towards Hallie, who shook her head to signify a vigorous no. Nick rolled his eyes and put the phone back to his ear.

'Hallie's asleep right now,' he said and Hallie nodded that yes, yes she was.

A deep and freezing silence followed.

'If you have an email, I can send you a couple of contact names and numbers and an address,' Nick offered.

'Or you can give them to me now.'

Nick tried to imagine the man behind that

lethally quiet voice. The image would have done his computer game proud. 'Our host's name is John Tey of The Tey Corporation. We're staying with John another two nights and heading back to London on Saturday.' Nick didn't wait for another serving of heavy silence; he just gave Jake Bennett the Teys' home address and John's business phone number.

'What's the flight number?'

Nick gave it to him. 'John's head of security is a man called Meng Kai. Wouldn't hurt you to have his contact details as well.' He rattled them off and then repeated it for good measure.

'Why does your host need a head of security?'

'He's an extremely wealthy man whose wife was kidnapped and killed many years ago. He has a daughter. He takes her protection seriously.'

More silence while Hallie's oldest brother digested that little morsel.

'Anything else I should know?' asked brother Jake finally, with enough bite to make a man bleed.

'No. I'm done with the sharing for now.'

'Do I need to know *you*?'

'Hard to say, but I'm going to go with yes.'

Hallie's brother either laughed or growled. Hard to tell. 'You have no idea what you're in for.'

'If, by that, you mean that I might not have encountered your sister's more impulsive tendencies, believe me I've met them.' Hallie was peeking out at him from beneath the Great Wall of China. Nick eyed her steadily and pitched his next words to her. 'Or are we talking about you and the protective tendencies of the rest of the brothers Bennett? Because your sister seems to think I'm going to take one look at you all and flee.'

'They usually do.'

'I'm heavily invested.'

'We'll see.'

'We'll be finished here in two days. Hopefully no one will need to be in touch.'

'You do want to hope that,' said Jake.

This conversation was going great.

'Nice talking to you,' said Nick and hung up, tossing his phone on the table and running a hand over his face.

'That good, huh?' said Hallie from the bed.

'The things I do for you.'

'I'm very appreciative,' she said. 'Heavily invested in what?'

'Hugging.'

'Ah.' Her smile came slow and sweet. 'Good to know. Come back to bed.'

'If I do that I'm likely to fall asleep in the meeting today,' he said. 'I don't want to fall asleep in the meeting today.'

'How's it going?' she asked.

'We're getting there.'

'And the telling John we're not married?'

'I'll try and get him alone some time today and tell him. I'll let you know as soon as it's done.'

'What if he pulls the contract?'

Nick leaned forward in the chair, elbows to his knees and rubbed both hands over his face this time. 'Yep.' He desperately didn't want that to happen, but if it did Nick would accept John's decision and take full responsibility for the breakdown in negotiations.

'What if we made up some story about my family not wanting me to marry, or me being already married but separated? Put the reason for us not being married back on me?'

'No. No more lies.'

'Honourable.'

'No,' he said wearily. 'I'm just sick of patching over old mistakes with new ones. It's time to come clean.'

'Sometimes honour's a little hard to define.' Hallie sat up, wrapped the sheet around her. 'You tried to spare Jasmine's feelings, you're about to come clean to John and you braved Jake and told him where I was. There's honour to be found in all of those actions.'

'Eye of the beholder, Hallie.'

'Yes.' Hallie smiled at him and damned if it didn't make him feel invincible. 'It is.'

'We could always get a hairdresser to come to us,' said Hallie as she surveyed her latest efforts to wind Jasmine's hair into a glamorous bun. 'I'm thinking we need a professional.'

'We can do that,' said Jasmine. 'Do we need to get our nails done too?'

'Well, it certainly wouldn't *hurt*,' said Hallie. 'Oh, and I have perfume for you too. A thank you gift for making our stay here such a memorable one.'

'Hallie—'

Jasmine paused and fell silent.

'What?'

'Tonight at the ball – how do I get Kai to notice me?'

'Really not going to be a problem,' said Hallie. 'He already notices everything about you.'

'Maybe notice isn't the right word,' said Jasmine. 'Maybe I want him to seduce me.'

'Ah,' said Hallie.

'Or I could take the initiative and seduce him,' continued Jasmine. 'Or at least try.'

'Or not.'

'You don't think I should?'

'Depends why you're doing it.'

'I'll be leaving here soon.' Jasmine looked close to tears. 'And I know you're going to say it's all for the best and that I need to grow up and that Kai needs to not be my paid protector... and I agree with all of that, but it's hard. Letting him go... Hallie, it's so much harder than I thought it would be.'

Hallie knew the feeling. The thought of having to uphold her end of the bargain and walk away from Nick once they got back to London made her feel hollow.

'I want to give Kai something to remember me by,' said Jasmine softly. 'Something to hold in his heart.'

'What about chocolates?' Empathy aside, Hallie was beginning to better understand the plight of older brothers and sisters.

'Why not give him me?' said Jasmine quietly. 'What if Kai's the right man but it's the wrong lifetime? What if I never get another chance with him?'

'Jasmine, you're very—'

'Don't say young.'

Hallie bit her lip and pulled that particular word out of her vocabulary. 'Okay, then, how about this? Giving yourself to someone is a big step. You need to be sure.'

'Was Nick your first?'

Hallie nodded.

'Did you wait for your wedding night?'

'No.' Not exactly a lie, but Hallie still felt the bite of it. 'But I still waited until I felt like I was with the right man and that it was the right time.'

Kind of.

'I wouldn't regret it,' said Jasmine stubbornly. 'Being with Kai tonight – if that happened, I wouldn't regret it. Not for one minute.'

'Okay. Let's assume seduction is a possibility,' said Hallie. No point rowing against the tide. 'How are we off for protection?'

'I have nothing.'

'Well, that has to change. You need to be prepared. You can't rely on stopping in the heat of the moment. Your brain may not be working – trust me on this.'

'Maybe I can send Kai out for some,' Jasmine's expression was deceptively demure.

'Yeah… *No*,' said Hallie. 'I vote we get the hairdresser to shop before she gets here.'

'He,' said Jasmine. 'The hairdresser's a he.'

'Even better. What else do you need for tonight?'

'I need to choose jewellery,' said Jasmine. 'I have all my mother's jewellery to choose from, and my own, but I was wondering about wearing this.'

Jasmine went over to a small wooden jewellery box and lifted out a long silver chain so fine Hallie could hardly see the links. There was a single teardrop pearl a shade lighter than the colour of her skin dangling from the end of it. 'I thought this. It's not expensive, more of a trinket really, but my mother gave it to me to play with when I was very small and then she let me keep it. There's no clasp; it slips over the head. But it's too long.'

'Not if you wear it backwards,' said Hallie.

'Oh.'

'With the front of it just skimming the bones below your neck. Pretty. 'And it'd work for Kai too, because it's not ostentatious. It won't remind him of your family's financial status, and that's important. Believe me, I've seen this one in action.'

Jasmine's bitter little smile looked out of place on one so young. 'It turns out Kai's family has wealth too.'

'Good news,' said Hallie. 'Makes you more equal.'

'You'd think so, wouldn't you?' said Jasmine quietly. 'So, about what we were speaking of before. Me seducing Kai. I don't suppose you have any tips?'

'Well, there's the dress that makes you look amazing,' said Hallie. 'And with your hair up, and all that skin on show…'

'I could ask him to dance,' said Jasmine.

'You could. It *is* a ball. You could wait for a slow dance. A waltz, so that Kai has to put his arms around you and deal with all that skin. And then you just kind of… feel your way from there. Although not literally. No inappropriate feeling of Kai on the dance floor or anywhere in front of an audience. That would be bad.'

'I'll be very discreet,' offered Jasmine.

'And, just for the record, I'm still of the opinion that there's nothing with giving the man chocolates to remember you by. Do it every Valentine's Day. There's nothing wrong with making your overall seduction routine last *years*.'

'You sound like my—'

'Friend,' said Hallie firmly. 'I am.'

Nick called Hallie in the lunch break of what

was turning out to be a very long day. He'd kept his mind on business all morning and he needed his reward. He didn't want to dwell on just how much he'd come to count on the support of one Titian-haired woman who sold shoes in her spare time. Nor did he want to dwell on his growing urge to lock her up so as to keep her safe. He just wanted to hear her voice.

'Nick!' she said when she picked up the phone. 'What are you up to?'

'Lunch break,' he said. 'You?'

'Hairdresser Wu is currently doing Jasmine's hair and telling us all about the fight he had with his boyfriend last night. It was a doozy.'

Nick laughed; he couldn't help it. 'Hallie, does the world ever stop giving you fodder for enjoyment?'

'Never,' said Hallie. 'Not ever. Hang on, I'm taking you out to the terrace. Are we still set for the ball?'

'So far.'

'Good, because this hairdo I'm wearing needs to be admired. 'Wu's a magician.'

'Glad to hear it. You on the terrace yet?'

'Just. Did you tell John about us not being married?'

'No. John and Kai have been out of the office

all morning. It's just me and the lawyers here today.'

'Why?'

'Don't know. But before he left, John gave his lawyers the go-ahead to wrap this negotiation up. John has extensive and impressive business interests. I'm not his only priority. I'm assuming something else came up that needed his personal attention.'

'Makes sense,' said Hallie.

'If he comes in this afternoon I'll tell him,' said Nick.

'You may have to wait until you get back here,' said Hallie.

'Why?'

'Because John and Kai just pulled up and John's getting out of the car and Kai's pulling back out. You know, maybe you could tell John *at* the ball. Find a quiet moment.'

'You just want to get *to* the ball.'

'This is true,' said Hallie. 'But I also have faith in your ability to make John understand why you told him we were married. It was a lie for a reason.'

'Hallie, I can't *tell* him the reason. That'd implicate Jasmine. No one wants that.'

'This is why I adore you,' she murmured. 'I've

been thinking up possible reasons for our deception all morning. Tell him I wanted a trial run.'

'A *what*?'

'A trial-marriage run, with all the trappings. It's what all the cool kids are demanding these days.'

'You *really* think he's going to believe that?'

'I'll have you know that people often think I'm nuts. It's not such a stretch.'

'You're not nuts.'

'Well, *I* know that.'

'You're too generous,' he said quietly and knew it for truth. Generosity of spirit had never been at the top of his list of qualities the ideal woman should possess.

But it was now. 'Henry from Tiffany's thinks you're exactly my type. He thinks I'm doomed.'

'Killjoy,' she said. 'Do *you* think you're doomed?'

'Nah,' he said gruffly. A little short on weapons with which to shield himself from her, maybe. But not doomed. He could still walk away at the end of this week if he wanted to.

Not that he…wanted to.

'Gotta go,' she said. 'John's here. I'll see you later.'

She made it sound like a promise and an adventure all rolled into one. Nick sighed and returned his phone to his pocket. It was entirely possible that he was a little bit doomed.

'Mr Cooper,' said one of John's lawyers from the doorway through to the conference room. 'Clause twenty-eight B has been revised. We're ready to continue when you are.'

Only five more clauses in two different languages to go. 'I'm on my way.'

'Your hair looks—'

'Magnificent,' said Hallie with an inward grin for the slightly perplexed expression on John Tey's face. Hairdresser Wu had twisted and pinned, cajoled and tucked, and the resulting upswept bun would not have looked out of place in a golden era Hollywood film. 'The rest of me does not match,' she said, referring to her ivory-coloured trousers, lime-green cotton Tee and flat pink sandals. 'But it will. Jasmine's inside getting her hair done too. We bribed the hairdresser here rather than go to the salon.'

'Resourceful,' said John. 'I'm sorry that your sightseeing has had to be curtailed.'

'These things happen,' said Hallie. 'Your daughter and I are still managing to have a very good day. Have you heard any more about the diner from the crab restaurant?'

'He died.'

'Oh. How sad.'

John inclined his head.

'So… he was poisoned?'

'We still don't know.'

'Do *you* think there's a threat to Nick's life?'

'It could be just coincidence,' said John. 'The extra security is staying in place, regardless. Hopefully, we are being over-cautious.'

Hopefully.

'Nick tells me that this is the first time you've chosen to venture into computer game distribution,' she said. 'Why now? Why Nick?'

'Diversification is always welcome,' countered John with a smile. 'Nicholas has developed an excellent and extremely marketable product and he's a very intelligent young man. He looks to the long game when it comes to building a business. I like that. Together we can make a lot of money.'

'You already have a lot of money. Why do you want more?'

'Men always want more, no?'

'Women too,' said Hallie. It hadn't escaped her notice that for all her and Nick's wheeling and dealing when it came to the terms of their 'wife for a week' agreement, she'd swiftly broken every one of those agreements in her haste for more of Nick.

'Perhaps it's our nature,' offered John.

'Yes. Perhaps it is.' Hence Nick's insistence on a bunch of rules to govern this week in the first place. Hallie shrugged off her sudden bleakness and offered John what she hoped was a corporate wife smile.

'Your daughter has been a marvellous hostess. Far better than I would have been at her age.'

'Ah, but you're not more than a few years the older.'

'Four and a half years,' said Hallie. 'We figured it out today.'

'My daughter tells me that you lost your mother at an early age too.'

'Yes.'

'What do you miss the most about her?'

'The softness she brought to things,' said Hallie without hesitation. 'The female point of view. My brothers... they've always been there for me – but they're not soft.'

'My daughter has bonded with you.'

Hallie smiled. 'Your daughter needs more friends.'

'Will you continue your friendship with her?' he asked.

'I'd like to.' Had Hallie been Nick's wife she would have been able to. But she wasn't and she didn't know what would happen next. Maybe Jasmine would understand and forgive Hallie and Nick the lie. Time would tell.

'My daughter tells me that she addressed an envelope for you, to one Jianne Xang of Shanghai,' said John. 'I know the family. Very good family. Very traditional.'

'So I've heard.'

'Jasmine says you're related.'

'Jianne married my brother. That relationship ended a long time ago and we never stayed in touch. I thought maybe I'd see how she was doing.'

'Ah.' John nodded. 'And were I to mention that Jianne's family have another marriage in mind for her? A notably prudent union for that family? Would you still want to get in touch with her?'

John Tey's eyes were very piercing. She'd never noticed that before.

'I'm not looking to disrupt Jianne's life,' said Hallie finally. 'I don't see how my contacting her will change Jianne's future plans. I mean her no harm.'

'I've also had dealings with the man Jianne's family has approved for her,' said John. He is a man of little honour. Jianne's family are in his debt.'

Hallie frowned. 'Meaning?'

'Meaning that an outsider might look at the situation Jianne Xang finds herself in and think that she too could use a friend.'

'Why are you telling me this?'

'I'm thinking that should you wish to contact your former sister-in-law, you might want to have my daughter address another envelope for you. One without your Australian address or your family name on it. It would stand a better chance of being delivered.'

'Nothing is ever simple, is it?' said Hallie bleakly.

'Life is complex, yes.'

'Anything else you want to tell me?' asked Hallie warily.

'That was it,' said John. 'Anything you want to tell *me* about my daughter's plans for the ball this evening?'

'Did you just make me indebted to you?' asked Hallie. 'And now you want me to share Jasmine's confidences in return? Oh, you're good.'

'Practice,' said John.

'Your daughter is in love with Kai,' offered Hallie bluntly. 'This can't be news to you.'

'It's not. Anything else?'

'Nothing I can recall. Decisions are complex.

Sometimes everyone just has to wait and see what happens.'

'Indeed.'

'Remind me never to play poker with you,' said Hallie. 'Or bridge. Or Mah Jong. Or anything else.'

'You flatter me.'

'I'm onto you.'

'Poor Nicholas.'

'He's not that poor.'

John Tey had started laughing. 'I envy him,' he said.

'He does have many fine qualities.'

'True, but that's not what I meant. I had the pleasure of sharing my life with a smart and joyful partner once and I do thoroughly recommend it.' John smiled wistfully. 'She was my wife.'

The afternoon passed slowly for Hallie, for all that she and Jasmine had tried to fill it. John spent the afternoon in his home office with the door closed. Kai and Nick returned to the villa just after six. Nick smiled when he saw her and Hallie tried not to remember that this time next week she would be back in London and Nick would no longer need her in his life.

Far, far easier to concentrate on the now.

'Work, work, work,' she said as Nick pulled her

towards him for a brief hug. He really had taken her request for hugs to heart. 'You ready to play?'

'I will be after a shower and a change of clothes. Care to shower with me?'

'What and ruin my hair?'

'Princess,' he said with a grin.

'Now you're catching on,' she said. 'Go. Have your shower. Jasmine and I are just putting together a tray of nibbles, and then I too will be heading upstairs to don my golden gown.'

'Anyone would think you'd never been to a ball.'

'And they'd be right,' she said. 'This is my first.'

'Cinders,' he said.

'Hallie,' she corrected him.

'Your hair looks beautiful,' he said and pressed his lips to her temple and headed for the stairs. 'I'll see you soon.'

By the time Hallie made her way to the guest room half an hour later, Nick was already showered and dressed for the ball; a handsome heartbreaker in an elegant black dinner suit that looked tailor-made for him and probably was. She should have been more immune to his looks by now, she desperately wanted to be, but there was something about the combination of dark hair, dark suit and a snowy white shirt that made her breath catch in her throat.

She picked up her gown and shoes and brushed past him on the way to the bathroom. She shed her clothes and slipped the gown on. Makeup came next and then the shoes – dainty stilettos that added a good couple of inches to her height. Next a dab of the perfume Nick had given her at her pulse points and finally a wrap of amber-coloured silk a couple of shades lighter than her gown.

Time to see if Nick approved of the way the corporate wife was packaged. She entered the bedroom regally, only to find him staring out of the window, trying hard to exude manly patience. 'I'm ready,' she said.

He turned, studied her from head to toe, and the purely masculine appreciation in his eyes was immensely gratifying. 'You're beautiful,' he murmured. 'But you're not ready.'

'I'm not?'

'You forgot your jewellery.'

She had her rings on, didn't she? Yep. Hard to miss them. 'I really hope you're not talking about the watch you bought me the other day.'

Nick pointed towards a grey velvet case sitting on the sideboard.

'Oh. You mean *that* jewellery.' The jewellery

she'd never seen. The jewellery he'd chosen without her. 'I forgot about it.'

'You *forgot* about it?' Nick appeared disbelieving.

'Maybe if I'd *seen* it I wouldn't have,' she told him sweetly.

'You can see it now.'

Hallie walked over to the sideboard and her hands came up, seemingly of their own volition, to stroke the long velvet box, but then she hesitated.

'What *now*?' said Nick.

'I've seen the necklace Jasmine's wearing tonight and it's very simple,' she said with a frown. 'I wouldn't want to go overboard in comparison.'

'Maybe this is simple too,' said Nick. 'Why don't you open it and see?'

Why didn't she? She was nearly bursting with curiosity, wondering what he'd chosen and whether she'd like it. Worried that she wouldn't. More worried that she would. There was only one way to find out. Hallie opened the box with careful hands. And gasped.

The necklace was like a pearl choker in design but where the pearls would have been there were diamonds, big carat-sized diamonds that glittered brilliantly in the light. As far as jewellery went it was exquisite, eye-popping even, because Hallie was pretty sure hers were halfway out of her head. But it wasn't simple.

'Do you like it?' he asked.

'Are you serious? It's absolutely gorgeous.' He was taking it from the box and putting it around her neck, his fingers warm and gentle against her skin as he fastened the clasp.

'It suits you. I knew it would.' He steered her towards the bathroom. 'Go take a look in the mirror.'

Hallie went and looked, made a minute adjustment to its position. There, now it was perfect and now she was thinking Audrey Hepburn in *Breakfast at Tiffany's* or Grace Kelly in anything, both of them as redheads, of course.

'What do you think?' said Nick from the doorway. He was leaning lazily against it, his smile indulgent and his eyes dark.

'It probably wouldn't do to bring it all this way and not wear it,' she said, while the diamonds around her neck blazed with every movement she made. They probably wouldn't overshadow Jasmine's teardrop pearl all that much, she decided a touch desperately. The diamonds were stunning in a different way, that was all. They might even *complement* Jasmine's pearl.

'There are earrings to match.'

'Oh, well…' Hell. May as well do things properly. A minute later she was wearing them too. 'Do you think it's too much?'

'You could always take the dress off,' he muttered. 'That'd work.'

'Focus,' she said sternly.

'I am.' Nick seemed to collect himself. He straightened and offered her his arm. 'Mrs. Cooper,' he murmured.

'Mr. Cooper,' she said. 'I do believe I'm ready. Shall we go?'

CHAPTER FOURTEEN

THE BALLROOM AT THE Four Seasons Hotel was where British Colonialism met Asian Affluence and a spectacle of such unbridled opulence that it left Hallie gaping. There were champagne-glass pyramids complete with nervous waiters, elaborately costumed opera singers with faces whiter than snow. There were five-tier chandeliers and peacock feathers by the bucketful. There was a dance band over by the dance floor, and there were Hong Kong's finest – dressed in their finest – mingling graciously.

'How on earth am I supposed to go back to selling shoes after this?' she murmured, desperately trying to commit it all to memory; the colours and textures, the scents and the sounds.

'Maybe you won't have to,' murmured Nick and Hallie felt her heart skip a beat.

'You'll have enough money after this to get through your diploma without selling more shoes, won't you?' he added.

Oh. *That* was what he meant. For a minute there, she'd thought that Nick had fallen in love with her and for a moment she'd wondered what it would be like to be Mrs Nicholas Cooper for real. For a moment there, she'd thought it would be just fine. But that was ridiculous. The whole point of agreeing to this charade in the first place was so she could focus on her real dream, the one that didn't involve Nicholas Cooper and fairy tale endings. The one that involved hard work, independence and the satisfaction that came with achieving one's goals. 'I'll make it enough,' she said firmly. 'You're right, selling shoes is over. Asian Art World, here I come. Here's to you for helping to make it happen.'

'I've watched you, Hallie.' There was a serious note in his voice. 'I've seen the enthusiasm and the energy you bring to everything you do and I know without a doubt that when you do decide on a career, be it in the art world or somewhere else, you're going to be a huge success. Don't ever doubt it.'

'Thank you,' she said quietly. For all his faults, and yes, not falling helplessly in love with her was one of them, Nicholas Cooper believed in her. Hallie felt her heart falter, felt it stumble before righting itself, and when it did it wasn't altogether hers any more. Some of it was Nick's. Not that she was inclined to let him know that.

So she pinned on a smile, a smile that became more genuine as she was introduced to friends and acquaintances of John and of Jasmine. She nodded to husbands and mingled with wives as they ogled the diamonds around her neck overtly, Nick covertly, and made laughing conversation with her.

Partnering Nick to a ball was easy. He was gorgeous, charming, and knew exactly when to leave her to her own devices and when to stay by her side. 'You're a very good escort, you know that, don't you?' she said as he whisked her half finished glass of champagne from her hand, handed it to a passing waiter, and snagged a cool glass of water as a replacement. It was exactly what she wanted. 'How did you know I wanted water?'

'I didn't,' said Nick. 'But you hadn't touched your champagne in over an hour and it's getting warm in here so I figured it was worth a shot.'

'Gorgeous, generous, *and* attentive,' said Hallie dryly. 'Is there anything you're *not* good at?'

'Rules,' he said, his eyes darkening. 'I'm not real good with rules. Dance with me.'

Hallie took a quick sip of her water, felt it slide, wet and cool, down her suddenly dry throat. Dancing meant touching, touching meant wanting, and when touching, wanting and Nick came together, she was inclined to forget the rules herself. 'I'm thinking we should forgo the dancing. If I dance with you and love it, I may never want to dance with anyone else.'

'There is that.' And with a charmingly crooked smile, 'Dance with me anyway.'

Jasmine watched Hallie and Nicholas take to the dance floor with something approaching envy. Hallie looked so beautiful in her gown, but it was the stars in Hallie's eyes that Jasmine envied most. The smile on Hallie's face that told Nicholas and the world that there was nowhere else Hallie would rather be.

Jasmine could think of dozens of places that she would rather be as she stood at her father's side and sipped her champagne and tried not to notice that Kai, who stood on her other side, was far too busy scoping the room to have eyes for her.

One long, penetrating glance at the beginning of the evening was all Kai had spared her. After that, he'd barely looked at her at all.

So much for dazzling him with her subtle beauty

and igniting his senses with the perfume Hallie had given her. So much for finding the courage to ask Kai to dance with her… Jasmine stared blindly down at the nearly empty champagne glass in her hand. Maybe if she had another drink…

Jasmine looked around for a drinks waiter and found one and caught his eye. He started towards her. The plan was to exchange her empty glass for a full one. Such a simple plan, only Kai had a different one and when the waiter had taken her empty glass, Kai sent him away with a glance. 'Two's enough for now,' he told her. 'I need you alert.'

Which, strangely, gave her more courage rather than less.

She may not have caught Kai looking at her this evening but that didn't make him any less aware of her.

'Dance with me,' she said.

'I'm working,' Kai said in reply.

'Can you not do both?'

'Not well.'

'You're still worried about Nicholas's safety?' she asked, with another glance in the Coopers' direction.

'Yes.' This time Kai did spare her a glance. 'Something feels off.'

'You also have four more security guards here

tonight watching them. Can you not survey the room from the dance floor?'

Kai said nothing. Silence was so often his defence.

'Bolin Sun is here,' she said finally. Bolin's parents were old family friends of her father's. 'Perhaps *he* will humour me with a dance.'

'He's here with someone.'

As far as Jasmine could tell, Bolin had arrived in a party large enough that Bolin's companion would not be short of company for the duration of one dance. 'Perhaps he'll humour me anyway. You wanted me to broaden my horizons,' she reminded him and made to move off, but before she'd taken two steps in Bolin's direction Kai was blocking her, his face set and his mouth a forbidding line.

'Not him.' The words came out clipped and low. Vicious, even, and Jasmine rode the thrill of knowing that Meng Kai was not nearly as composed as he seemed. 'Pick someone else.'

'Dance with me,' she said.

And this time Kai held out his arm for her to take and led her onto the polished wooden floor.

Hallie frowned when Kai and Jasmine finally took to the dance floor. The body language was all wrong – Jasmine looked strained, Kai looked stiff and far too formal, none of his catlike grace in evidence now. 'Look at them,' she said in exasperation. 'How does Kai even expect to dance with Jasmine when he's not even touching her? Anyone would think he doesn't *want* to dance with her!'

'That would be my call,' said Nick as he whirled her around the dance floor and Jasmine and Kai disappeared from view.

'Not that I have anything against you being right in general but in this particular case I really hope you're wrong.' Matchmaking really wasn't Hallie's forte. What if Kai *wasn't* in love with the younger girl? What if she'd given Jasmine the wrong idea altogether? 'What are they doing now?'

'Jasmine's just put her hand on Kai's shoulder,' said Nick and whirled her back around. 'See for yourself.'

Hallie glanced, and then groaned. The only thing between the other couple was tension. 'I can't watch.' She turned away abruptly and came nose to chest with Nick's shirt. 'Out of my way. I'm going to go and shoot myself for interfering.'

'Wait,' said Nick, his movements smooth as he swung her back around so that they could both look.

The other couple had started dancing and if

Kai had thought to keep Jasmine at arm's length, Jasmine had other ideas. She stepped in close. Kai's hands rather unwillingly slid to her waist, his fingertips brushing bare skin, and then, as if he couldn't help himself, he gathered her closer still, the longing in him unmistakable.

'My parents used to dance like that,' said Nick. 'They always gave each other room to move, to be themselves, but then when they came together you could tell that at that moment in time there was nowhere else they'd rather be. It was like… magic.'

'Nick, you're a romantic!' Hallie was thoroughly enchanted by his words. 'Do you think *we're* ever going to dance like that?'

'No.' His voice was firm but his eyes were warm as he swung her smoothly away. 'We are going to avoid dancing like that at all costs.'

No one had ever told Jasmine that dancing could set a body to burning. Every breath, every slow glide of her body against Kai's. The warmth of his fingertips on the skin at her back and the strength in his arms as he guided her over the dance floor. She wanted to remember the music that was playing and the scent of him. She'd rarely been this close to him before and not sparring. And whatever they were doing at this moment – it wasn't fighting.

Jasmine didn't care that her father would only have to take one look at her to know that her heart was not her own. She didn't care that other people might look her way and see a foolish young girl who hadn't learned how to hide her feelings.

She was growing up and owning her emotions. Letting them show, finding her way.

Seduction didn't have to be all about the fast tumble, Hallie had told her, and Jasmine believed her.

Sometimes seduction could be tremblingly, exquisitely, slow.

'How long have you known of my feelings for you?' she asked softly and when Kai ducked his head the better to hear her, she filed the brush of soft hair against her cheek away for future reference too.

'Don't ask me that,' he said.

'You recognised them before I did,' she said, and willed the heat in her cheeks away. 'You argued with my father the day before my sixteenth birthday. You fought for my freedom.'

'Jasmine, I had to. I was there to *protect* you. Not—'

'Not what?'

'Not take advantage of you.'

'And now? Would you take advantage of me now?'

'No.'

'What if I asked you to? *Wanted* you to?'

'No.' His voice was little more than a tortured whisper. 'Jasmine, no.'

'How about in three years' time?'

Kai closed his eyes and rested his forehead gently against hers. 'Maybe.' They barely moved, little more than a shuffle, but this was the dance that Jasmine's girlish fantasies were made of. This man, holding her. 'If that's what you want.'

'You keep implying that my feelings for you will change,' she murmured. 'Why is that?'

She could feel the tension in him, the tremor in him as she touched gentle fingertips to the skin of his neck.

'I'm easily discarded,' he said.

'No,' she said fiercely. 'You're not. Don't think like that.' She knew where some of this was coming from – so easy now to see the damage his father and hers had done to this man's sense of self-worth. 'To hell with them,' she said raggedly. 'I value you, Meng Kai, and I always will. Ask me who taught me about compassion and understanding. Because it wasn't my parents.'

'Don't,' he whispered.

'It was you. Ask how I learned about honour and strength of purpose.'

'Jasmine, please—'

'I watched you. Who do you think instilled in me the courage to leave this gilded cage?' She didn't wait for his response this time. 'It was you.' She'd told him these next words before, but maybe he needed to hear them again. 'And when I return in three years' time, all worldly and wise—' Jasmine tilted her lips forward and let them whisper across his cheek. Words to remember her by and the actions would follow. '—I'm coming for you.'

Hallie danced like a dream. Like Nick had held her in his arms a hundred times before. He lost himself in the feel of her, the brush of a thigh, fingertips on bare skin; it was like foreplay, like flirting, and Hallie was a natural at it. He'd never known anyone who delighted in the moment as much as Hallie, and when a slow number began she snuggled in closer, with fire in her hair and stars at her throat.

Just his type, Henry had warned Nick, only Henry hadn't known just how perfect a fit Hallie Bennett would turn out to be. It was so easy to spend time with this woman. To let her into his head and to be drawn into hers and delight in the being there.

Not his doing, when Hallie slowed the dance way down, but Nick took full advantage of it and let his body savour the feel of flesh on flesh and the unspoken knowledge in her touch. She knew how to hook him, how to please him and Nick had never taken so much delight in being played.

'Is Hong Kong everything you thought it would be?' he asked her.

'Yes.'

'And the ball is to your liking?'

'Everything is to my liking,' she said and lowered her lashes and the dazzling smile she'd given him moments before started to fade. 'Let's just call it a week out of time and place. An experience I will never forget.'

She was talking as if it would all be over soon and, somewhere in the dim recesses of his mind, Nick thought he should have been glad that Hallie hadn't forgotten their deal. The 'I only need a wife for a week' deal and that in a couple more days that week would be up.

He should have been glad that Hallie wasn't pushing for more of his time in a different place. He should have been relieved.

Yes, he was temporarily besotted with the woman in his arms. Yes, she was a match for him in bed and out and he kept finding more things to like about her. That didn't make her The One. He wasn't ready to wrap his life around someone else's and line their needs and goals up alongside his.

Was he?

It could have been fifteen minutes later, it could have been fifty, when the music stopped and Nick peeled her out of his arms.

She had a dreamy look about her and then she blinked, and then she was back.

'Where were you?' he asked.

'Fantasy land,' she said as warmth crept into her cheeks and she shot him a half-embarrassed smile. 'I was having my Cinderella moment. It's possible I got a bit carried away.'

It was entirely possible that they both had. He looked around for John but their host was nowhere in sight. Neither were Jasmine and Kai. 'Would you like to go out to the balcony?'

Where there was bound to be a night time Hong Kong skyline to be dazzled by, rather than the woman beside him. Hallie nodded. 'Can you see Jasmine and Kai anywhere?'

'They left the dance floor half an hour ago.'

'Hopefully this is a good thing,' murmured Hallie.

'Why? What did you do?'

'Nothing.' The angelic look she sent him was in no way reassuring. 'Nothing except dispense sound advice when it comes to dealings with the opposite sex. The kind of advice my brothers have always given me.'

'Namely?'

'Take your time. Be sure. Make sure the family approves. That kind of thing. My brothers would have been proud.'

It hadn't escaped Nick's notice that when it came to interacting with *him*, Hallie had broken all those rules and more. 'So what happened with me?'

'You?' Nick couldn't see Hallie's face, but he thought he detected a hint of strain in her voice. 'You kind of don't count.'

'Because I'm your little rebellion against your family's over-protectiveness?' He couldn't keep the edge from his voice. Hell if he wanted to.

'Nah.' She still wasn't looking at him. 'Because you're you.'

There were almost as many people on the balcony as there were inside. The air was cooler, the faint breeze a welcome surprise. 'What time is it?' she asked him.

'Ten past eleven. Not long to go now.'

No, it wasn't. Not to midnight. Not to the end of their time together. Hallie smiled but it wasn't a real smile. It was going to hurt to say goodbye to this man in two days' time; she'd always thought it might. She just hadn't realised how much.

And then the thunder of drums sounded from inside and people turned and started heading inside, Jasmine amongst them. 'Lion dancing,' said the younger girl, linking arms with her as they fell into step with the slow-moving crowd.

'How was *your* dancing?' she asked and laughed when Jasmine blushed.

'I took your advice,' said Jasmine shyly. 'I chose the slow hand, and found my way.'

'Good for you,' said Hallie fiercely and drew the younger girl against her for a fast hug. 'That man is toast. Speaking of which… Where is he?'

'He's gone to the kitchen. Something to do with checking out the wait staff.'

The drums settled into a steady, driving rhythm and a magnificent Chinese lion appeared, bigger and more elaborate than Hallie had ever seen. He strutted, roared, and considered the poles set out before him, each pair of poles that little bit higher than the next. He disdained the lowest poles, sniffed at the next, wove his way through the third, and sat before the fourth. He groomed himself lazily as he studied the tallest of the poles, poles that were taller than Nick, and then with a flick of his tail and an unbelievable leap he was standing on top of them and along with it all came the bold beating of drums. The colour red was everywhere; on decorations, on dresses, on the jackets of the wait staff who circulated with a never-ending supply of drinks and finger food. The wait staff. Hallie stared hard at a waiter heading towards them with an empty tray. He looked familiar, irritatingly familiar.

'Nick,' she whispered, disengaging her arm from Jasmine's and tugging on his sleeve. Wasn't that the waiter from the restaurant? The one who'd served the poisoned crab? 'Nick!' But Nick was engrossed in the lion dancing. And then the waiter was almost upon them, one hand holding the tray aloft, his other hand close to his side and in it was something that gleamed with a dull black shine. Nick was turning towards her now but it was too late to warn him. If it was a gun, the waiter had a clear shot. Hallie did the only thing that came to mind.

She charged the approaching waiter and tackled

him, gridiron style, and they went tumbling to the ground, both of them, the crowd parting as onlookers scrambled to get out of the way. Some were quick enough, others weren't. Two other guests hit the ground, both of them men, both of them cursing, but not nearly as much as Nick, who was wading through the wreckage, trying to get to her. The waiter scrambled to his feet and rabbited his way through the crowd, his tray and whatever had been in his hand lying forgotten on the floor.

'It was the waiter from the crab restaurant! He was aiming something at you,' she said breathlessly as Nick helped her to her feet. Kai was beside them now, barking orders into a cell phone. 'I thought he had a gun!'

'You mean this?' said Kai, picking up a small black cylinder that gleamed dully.

It was metal. It was black. It looked like the barrel of a gun. But it wasn't a gun. She glanced at Nick to see how he was taking this latest development. Not well. 'It certainly *looked* like a gun,' she said with a cheesy smile. 'From a distance.'

'Actually, it is a gun of sorts,' said Kai. 'It dispenses darts.'

'Ah,' she said. 'Good to know.'

'Are you hurt?' asked Nick grimly.

Her head was pounding, her arm aching. It was five minutes to twelve. 'Hurt? Me? Of course not.'

Kai was making sure no one else was injured. Jasmine was soothing ruffled tempers. Nick was looking at her, his face set. 'I can't believe that you crash-tackled him,' he said at last. 'Don't you have any concern for your own safety whatsoever? What were you *thinking*?'

'I was thinking of you!' she said heatedly. 'I thought he was going to shoot you! I couldn't just stand by and do *nothing*.'

'Hallie, excuse me,' interrupted Jasmine tentatively. 'But I thought we might go and find my father and then get you both home. He's probably out on the balcony waiting for the fireworks to start.'

'Who needs to go outside?' muttered Hallie. 'They've already started in here.' But she followed Jasmine and Kai out to the balcony with Nick at her side and stood where Kai decided it was best to put them, backs to the wall in an alcove.

'*Another* attempt?' said John when he joined them and Kai told him of the waiter and the dart gun. 'I had hoped we were being overly suspicious.'

'I wish I knew who was behind it all,' said Nick.

'Yeah,' said Hallie glumly. 'Pity the waiter got

away.' Lara Croft wouldn't have let the waiter get away. Lara Croft would have nailed the waiter and then they'd have *known* who was behind the attempts on Nick's life. 'I wasn't really thinking straight when I tackled that waiter,' she told Nick apologetically.

'Finally, she sees reason,' he murmured.

'I should have pinned him down.'

Nick stared at her incredulously. John Tey smothered a chuckle.

'I have our people looking for him,' said Kai. 'We'll find him.'

People were crowding onto the balcony. It was almost midnight, and the fireworks were due to begin. As far as Hallie was concerned it was the end of a long day with more ups and downs in it than a triple loop roller coaster. 'Two more minutes,' she said, glancing at the glowing neon clock set high on the hotel wall.

'I shall wish for a better tomorrow for you,' Jasmine told Nick earnestly. 'One without assassins.'

'Thanks, Jasmine.' Nick's features softened before hardening again as his gaze rested challengingly on Hallie. 'You could try wishing for some more sense.'

Ha! Hallie smiled sweetly. 'My wish is that the

vase I bought you turns up tomorrow.' Then she could stuff him in it.

'What vase?' said Kai, his head snapping round as he pinned her with his gaze.

'The one I bought for Nick at Lucky Plaza,' she said. 'When you and Jasmine were in the bathroom.' Kai was looking at her in disbelief. 'Separate bathrooms,' she added hastily. 'As opposed to being together in the same bathroom.'

'You bought a vase,' said Kai flatly. 'For Nick. From the corner shop near the bathrooms in Lucky Plaza.'

Hallie nodded.

'A funeral vase.'

Hallie nodded again. 'Yes, that's right. The one in the window.'

'And the salesman *let* you?' said Kai.

'Well, he took some persuading, but yes. I arranged to have it delivered before the end of the week but it hasn't arrived. Hopefully tomorrow.'

Kai was turning to John, shaking his head and muttering something. John was staring at her, open-mouthed, as if frozen to the spot. Nick and Jasmine looked as baffled by their reactions as Hallie felt. 'What?' she said uneasily. 'What's wrong?'

Ten. The countdown to midnight began, in Cantonese.

Nine. 'The shop you speak of sells funeral vases sure enough,' said John.

Eight. 'But they don't sell them empty.'

Seven. 'What do you mean, not empty?' she said.

Six. 'The one I bought was empty.'

Five. 'Well, they don't deliver them empty,' said Kai.

Four. 'When you bought Nick that vase—'

Three. '—you ordered his execution.'

Two. 'I *what*?'

One. 'That's why someone's been trying to kill him.'

Oh dear. The crowd roared as fireworks erupted in the sky, huge blasts of colour raining down from the heavens, each one more spectacular than the last and all around them people were laughing and embracing, kissing and shaking hands, their faces alight with pleasure and the glow from the fireworks.

Hallie opened her mouth to speak but no words came out. They were all staring at her; Jasmine, Kai, Nick and John; all waiting for her to speak but she had no idea what to say. Her hands were trembling, hell, her entire body was trembling with a mixture of fear and disbelief. This was a joke, right? It had to be a joke. But the expression on Kai's face assured her it wasn't.

A fresh blast of fireworks opened up the sky with a crack that made her jump; a kaleidoscope of red, green and gold, while her gut roiled and her head ached with the sure knowledge that in buying Nick that damned vase she'd made a huge and deadly mistake.

'I—' What on earth could she say? She looked to Nick. 'You—' Nope, she still couldn't find any words. She put a hand to her aching head and shrugged, still helplessly enmeshed in Nick's gaze. Good Lord, she'd put a contract out on him. How the hell was she supposed to explain *that*?

She couldn't. Not now. Maybe not ever. It was just too bizarre.

But they were all still waiting. Waiting for her to say something. Anything. She opened her mouth and took a deep breath. 'Sorry about that,' she said finally.

CHAPTER FIFTEEN

HALLIE HAD NEVER PEGGED Nick as the coldly furious type and he wasn't. His was more of a simmering, bubbling fury and only his iron control, and quite possibly the presence of Kai and the Teys, kept it contained. They'd left as soon as the fireworks were over and the drive home had been mercifully conversation free. Once at the villa she and Nick had said their 'Thank You's and their 'Goodnight's and headed for the bedroom, and once they were *there*, Nick wasted no time in shrugging off his jacket and tie and opening a couple of shirt buttons.

Hallie eyed him warily as she set her purse down on the counter and folded her wrap. Her brothers had tempers, all of them. She was no stranger to eruptions of the masculine variety. Pete's was like a summer storm, all noise and flash and gone in an instant. Luke's involved pacing, pointing, and a great deal of arm waving. Jake's was controlled and biting, and Tris… Tris didn't do temper very often but when he did he flayed people raw. Hallie was hoping, really hoping, that Nick was going to be a little less like Tris and a lot more like any one of her other brothers in that regard.

A timid knock sounded on the door and Hallie opened it to find Jasmine standing there holding a tea tray.

'Peppermint tea,' said the younger girl, pressing the tray into her hands. 'It's very soothing,' she added, and fled.

'I knew it,' said Nick as Hallie nudged the door closed and set the tea tray on the sideboard. He was pacing now, from one end of the room to the other. This was good. Pacing she could deal with. Pacing expended energy that could otherwise be used for yelling. Tris never paced.

'I should *never* have gone shoe shopping with my mother,' he was saying now. 'She's a bad influence. I should have gone to the country club and found Bridget instead. Bridget would have pretended to be my wife for a week. She'd have ripped Jasmine to shreds, alienated John, tried to seduce Kai, and driven me insane, but so what? At least she wouldn't have *ordered my execution!'*

Uh oh. He'd stopped pacing. 'Tea?' she offered.

'Why me?' he roared. 'Why you? Why *now*?'

'I have a plan,' she said quickly.

'No! No more plans. I know your plans and they *never ever work!*'

'Are you sure you wouldn't like some tea?' Hallie sniffed a steaming cup. 'I think she put alcohol in it.'

He stared at her. Stared at the tea.

'I'm calling your brothers,' he said abruptly. 'I'm going to tell them all about this man, wife and funeral vase fiasco and then I'm going to get them to come and take you home.'

'You can't,' she said pleadingly. 'You need me.'

'To do *what*?' He was back to roaring.

'To go back to the shop and cancel the hit.'

He stared at her in disbelief. And then, 'No! Absolutely not! These people are professional killers, Hallie. They're not going to be impressed by you saying you made a mistake and didn't realise you were ordering my execution after all. They'll kill you to keep you quiet.'

'I'm not going to tell them I made a mistake,' said Hallie. 'I'm going to tell them I needed the job done before the end of the week and that they failed to deliver. I'm going to tell them that the terms of our contract have been breached and that I no longer need their services.'

'You're going to *fire* them?'

'Yes.'

'I don't believe this,' he muttered. 'It's like living in a black comedy.'

'Listen to me, Nick. I can fix this. First thing in the morning I'll cancel the hit. Kai will know how to contact them. Easy as.'

'This would be the Kai who took you to the plaza and let you buy the vase in the first place.'

'To be fair, he didn't know I'd bought it,' said Hallie. 'He's Jasmine's bodyguard, not mine. But I'm sure he'll agree to help.'

Nick was pacing again. Muttering beneath his breath and raking his hand through his hair. Very Luke. She opened her mouth to explain her idea some more.

'No.' He held up his hand for silence. 'Don't talk. Don't say another word. Let me think.'

So she closed her mouth and concentrated on pouring the tea and stirring in sugar, lots of sugar, to help with the shock. She was shakier than she wanted to admit. Horrified by the notion that she'd inadvertently ordered Nick's execution. She'd wanted to make her own mistakes, sure enough, but she'd wanted to make her own *little* mistakes. Not huge, deadly ones she wasn't at all sure she was going to be able to fix. 'I'll call Tris if that's what you want,' she offered quietly. 'He's the best one for this. I can call him now.'

Nick shot her a hard-eyed glare and Hallie looked away, looked at her tea. She was going to cry, dammit, she could feel the tears building behind her eyes. She put her hand to her cheek and hastily wiped away the first escapee. Another followed.

'No crying!' said Nick hurriedly. 'I don't do crying.'

'I'm so sorry, Nick. I've ruined everything for you.'

'Not yet, you haven't. Let's think about this. Maybe it *is* as simple as cancelling the contract. We could get John to call ahead to the shop. Let them know we're coming in and that plans have changed.'

'We? What we? There is no *we* because *you* can't come!' She wouldn't let him come. 'If I walk you into that shop they'll shoot you on the spot and *stuff* you into that vase before I can say good morning. I need to go there alone.'

'No.' One word, simple and irrevocable.

'You can't come,' she pleaded. 'You have to pretend you don't know anything about it. If they think I'm cancelling their services because they botched the job and you discovered I ordered your execution, they may well kill you anyway. Out of sheer professional pride.'

'How much alcohol did you say was in that tea?' he asked.

Hallie passed him a cup and he swallowed the contents in one go.

'I hate this,' he muttered.

'Yes, but it'll work,' she said with far more confidence than she felt. 'Trust me.'

'I do trust you,' he said. 'It's the bad guys I don't trust. What if your luck runs out? What if you get hurt? I'd never forgive myself.'

'You have to think positive,' she said. 'Think Lara Croft in Tomb Raider.'

'Lara Croft has big guns and multiple lives. You have no guns and one life.'

'To live the way I choose. I choose to do this, Nick. This is my mistake. I want to fix it.'

He was closer now, close enough to reach out and touch, and the conflict between wanting to keep her safe and wanting to agree with her plan was there in his eyes. He lifted his hand to her cheek, his eyes almost black, his tension a living thing.

'I can't do this,' he muttered roughly.

'Which *this* are we talking about?' she whispered as his lips came closer to her own and his hand slid from her cheek to cup the back of her head. 'This as in kissing or this as in agreeing to my plan?'

'Any of this,' he said, and captured her lips with his own.

She expected anger from him, the remains of it at any rate, but his kiss was unexpectedly sweet, his hands in her hair so very gentle as he traced the bump on her head.

'Does it still hurt?' he murmured roughly.

'No.' She slid her hands over his chest, luxuriating in the feel of him, so warm and solid and, above all, alive. He kissed her again, deeper this time, with a needy edge to it that she matched with a helpless, aching need of her own.

'How about now?'

'No.' With her hands digging into his shoulders and her skin on fire from his touch.

His hands slid to her shoulders and his long, sure fingers started toying with the straps of her gown and then he bent his head and set his lips to her shoulder in the exact place her straps had been.

Hallie gave in, gave up, shivering in pleasure as his mouth feathered over her shoulder, tracing a slow torturous path along her collarbone. He lifted her effortlessly onto the sideboard and found her nipple with his mouth, through the thin barrier of silk that her dress afforded her, but it wasn't enough, not nearly enough. She wove her fingers through his hair, revelling in its soft, silky texture as she arched back and he slid the straps of her dress down her arms. The bodice followed and then her breasts were bared for him and his fingers grazed her puckered nipples with a touch so gentle she didn't know whether to weep with pleasure or scream with frustration. 'I won't break,' she said huskily, by way of a hint.

'I know.' His smile was crooked. 'You're probably indestructible. I noticed that today. It's just that you look so damn fragile.'

'I'm not fragile,' she said. 'I'm not even a virgin any more.' And then he bit down on her aching, swollen breasts and she screamed her approval as sensation shot through her.

'God help us,' he said fervently as he swept her into his arms and carried her over to the bed.

Hallie clung to him as they tumbled onto the pillows, wanting him over her, inside of her, wanting it now. Her heart beat wildly and her breathing was fast and urgent as she undid the buttons on his shirt, pushed it aside, and surged against him, glorying in the rasp of skin on skin as her nipples pressed hard and tight against his muscled chest. More, she craved it, demanded it, fumbling with his belt, with the fastening of his trousers, only to have him push her hand aside with a half strangled laugh.

'No,' he muttered. 'Ladies first.'

'Whatever happened to equality?' she grumbled.

'Equality is overrated.' His smile was slow and wicked as he eased her gown from her body and then her panties. 'Ladies first is a good option for you right now. Trust me.' He took her hands and drew them above her head and she let him do it, let him do whatever he wanted. She was naked for him, utterly naked except for the diamonds at her ears and around her throat. She felt completely exposed, utterly vulnerable as he loomed over her, his eyes intent. 'Close your eyes,' he whispered and she did as he commanded, whimpering with pleasure as his lips traced a path from her wrist to her elbow. He stopped when he reached her elbow, stopped to curse beneath his breath before tracing the area surrounding the angry red graze with gentle fingers. Hallie shivered hard and he moved on, his hands tracing a path down her body for his lips to follow, the soft underside of her breast, the slight curve of her stomach, and everywhere he touched her muscles contracted and the pleasure built. She knew what was coming when he spread her thighs wide and moved lower, knew it and craved it but he made her wait, made her plead while he scattered tiny kisses over her hips and his thumb circled the sensitive folds of her flesh.

'Please!' As his mouth moved closer and his hands held her firm. She strained against him, clutched at the sheet above her head, and finally, finally, he licked into her. She couldn't breathe, the heat of his mouth was divine, the rhythmic stroking of his tongue an unbearably exquisite torment. He knew exactly where to lick, exactly how to please her, and she writhed beneath him, riding the wave of anticipation he built so cleverly, riding it hard. And when she didn't think she could stand any more, when she was slick with sweat and just about to shatter into a million pieces, he concentrated his efforts and the world exploded inside her, all around her, as she shuddered her release.

'Oh, my God!' she gasped.

'Told you so,' he muttered, shedding his trousers and moving over her as she brought her hands to his hair and his lips down to hers for a feverish kiss that had nothing to do with tenderness and everything to do with raw driving need. It was his turn to groan now, his turn to shudder as he settled himself between her legs. His turn to whimper as her need for him turned savage.

'Ssshhh,' he muttered. 'Easy.'

Nick inched slowly into her, inexorably penetrating her hot, slippery flesh as her body stretched to accommodate him. He slid his fingers between them to further coax her taut, tight muscles into submission. And then he was seated in her up to the hilt, exactly where he wanted to be, his entire body on the verge of exploding as her hips slammed into his and her body climaxed around him again. He'd never seen anything more wanton, more beautiful, than Hallie lost in passion. So fearless, so utterly open for him, as he spread her legs wide, cupped his hands around her buttocks and surged into her, glorying in his possession, in the scent of sex, and the tight slickness encasing him.

'I've decided that sex is better than dancing,' she whispered as her legs encircled his waist and her nails raked his back.

'This isn't sex.' He was spiralling out of control, seconds away from his own pulsing release. 'This is madness.'

Hallie woke just before dawn, too worried about what the day held to go back to sleep. She slid out of bed and padded to the window to look down on the Teys' tranquil garden, wondering if John would be up soon and out there practising t'ai chi. Wondering if he did and if she watched, would some of his calm feed through to her. She shifted the curtains aside to lay her palm on the windowpane, and reached for the confidence she knew she had to have if her plan was ever going to work.

Nick stirred and she turned to watch him; saw him reach for her, and wake when he couldn't find her. She felt the moment he saw her, felt it as a heat that licked over her entire body, and then he was out of bed and heading towards her, beautifully, magnificently naked. She knew that body now, had loved every inch of it during the night. She knew his scent, the taste of him on her tongue, the playful edge in him and the fire.

What she didn't know was the workings of his mind. What he wanted from her and whether he was going to regret the week he'd spent with her. She didn't want him to have regrets. She looked to his eyes to see if they were cool, to his mouth to see if it was stern, and to his jaw to see if it was set, but Nick was none of those things this morning. He snaked an arm around her waist and drew her into his warmth and his hardness, resting his chin on her head, saying nothing as he too stared out at the wakening day.

'I couldn't sleep,' she murmured.

'I noticed,' he rumbled, his voice working its usual magic on her skin. 'Ready to save the day?'

Not yet. But she would be. 'Sure.'

'Liar,' he countered, with a gruffness that spoke of worry. 'You don't have to do this, you know. It's not too late to change your mind. We can find another way. A safer way.'

'There is no safe way. This is a good plan, Nick. You know it is. I want to give it a try. I want to fix this my way.'

'Why? So you can prove to your brothers that you can?'

'No. It's not that.' All her life her brothers had fixed her mistakes when she'd made them. They'd done it out of love for her, she knew that. They'd done it because they considered her upbringing their job and they took their work seriously. But hadn't they seen? Hadn't they ever looked beneath the protests and seen how they were eroding her confidence and her self-belief? 'This isn't about my brothers,' she said quietly. 'It's about me. I need to prove to myself that I can do this.'

Nick sighed heavily, his arms tightening around her. 'Can't we just take that as a given?'

'No.'

'Damn.' He turned her in his arms, turned so

that she was facing him, then lifted his hand to tuck a stray strand of hair behind her ear. 'How can I help?' he murmured. 'What do you need?'

No more questions, no more protest, just simple support and it flew like a shaft, straight and true, to lodge itself in her heart. She'd been walking a tightrope ever since she'd met this man. She'd resisted his warmth and resisted his wit. She'd even resisted his lovemaking for a while. But she couldn't resist his belief in her. There would be no more balancing on the high wire, not with this man. Silently, willingly, Hallie tumbled into love.

'What do I need?' Her lips curved as she wound her hands in his hair and pulled his lips down to meet her own. The answer was obvious.

Right now, right this very minute, she needed him.

CHAPTER SIXTEEN

'YOU SHOULDN'T BE OUT here,' Kai said to her from the shadows of the yellow cassia tree. It wasn't even dawn, the first slivers of grey had yet to grace the sky, but Jasmine hadn't been able to sleep and this garden had always been a place of refuge.

She'd known he was there well before she stepped down into the lower garden – Jasmine had a sixth-sense when it came to knowing Kai's whereabouts, but her eyes confirmed the shadow of him leaning against the tree trunk and his words made his presence unmistakable. 'It's not safe.'

'There's security everywhere, I'm behind a tree and I'm not the target,' she said as she too let the shadows cloak her. 'You simply don't want me here.'

Kai said nothing but the tension in the air around

them kicked up a notch. 'Why *are* you here?' he asked finally.

'I couldn't sleep. I was worried for Hallie and for Nick. Hopeful for myself and what the world will bring once I start exploring it. Worried about you.'

'Why would you worry about me?'

'Because you're not free. And you should be.'

'Your father offered me a senior position on his executive board yesterday,' Kai said. 'It's a generous offer. He seems to think that the key to my future is for me to wield as much legitimate power as possible. And that the next step is for me to have my father bargain on my behalf for immunity from Triad interference.'

'Would your father do that?'

'John thinks yes.'

'What do you think?'

'I think my father owes me. Whether his indebtedness will stretch that far, I don't know. We're not close any more. Not in the way we once were.'

Regret in those softly spoken words, and a weariness that went soul-deep. 'Kai, this position on my father's executive board... This further distancing from your family... Is this what you want?'

Kai shifted his weight from one foot to another. 'Yes.'

'Then do it,' she said softly. 'Make it happen and know that you have my support, now and always, irrespective of any romantic love I might feel for you. I would see you free to do as you please.'

Stillness was Kai's last retreat; she realised that now. When there was nowhere else to go, when the present held too much pain in it he simply locked down deep inside.

One day – some day – she wanted to shatter that control, she wanted him naked and sweaty against her, lost in her and spinning towards release. Some day up ahead.

'They haven't been bad years for me, these past years,' he said gruffly. 'There was laughter in them. Pleasure in them. There was you.'

Impossible to untangle, these ties that bound her and Kai together. Maybe they simply needed to be acknowledged and accepted for what they were. 'I have a gift for you,' she said. 'Will you accept it?'

'I would see it first.'

So careful, she thought. Always looking for the trap. She would see that instinct lessened too – some day, up ahead.

Jasmine dug into the pocket of her sweat pants for the trinket he'd once bought for her, wondering if he would recognise it. A little plastic turtle hanging from a woven black leather cord. It seemed fitting. It harboured the memory of a thousand fragrant flowers and a gentle, fleeting touch. That was the moment…if such a big feeling could be crammed into so short a time.

That was the moment when she fell.

Jasmine held out her hand and the little turtle rested in her palm. Hard to see it in the darkness. Hard to recognise until Kai's fingers closed around it and began to learn the shape of it. Heaven and earth; that was what the little turtle symbolised. Heaven on earth was what she wished for this man. From her heart to his hand.

She saw the hesitation in him, felt the ripple of it, and then he separated the leather cord and slipped it over his head and tightened the cord back up until the turtle came to rest just below his throat.

'I love it,' he said simply, and leaned forward and pressed his lips to hers, chaste and reverent.

The long seduction had its moments. And this was one of them.

Jasmine pulled back reluctantly and leaned against the garden wall, taking care to remain in the deeper shadow of the tree. It would be dawn soon. A new beginning. A gift well received.

Three years. Three years learning everything

she could about the world she lived in and then she would be back for this man and then…

Then they would see.

'Do you think you'll be able to cancel the contract Hallie put out on Nick?' she asked with a tiny grin for the absurdity of the situation.

'I think so, yes. Contact has already been made. It can be done but I'm going to need help.'

'Whose help?'

'Hallie's.'

'I hate this,' said Nick five hours later as everyone gathered in the Teys' kitchen for a final briefing of the plan. 'I can't believe I'm letting you do this.'

'It's the only way,' said John. She's the only one who can cancel the contract. I'm afraid your accompanying her is out of the question.'

'Why is it out of the question? You organised this. Surely you can arrange for them to meet with *me*.'

'No,' said John firmly. 'I'm afraid we can't.'

Nick scowled. The thought of Hallie facing down professional assassins without him ate away at his stomach like acid.

'I still think I should be going there on my own,' said Hallie. 'Completely on my own.'

'No,' he said curtly. 'You are *not* going there alone. If not me, then Kai.'

'Why drag Kai into it? Or John for that matter? This business has nothing to do with them.'

'No,' he repeated. 'You take Kai or you don't go at all.'

'Kai will accompany you,' said John Tey.

'He's very capable,' said Jasmine earnestly.

Hallie sighed and glared at him, glared at them all. 'Fine, I'll take Kai.'

Nick met Kai's steady gaze and a look of silent understanding passed between them. Kai would do everything in his power to protect her. Everything. He'd better.

'Stop that,' Hallie told him sharply.

'Stop what?'

'That look. The one that says you're going to tear strips off Kai's hide if he lets anything happen to me.'

'You *know* that look?'

'I have four brothers,' she reminded him darkly.

'And I can honestly say I don't know how any of them survived your adolescence,' he snapped.

John Tey smiled. Kai's cough sounded suspiciously like laughter.

'I've phoned ahead. The meeting is set,' said John. 'They'll be waiting for you at the shop.'

'Ready?' Nick asked, quieter now. Quietly concerned.

'Ready,' she said with far more confidence than the situation warranted. 'My negotiating skills are honed and ready to go.'

They ought to be. He, Kai, John, and Jasmine had spent the last two hours firing every conceivable question or objection the bad guys might come up with at her and coaching her on her reply. 'Stick to the plan,' he said gruffly. 'Stay with Kai.'

'Of course.' Hallie smiled at him reassuringly.

'And don't do anything stupid.'

Her eyes narrowed. Her chin came up. He loved that look. 'Was there anything else?' she said, heavy on the sarcasm.

'Yeah.' He strode over to where she was standing, took her face in his hands and kissed her with enough heat to light up half the city. 'Be careful.' He put his hands in his pockets and took a step back before he grabbed her again. Because if he did he knew he'd never let her go.

'It'll take twenty minutes to get there,' said Kai. 'Another twenty, perhaps, to complete the negotiation. I'll call when we're done.'

Nick nodded and watched in tight-lipped silence as they headed for the door. Watched while his stomach roiled for fear she'd be hurt and his brain informed him that letting her attempt to cancel the hit out of some crazy desire to prove her worth was undoubtedly the worst decision he'd ever made.

It was going to be the longest forty minutes of his life.

It was early in the day and many of the shops were still closed. Lucky Plaza was closed as well but Kai drove directly to loading bay entrance number five, parked the Mercedes beside the huge corrugated roll-a-door and cut the engine.

'They're meeting us here,' he said, nodding towards a wall-mounted security camera. 'They'll have seen us arrive. Are you ready?'

Hallie nodded. Her heart was beating a furious tattoo, her hands were clammy, and her lipstick had doubtless been chewed away completely, but she was ready. 'Wait!' Her lipstick. She flipped the sunshield of the car down to reveal the small mirror on the other side, fished her lipstick from her Hermès handbag and carefully applied a fresh coat to her lips. *Now* she was ready.

Kai gave her one of his rare, slow smiles and then the loading bay door opened and two suited sentries stood waiting for them. Hallie took a deep breath and then another before reaching for the door handle. She could do this. Would do this, dammit, because this little catastrophe was of *her* making and *she* was going to fix it. What's more, Nick *trusted* her to fix it.

It was time to go do business.

The plaza was deserted and eerily quiet but the door to the little corner shop was open, the lights inside were on, and the young salesman she'd bought the vase from stood waiting by the counter. He wasn't alone. An older man with greying hair and hard black eyes stood beside him. Whoever he was, and she really wasn't inclined to ask, he wore authority like a cloak and power like he was born to it. Maybe he was.

'Thank you for agreeing to see me at such short notice,' she said politely.

'We have no quarrel with the Tey Corporation,' the older man said in heavily clipped English. His cold black gaze shifted from her to Kai. 'And we certainly have no quarrel with you. I am at your father's service.'

Kai had a father, thought Hallie. And designer suit clad assassins bowed to him.

Something to remember.

The older man turned his reptilian black gaze back on Hallie. 'You have business with us?'

'Business that should have been concluded by now,' said Hallie, knowing instinctively that this man would not tolerate weakness. 'I now find myself in the rather unfortunate position of having to change my plans.' She smiled, a careful, charming smile. 'I'm afraid your services are no longer required.'

'I'm afraid, Mrs Cooper, that we do not renegotiate contracts. Not even with those who place them,' said the older man with a charming smile of his own. 'It's bad for business.'

Nick kept himself occupied by pacing from one end of the Teys' long living room to the other. Jasmine had made tea, two lots of tea, and thirty minutes had come and gone. The first twenty had been bearable. The first twenty minutes had involved Hallie and Kai getting to where they were going. Now it was different. Now, thought Nick grimly, Hallie was meeting with contract killers, firing them, to be precise, and Nick's nerves were stretched to breaking point. Any time now, they'd call.

'Your wife is a very resourceful woman,' said John. John, who had been a quiet, reassuring presence throughout the entire debacle. 'I'm confident she'll succeed. And Kai is with her. They will not dismiss him lightly. Not the man, nor the organisation he represents.'

Nick sighed heavily and ran a hand through his hair. His primary concern was for Hallie's safety. Once she was safe he would worry about the next problem, namely that Kai's presence at the meeting and the implied involvement of the Tey Corporation would have unwanted consequences for the older man. 'How far will this place you in their debt?'

'Not that far,' said John with a slight smile. 'We are neither enemies nor allies, our two organisations, even though both wield a great deal of power. We co-exist. We are respectful of each other. I do not believe this small transaction will upset that balance.'

Nick didn't know whether to believe the other man or not. His explanation sounded too simple and far too easy, given what he knew of Chinese culture. 'I couldn't let her go alone.'

'Nor I,' said John. 'I am your host. I allowed my daughter to take your wife to Lucky Plaza in the first place. My conscience would not allow it.'

'Thank you,' said Nick quietly. He appreciated everything the older man had done for them. He really did.

'Your wife made a simple mistake,' said John magnanimously. 'It could have happened to anyone.'

Nick just stared at him.

'Okay,' said John. 'Maybe not anyone.'

'Of course you don't renegotiate contracts,' said Hallie, deciding it was time to examine a magnificent porcelain vase displayed on a marble pedestal. 'These really are the most exquisite pieces,' she said admiringly, and then, on a more businesslike note, 'I understand your position perfectly, but I'm not here to renegotiate. The delivery was not made in the specified time. Our contract is void. I have no need of another.' She was politeness itself. Tris would be proud of her. Nick would be amazed. 'I simply wished to let you know in person that I consider our business complete.'

He wasn't going to go for it. Hallie held the older man's gaze, knowing in her bones that he was going to say that he didn't do this either. That the contract was complete when the delivery was made and not before. That was good business too.

'This is the first time we have had such a problem,' said the older man bleakly as he looked to the young salesman. 'Make it the last.'

The young crime lieutenant nodded respectfully.

The old general studied her thoughtfully before

glancing once more at the silent Kai. 'So be it,' he said, with a dismissive wave of his hand. 'Give my regards to your husband. Our business is complete. My assistant will see to the details.'

'Thank you,' said Hallie and bowed her head in acknowledgement because, frankly, it seemed the thing to do. She waited until the older man was gone before straightening and turning towards the salesman who'd sold her the vase in the first place.

'You're a very fortunate woman, Mrs Cooper,' he said dryly. 'He let you live.'

'He let you live too,' said Hallie. 'Bonus.'

The young salesman smiled his crooked smile. 'I like you,' he said.

'Be grateful you're not married to her,' said Kai.

'True.'

Hallie ignored their bonding banter completely. She wasn't done yet. 'Can you see to the details today?' she asked the salesman. 'Can you see to them now?' She watched as he whipped out his phone and started texting.

'No problem,' he said. 'Doing it now.'

'Thank you,' she said, bestowing a brilliant smile on him, and then, as a new thought occurred to her, 'I wonder…'

'No!' said Kai. 'No wondering.'

'No refunds either,' said the salesman.

'Of course not,' said Hallie. 'That would be tacky. I was just wondering about the vase. The vase in the window. After all, it *was* part of our arrangement…'

'They haven't called,' said Nick. 'What's taking them so long?' He was on his fourth cup of sugar-loaded green tea and the sugar was starting to take effect. Soon. They would call soon. Meanwhile Nick paced. Pacing was good. Pacing and waiting was far better than sitting and waiting and he wished for the hundredth time that he could have gone with her. Dammit, he *should* have gone with her, regardless. Because if anything happened to her…

The muffled ringing of John's cell phone interrupted his latest what if. Nick felt the blood drain from his face, felt an icy calm steal over him as John took the call. It was brusque, it was brief, it was in Cantonese. And then it was over.

John Tey pocketed his cell phone and turned towards him, a broad smile on his face. 'The meeting was a success. The contract has been dissolved.'

Nick felt the breath he'd been holding leave his

body, felt the blood in his body start to move again as relief washed through him. Hallie was safe, that was all that mattered. His hands were trembling so he put them on the counter to make them stop, his legs were shaky too, nothing he could do about that other than pray they held him up until the sensation passed.

'Here,' said John, pressing a squat glass of clear liquid into his unresisting hand. 'You love her, you feared for her. It's a perfectly normal reaction.'

Nick drained the contents of the glass, almost choked on the fire of it. 'What *is* this stuff?' he spluttered between gasps.

'Cheap Russian vodka,' said John Tey with a chuckle. 'Very good for shock. Very good reminder that you are alive.'

'She did it,' said Jasmine joyfully. 'She's a hero.'

'Crazy, reckless woman,' Nick muttered beneath his breath. 'I should *never* have let her even attempt it.' Just wait until he got his hands on her. Wait till she walked through that door. Hero or not, he was going to lock her up and throw away the key until she *swore* she'd never put him through anything like that again!

'Of course, you're a hero too,' said Jasmine

thoughtfully. 'You may actually be the biggest hero here today.'

'What?' Nick blinked. How could *he* be a hero? He'd done *nothing*! Nothing but wait and in waiting go slowly insane.

'You didn't interfere,' said Jasmine. 'You let her go even though it went against your nature to do so and you trusted her to fix the problem herself. I think that was very heroic.'

'You're a sweetheart,' he said gently as he held out his empty glass for another hit. 'But I think you're confusing heroism with lunacy.'

Twenty minutes later Hallie and Kai walked through the door and Nick managed to greet them civilly enough, thanks in no small part to John's most excellent cheap Russian vodka.

'All done,' said Hallie, all smiles. 'I told you it would work.'

Nick sighed, reached for her and held her close to his heart and she sagged against him, not quite as nonchalant or as confident as she seemed.

'Don't you ever put me through that again,' he said gruffly. 'You hear me?'

Hallie hugged him hard and pulled back a little self-consciously.

Jasmine, he noted, was playing it far cooler with

Kai. She'd waited until he set the large parcel he was carrying down on the sideboard before crossing to greet him, a fragrant cup of tea held carefully in both hands. He watched as Kai took the tea with a wry smile on his face and a gentle meeting of hands and knew Hallie had been right about that too. Jasmine and Kai were in love.

It was a pretty sight, two dark heads bent over an offering of tea, with whitewashed walls, dark wooden furniture and a hastily wrapped parcel in the background. A hastily wrapped *vase-* shaped parcel in the background.

No. No way. She wouldn't have dared. Temper licked through him, hot and swift. It couldn't possibly be what he thought it was. Could it? He glared at Hallie and she smiled back at him, the picture of innocence. He didn't trust that smile, not one little bit.

'What the *hell*,' he said, pointing towards the parcel, 'is *that*?'

Nick accepted John's rather hasty offer to complete their business directly. It was either that or blow a fuse over how and why Hallie came to be in possession of that damned vase and he suspected the older man knew it. So they were in John's study, the contract papers spread out on the desk, having just been signed by the older man and just about to be signed by him. Trouble was, he couldn't do it.

'Is there a problem?' asked the older man.

'Yes,' he said.

'We have agreed that the terms are fair.' John's voice was cool.

'And they are,' Nick was quick to say. 'That's not the problem. The problem is that a contract is based on trust and understanding. Honour. You've always been honourable in your dealings with me. I, on the other hand, have not been completely honourable in my dealings with you.'

John Tey sat back in his chair and regarded him steadily.

Nick took a deep breath and prepared to tell it like it was. 'I'm not married. Hallie isn't my wife. She's only pretending to be my wife.'

'I know,' said the older man, and at Nick's open-mouthed astonishment, 'I've always known.'

Maybe it was the vodka, maybe it was this latest shock coming so close on the heels of the appearance of the vase, but Nick didn't know what to say. Or do. He wasn't entirely sure he still had the power of speech.

'You don't really think I'd sign a hundred-

million dollar deal with a man and not run a background check on him, do you? It's standard company procedure.' John Tey smiled. 'Given that the
company details you provided were accurate to the
last cent, I would, however, like to know why you
felt it necessary to lie about your marital status.'

Ah. 'A misjudgement on my part,' said Nick
uncomfortably. He really didn't want to go into the
why of it.

'I believe that at one stage my daughter viewed
you as a prospective husband,' said the older man
shrewdly. 'And that you invented a wife because
you wished to spare her feelings.'

'I invented a wife because I wanted to secure
this deal,' corrected Nick, with a self-mocking
twist of his lips. If he was going to tell the truth it
may as well be the unvarnished truth. 'I couldn't
afford to offend you. Trust me, there was far more
self-preservation involved than chivalry.'

John Tey conceded the point with a shrug.
'Then there's Hallie.' He shook his head, smothered a chuckle. 'You may not be married to her
yet, Nicholas, but it's clear you've given her your
heart.'

'What?' spluttered Nick. 'You can't think… I'm
not….' Oh, hell! He was.

He was foolishly, undeniably in love with Hallie

Bennett. She of the Titian hair, golden-brown eyes and God-given *talent* for finding trouble.

'I think you're going to have your hands full there, son.'

Nick groaned. He could see it all so clearly. Hallie in his bed, sharing his life, and him never wanting, never even *looking* at another woman because this one filled him so completely. He could see it now. A house brimful with ancient wonders and rambunctious sons, and a tiny daughter with flyaway black hair and golden eyes and the ability to wrap her daddy, uncles, and all of her brothers around her dainty little fingers. He'd be buying shotguns by the dozen. Valium by the caseful. What if – and here was a truly terrifying thought – what if they had *two* daughters? 'Shoot me now,' he told John. 'It'll be quicker and far less painful.'

'Oh, I don't think so,' countered John. 'I think you'll find yourself well satisfied with your choice of life partner. Besides, I can hardly do business with a dead man, now can I?' John Tey picked up the pen and passed it to him. 'My signature is already on the papers, Nicholas. Honour has been satisfied. Sign.'

Hallie left Nick and John downstairs finalising

the distribution deal and headed to the suite to start packing for the trip home. The packing could have waited until later in the day, hell, it could have waited until tomorrow but she was too wired to rest so she started on it with a vengeance. The plan had worked beautifully, Nick was safe, and there was a quiet satisfaction in knowing that no one had pushed her aside and stepped in to save the day. She could be proud of that. Would be proud of it, dammit, and not apologetic as Nick seemed to think she should be, although, to be fair, it wasn't the successful cancellation of the hit that had sent Nick into orbit; it was the presence of the vase. Nick wasn't real happy about the vase.

Truth be told, Nick wasn't real happy with *her*. She'd been a lousy corporate wife, distracting him from his work, arranging to have him killed, and bringing his contract negotiations to a standstill. He was probably counting the hours until they touched down in London so he could pay her and be rid of her. Not that she blamed him.

For her part, saying goodbye to Nick and watching him walk away was going to be the hardest thing she'd ever done. One step forward, two steps back. For all her newfound self-confidence, she knew instinctively that letting Nick go was going to break her heart.

But she was determined that there would be no tears, no telling him she loved him. No. She wouldn't do that to him. He'd wanted a wife for a week and after that week was over, he wanted that wife to leave. That was the deal they'd agreed on; she could at least get that right.

She was still packing ten minutes later when Nick came up to the room and was composed enough to greet him with a tentative smile, a smile that faded when it wasn't returned. She watched him cross to the window and stand there, grim and preoccupied, with his hands in his pockets and his back towards her. Oh, hell. Something was wrong. She waited for him to say something, *anything*, but he remained ominously silent.

Hallie picked up a shirt and attempted to fold it but her fingers wouldn't co-operate. She had to know. 'Did he sign?'

'Yeah, he signed.'

'Yay.' Hallie let out the breath she'd been holding. For a moment there she thought she'd sabotaged his business deal completely. But if that wasn't it, then why the silent treatment?

Oh, yeah. The vase. 'I, ah, packed the vase for you. I thought I'd carry it in my hand luggage. It's very fragile.'

He closed his eyes, muttered a curse.

'And very good value as well,' she said in a rush. 'I think when you have it valued, you'll be pleasantly surprised. It's functional too.'

At this, his eyes opened and fixed on her, thoroughly disbelieving.

'Not that I expect you to, ah, use it in that way. You could use it as a regular vase. You could put flowers in it.'

'Flowers,' he repeated.

'Maybe a dried arrangement of some kind,' she suggested.

'I'll keep that in mind.'

She nodded. 'Yes, well, I'm really glad the whole funeral vase shambles didn't ruin it for you. I think, given the circumstances, that it might be better if I don't take your money. I mean, what with the clothes you provided and the trip itself...'

The contract hit...

'What do you mean *not take the money*? You have to take the money.' Nick pinned her with an angry gaze. 'We had an agreement.'

So they did. Hallie bit her lip and looked away.

'You need that money to finish your diploma.'

The diploma. Hallie sighed. Right now the diploma didn't seem to be very important at all. Maybe it wasn't. 'I'm thinking of putting my studies on hold.'

'Why?'

'I've had an idea.'

'God help us all,' he muttered. And then, as if bracing himself for a hurricane, 'Continue.'

'I'm going to start my own business.'

'What kind of business?'

'I want to start dealing in Asian antiquities, ceramics to be more specific. I have the knowledge. I know what I'm looking for. Not quite tomb raiding, I know, but I think I'd be good at it.' She waited for a great guffaw of mocking laughter but it didn't come.

'Will you have enough start-up money?' he asked. 'Will ten thousand pounds be enough?'

'I'm going to start small. Approach a few collectors and find out what they're buying. Then see if I can find it for them.'

'Because if you need more, I'd be more than willing to back your business venture.'

'You'd do that? Even after all the trouble I've caused you?'

'Yes. You're smart, you think on your feet and you make the world around you a brighter place. I'll back that any day. I'll back you.'

Hallie's eyes filled with tears. He was making it hard, so hard, for her to let him go. Not like her brothers at all, this man before her. Freedom, equality, respect; he'd shown her them all. If he'd only fallen in love with her as well…

But he hadn't. And if they became business partners she'd never be able to keep her feelings for him a secret and *then* where would they be? 'Thank you,' she said huskily. 'Your support means a lot to me but I need to do this on my own.'

Nick nodded. 'I can understand that. But if you ever need help you'll call me.'

'Sure.' Never. She closed the lid on her bulging suitcase. She was all packed. 'I'm going to miss Kai and the Teys. And you.' Her heart was close to breaking with just how much she was going to miss Nick but she summoned a smile. 'I've enjoyed our stay. It's been quite an adventure.'

'Very Lara Croft,' he said.

'I'd rather be Indiana Jones.' And when he lifted a questioning eyebrow, 'It's the hat.'

'I can see you in the hat,' he said, his eyes darkening. 'I can see you in nothing but the hat.'

'First the necklace, now the hat.' She could do this; get through this. 'Maybe you're developing an accessories fetish.'

'The necklace was spectacular,' he said with a wistful sigh. 'The necklace will haunt me until the day I die. Now, so will the hat. Thank you so very much.'

'Definitely an accessories fetish,' she said. 'I'm thinking shoes now. Stilettos. That might work for you too.'

'It's not the accessories.'

'It's not?'

'No.' He was close, very close. 'You're not wearing your rings.'

'They're in the bathroom. I hadn't forgotten them. I just….' Hadn't had the heart to leave them on. Hadn't been able to bear the pretence any longer. She didn't finish her sentence.

He went into the bathroom, came out with them in his hand.

'You want me to wear them,' she said, and felt her heart shatter into pieces. Of course he did. They weren't done here yet. Not quite.

'No. You don't have to wear them if you don't want to,' he said quietly. 'The thing is, I've been thinking about what I'm going to do next too. I have a plan as well.' And with a deep, ragged breath, 'I want you to keep the rings.'

'You're giving them to me?' Fine tremors racked her body as she looked away. 'You know I can't accept them.'

'I'm not giving them to you.' He put his hand on her shoulder and turned her back to face him, and now he could feel her trembling too. His eyes widened, and he stroked his hand down her arm as if to soothe her but he didn't let her go. Instead, he captured her hand in his and traced the knuckles of her wedding finger with his thumb. 'Actually, I suppose I am giving them to you, technically speaking, even though there's another one waiting for you at a certain store in Bond Street that would suit you more, but there's a catch.' His smile was crooked, his eyes uncertain. 'You have to take me too.'

'I….what?'

'I can't let you go,' he said quietly. 'I won't. So the way I figure it, you're going to have to marry me for real.'

'I…you want to marry me?'

'That's the plan,' he said. 'Of course it does depend on you saying *yes* to the plan. And it would really help my confidence if you stopped shaking.'

'My brothers are going to kill you,' she said faintly. 'We've only known each other a few weeks.'

'Was that a yes?'

'I'll drive you crazy.' She couldn't think straight, couldn't break free of the blossoming joy that threatened to engulf her. Nick loved her! He wanted to marry her. If anything, her trembling increased.

'Was *that* a yes?' he wanted to know. 'I'm taking that as a yes. But I'm going to need a declaration of love as well. Just to be sure.'

'You want to hear me say I love you?'

'It's a crucial part of the plan,' he said gruffly.

'I love you,' she said, bringing her hands up to frame his beautiful, beloved face, laughing when his arms came around her as if he'd never let her go. 'Yes, I'll marry you. I'm going to be the best corporate wife you've ever seen.'

'No!' He was half laughing and wholly alarmed as he picked her up in his arms and headed towards the bed. 'I don't want a corporate wife.' And with a catch in his voice that pierced her to the core. 'All I want is you.'

Jasmine, John and Kai were on hand to farewell them as they left for the airport the following morning. They didn't feel like business associates these lovely, generous people, thought Hallie, they felt like family. 'Thank you,' she said warmly, holding out her hand to John. 'For your hospitality and your kindness. It was a pleasure meeting you.'

She turned to Jasmine next as Nick shook hands with John and added his thanks to hers. 'I'm going to miss you,' she said as she embraced the younger girl. 'Keep in touch. Let me know your plans. And don't forget to come and visit.'

And then there was Kai, standing by the front door, a little apart from Jasmine and her father as he waited to drive them to the airport. He wore the same dark plain clothes he always wore and he was once again carrying concealed. The odd little green pendant around his neck was new. 'Thank you,' she said simply. 'For everything.'

'Stay safe, Hallie Cooper.'

'You know, once Jasmine goes, you'll have nothing to do,' she murmured. 'You might decide to travel, and if you do you may decide to visit us too. My door will be always open to you. I have brothers who'd really like you. And you'd like them.'

Kai just smiled.

Hallie watched as Nick completed his farewells, an affectionate hug for Jasmine and a simple heartfelt thank you for Kai. They'd been through so much together - all five of them- that lies and half-truths no longer seemed appropriate. Had never been appropriate, thought Hallie wryly, not really. But she had no wish to upset things just as they were leaving. No wish to watch this comfortable intimacy turn to wariness and suspicion so she kept her mouth firmly shut on the subject of her fictitious marriage to Nick and comforted herself with the knowledge that next time she saw them she *would* be married to him.

Nick joined her by the door and Hallie would have turned to leave but for Jasmine who'd retrieved a bright red parcel from the entrance table and was holding it out towards her. 'For you and Nick,' she said impishly. 'From my father and I.'

Oh, dear. With all the excitement of the past couple of days she'd completely forgotten to get a parting gift for them. The corporate wife had slipped up again. 'I, ah, really wasn't expecting a parting gift,' she said awkwardly.

'Open it,' urged Jasmine.

So she opened it and stared down in astonishment at the little jade horse she'd so admired the first time she'd met John. 'Oh, my Lord,' she whispered, looking to Nick for explanation but he looked as baffled as she was. What kind of parting gift was this? Had they gone nuts? Parting gifts were small, inexpensive mementos of a person's stay. Chopsticks were parting gifts, or a pretty silk scarf… Nothing wrong with a packet of fragrant green tea leaves either, come to think of it, but this… This was crazy. She didn't understand the gesture at all. 'I don't know what to say,' she said frankly. 'It's absolutely exquisite. But it's not a parting gift.'

'Of course not.' John Tey's mischievous smile was remarkably like his daughter's. 'It's a wedding present.'

CHAPTER SEVENTEEN

FLIGHT 124 FROM HONG Kong to Heathrow touched down with a screech and a swerve at five p.m. on a grey and blustery afternoon but neither the weather nor the bumpy landing could dim Hallie's happiness. She was manicured, pedicured, pampered and polished and was corporate wife chic in her lightweight camel-coloured trousers and pink camisole and jacket. Her shoes matched her top, her handbag was Hermès, and Nick was at her side, thoroughly eye-catching in his grey business suit and crisp white business shirt minus the tie. She was the woman who had it all and it was all she'd ever dreamed of.

That didn't mean she was a pushover.

'I still can't believe you didn't tell me you told John we weren't married,' she said as she stared down at the little jade horse in her handbag. What with that and the funeral vase, customs was going to be a real treat.

'I was going to tell you,' said Nick. 'Right after I proposed and you accepted but I figured I'd leave it a few minutes on account of the timing not being quite right. I wanted you to be quite sure I was proposing because I wanted to and not because I'd just blown our cover.'

Ah. It was slightly disconcerting just how well Nick knew her.

'Then, when I was just about to tell you, I got distracted.'

'By what?'

'You don't remember?' He sighed heavily but his eyes gleamed with lazy satisfaction. 'How soon a wife forgets.'

Hallie did remember. And blushed at the memory of their fiery lovemaking. 'After <u>that</u>.'

'After that my brain had turned to mush,' said Nick and it was Hallie's turn to sigh. It was almost impossible to stay angry with Nick when he was being charming, which was most of the time, but she didn't want to set a precedent.

'We're partners,' she said firmly. 'I expect you to share these little details with me.'

'Ah.' It was a very uncomfortable sounding 'Ah'. 'There's something else I should probably mention before we go through customs and out into the arrivals terminal,' said Nick.

She stopped mid-stride, and eyed him narrowly. Nick's mouth twitched as he pulled her into his arms and his mouth descended on hers, regardless of the people streaming past them. By the time the kiss ended, she was dazed, aroused and doubtless dishevelled, but she wasn't distracted. 'You were saying?' she said smoothly.

'Clea's meeting us here.'

'So?' To Hallie's way of thinking that was hardly a problem. 'I like your mother.'

'So do I,' said Nick, and then they tackled customs and stepped through the final set of doors and out into the arrivals area. 'But she said something about Valentine's Day being good to me, and I'm really not sure if there are going to be cupids and shiny red heart-shaped balloons involved. It's possible.'

'And it would be awesome,' said Hallie. 'I have a new role model.'

'No,' said Nick hastily. 'No you don't. Resist.'

'There she is,' said Nick a few steps later, and there she was, a vision splendid in magenta and lime chiffon with a leopard-print handbag that matched her shoes. No Valentine's Day accoutrements were in evidence. Yet.

'I knew it!' said Clea when they reached her. 'I knew you'd be perfect together. Mothers can sense these things.'

Hallie snickered as Nick suffered his mother's enthusiastic embrace and then she too found herself enveloped in a fragrant cloud of Clea.

'You *are* going to marry him, aren't you, dear? Let me look at you. There, of course you are!'

'Did you tell her?' muttered Nick. 'I didn't tell her.'

'Apparently mothers can sense these things,' said Hallie.

'Wait until you have children of your own. You'll see,' said Clea. 'Oh, you're going to give me such beautiful grandchildren!'

But Hallie didn't appear to be listening. She was looking past Clea, her startled gaze fixed on a dark-haired man leaning against a column some distance away. He was big and lean and all muscle, his hair was shaggy, and he was looking their way, his focus absolute. Nick watched with fatalistic calm as the man dislodged himself from the column to stand and glare at him with amber eyes as fierce and untamed as a mountain cat.

'I think you're about to meet Tristan,' said Hallie.

He'd figured as much. 'He looks a mite put out. Are you sure you left him a note?'

'Right there beneath the toaster. I swear.'

'I see.'

Tristan had finished taking his measure and was now staring at the hastily re-wrapped funeral vase tucked beneath Nick's arm, his expression grim.

'He knows about the vase,' she muttered.

'That's Interpol for you.'

'You're not taking this seriously enough, Nick.'

'Trust me, I am.'

From what Hallie had told him, her brothers were protective of her. And regardless of him wanting to marry her *now*, there was no denying he'd carted her off to Hong Kong under false pretences, had his wicked way with her, and allowed her to waltz, practically unprotected, into the lair of the local warlord.

Tristan started towards them.

'You're going to run, aren't you,' said Hallie morosely. 'They always run.'

'Absolutely not,' he said, tearing his gaze away from her brother to send her a reassuring smile, and then Tristan reached them, nodding politely enough to Clea before shooting his sister a wrathful, baffled glare that Nick could identify with. Then it was his turn to meet that flat golden gaze.

'So…' Tristan let the word trail off ominously. 'How was the trip?'

'Stop that!' Hallie stepped forward to stand protectively in front of him, hands on her hips, eyes flashing. 'You be nice to him!'

Tris's gaze cut to his sister, to the wedding rings already on her finger, and Nick saw a familiar wilfulness there along with no small measure of love. 'Why?'

'Because he's mine, that's why! Because I love him and I'm going to marry him and we're going to have beautiful babies together, so back off!'

'Babies?' echoed Tristan.

'Gorgeous, adorable babies,' said Clea, throwing in a grandmotherly smile for good measure. 'Soon.'

'How soon?' Tristan's searing gaze cut to Clea. Nick rolled his eyes in disbelief.

'Not that soon,' he said firmly, 'Later.' He reached out to pull Hallie back until she was once more standing by his side. 'Please,' he said dryly, 'don't try and help me.'

'But—'

'No.' He silenced any further protest with a warning glance. 'I let you call the shots in Hong Kong but you don't have to rush to my defence here. I don't need your protection,' he said softly. 'I don't *want* your protection. Not this time. You of all people should understand that.'

'Fine.' She sent him a glance that held equal measures of self-mockery and frustration. 'He's all yours.'

'Hard, isn't it.' Nick leaned down and kissed the generous pout of her mouth because he couldn't resist. 'Have a little faith. Maybe we'll bond.'

'Tris doesn't bond all that well,' said Hallie, shooting her brother a dark glance.

'Don't push him, Hallie. Your brother loves you. He only wants what's best for you.'

'That would be you,' she said with quiet certainty.

Nick looked down into Hallie's vibrant, beloved face, a smile on his lips and in his heart. 'Hold that thought,' he said. And kissed her again.

EPILOGUE

Three years later...

Hallie Bennett-Cooper hadn't insisted on a Valentine's Day gift from Tiffany's because she was in love with shiny baubles. She did it because she was madly in love with her husband, he loved being tortured, and who was she to deny him?

She'd taken to torturing Nick lovingly and often – there was the 'I bought you a new vase' torture – Nick had quite the collection these days. There was the 'Clea and I are having lunch today' approach – that was happening today *after* the trip to the jewellers. Nick didn't know it yet, but Clea was bringing a Valentine's Day date. Hallie didn't know who, but she was looking forward to it.

Entertainment was Nick's business, a big and astonishingly lucrative business, and Hallie and Clea did their damnedest to keep the man inspired.

'Henry,' murmured Hallie as she stepped through the doors of the jewellers and landed in another world. She walked in a lot of worlds these days, because of Nick, and she loved each and every one of them.

'Mrs Bennett-Cooper.' Henry's wide smile encompassed both Hallie and Nick. 'Looking as vibrant as always. More so, actually.'

'Why, *thank* you, Henry. I was hoping someone would notice.'

'I noticed,' said Nick. 'I just haven't commented yet.'

'Henry, we're in need of a little Valentine's Day trinket to make me feel truly appreciated.'

'I have just the thing,' said Henry.

'I knew you would.' Hallie beamed.

Henry brought his heels together and bowed, ever so slightly, in his Friday-night-poker-buddy's direction. 'I've been saving it for you at Nick's request.'

'Henry, did you just bow to him?' said Hallie. 'Something new in the service manual?'

'I'm making him feel special. Of course, it's now up to me to make *you* feel even *more* special,' said Henry as he led them to a viewing area and signalled discreetly to an assistant. By the time they were all seated, the assistant was handing Henry a slim presentation box that Henry opened with exquisite ceremony and set on the table in front of them.

Hallie leaned forward and gasped at the pair of antique silver and jade hair sticks nestled on plush white velvet.

Nick leaned back and smiled.

'They're not new,' said Henry. 'But we do have provenance and they're perfectly wearable.'

'Do you like them?' murmured Nick. 'Not too bland? Because I wouldn't want you to feel unlike yourself while wearing them.' Nick's drawl was lazy and his eyes were smiling.

'They're exquisite.' Hallie wondered if now was the time to mention her gift to him. Maybe it was.

'I have a gift for you too,' she said and took Nick's hand and threaded his fingers through hers. 'It's just that I can't let you have it just yet. You're going to have to wait another five months, three weeks and six days before you can hold this particular gift in your hands. Give or take.'

Nick paled. 'You're not—I mean—we—*what*?'

Maybe this wasn't the time and place after all.

Hallie took his hand and placed it gently against her stomach. 'We're going to have a baby.'

'That's what I thought you said.'

'You did say you *wanted* children.'

'I do,' he said instantly. 'I do. I just…' Nick passed a big hand over his face and looked towards Henry.

'Clea for a grandmother,' murmured Henry, well and truly intent on torture. 'A daughter with your recklessness, her mother's imagination and looks, and unlimited choices when it comes to what she'll grow up to be and do. You really didn't think this through, did you?'

Hallie grinned, patted Nick's hand, and reached for one of the hair sticks. Nick still looked thunderstruck, but she could see the news sinking in. The tiny tilt of his lips and the growing awe and satisfaction in his eyes. Oh, yes. As far as reactions went, that would do. She wound her hair around her hand and pinned it atop her head. 'Stop scaring him, Henry.' And to Nick, 'Does this make me look like a Madonna with child?'

Nick opened his mouth and shut it again with a snap. He tried again.

Nope.

'I may need one of those floaty Goddess-of-Fertility dresses,' said Hallie.

'You're beautiful and I love you.' Finally Nick found his voice. 'And I may need to take up meditation in order to stem the rising panic. Because my first instinct is to buy my daughter a gilded cage. You have those here, right?' he asked Henry.

'Special order.'

'Our children won't need a gilded cage, Nicholas. Wise and loving counsel will do.'

'Yes, but where are they going to get that?' Nicholas grinned suddenly, and Hallie blossomed beneath the enveloping warmth. She could do this. They both could.

'Don't make me poke you with my hair stick,' she warned him. 'It could be dipped in dragon venom. You never know.'

Hallie watched as Nick's eyes grew dreamy again. He was probably adding hair ornaments to game girl Xia's weapons arsenal. Or maybe he was thinking about fatherhood. Multitasking mastermind that he was, he was probably thinking about both.

'I don't suppose you have any hair stick daggers in the shop?' she asked.

'It's not that kind of shop,' said Henry, eyeing Nick warily. 'Has he just gone into shock? Should I bring out the Scotch?'

'He's not in shock. He's just busy.' Hallie picked

up the other hair ornament, tucked it haphazardly into her hair and smiled at Henry. 'Do your customers go into shock a lot?'

'Usually over the price.'

'Understandable, really.' Hallie waved a bejewelled hand in front of her husband's face. 'Hey, Nick. Daddy of the future.' *That* snapped him back to the present. 'Maybe you could build a gilded cage for our children in fantasy land and set a gorgon or two to guarding it. Treat it the way you would a therapy session with a good psychiatrist.'

'Maybe I could consult with your brothers over the best way to protect our child,' countered Nick.

'You really don't want to be doing that.'

'Oh, but I do.'

There was the tiniest chance that Nicholas was serious.

'Oh, this is going to be good,' said Henry. 'Shall I bring out the silver spoons?'

Two hours, a silver spoon and one double Scotch for Nick later, Hallie and Nick walked into the dining room of one of London's landmark hotels and found Clea and her mystery guest already seated and enjoying pre-luncheon drinks. Clea's mystery guest was Jasmine Tey.

'This is why I love Valentine's Day,' said Hallie, when hugs had been exchanged all round. 'Always the unexpected delight.'

'Same as every other day she wakes up in,' murmured Nick as he kissed first Jasmine's cheek and then his mother's. Clea smiled. Jasmine regarded him fondly.

'Why didn't you tell us you were in London?' Nick demanded of Jasmine. 'Does your father know you're here? Please tell me your father knows you're here.'

'He's practising,' said Hallie. 'Ignore him.'

'I only arrived two days ago,' said Jasmine. 'I applied for a semester exchange between my university and Oxford and got it. I'll be studying here for the next six months.'

'Practising for what?' Clea eyed her son narrowly.

'Fatherhood,' said Nick, and if his chest expanded and those glorious blue eyes shone brighter than usual, well, Hallie could get used to that. 'It's pending. I'm adjusting. We're going to have a baby.'

Clea smiled. Then she laughed until tears threatened to spill. Then she ordered champagne all round, except for Hallie who had bubbles in her water instead.

'How's your father?' Hallie wanted to know of Jasmine. 'What's Kai doing?'

'My father's well – he has a lady friend,' said Jasmine, with a nod for Hallie's wide- eyed response.

'And do we approve?'

'We do,' replied Jasmine. 'As for Kai, he's currently overseeing the Tey Corporation's expansion into Northern China. He bought himself a house in Harbin in Heilongjiang Province.'

'What does that even mean?' asked Hallie.

'It means that he's finding his way,' said Jasmine and reached into her bag for her phone. Moments later she handed it to Hallie.

The house in the photo had been influenced by Russian architecture more than Asian. It wasn't small. The quiet pride in Jasmine's eyes spoke volumes. 'Do you have Kai's number?' Hallie asked. 'May I text him with our news?'

Jasmine nodded. Hallie found the number, keyed in the message and then got a passing waiter to take a picture of them all before pressing send. 'I hope you sent chocolates to Kai at his beautiful new house today,' she said.

'But no.' Jasmine smiled serenely. 'I sent them to his office, where they will be seen and commented upon, and I signed my name to them because my admiration for him is certainly no secret and hasn't exactly faded. Give it another year or so and Kai might even believe it.'

'Good things do come to those who wait,' said Hallie as the phone in her hand trembled in response to an incoming message. 'Huh. Look at that. Kai sends his congratulations. He wants to know where we are.' Hallie felt altogether inclined to tell him. Another message came in as she was doing just that. 'Jasmine, he wants you to avoid the crab and apparently I need some bird's nest soup. That is so sweet.' Hallie handed the phone back to Jasmine. 'We should take a photo of the smorgasbord for him. Tell him we wish he was here.'

'Not too forward?' asked Jasmine.

Not forward at all, decided Hallie, Nick and Clea. More like playful. 'Although you *could* initial that message personally,' murmured Hallie.

So Jasmine did.

Halfway through their meal a small army of wait staff arrived at their table. The bright-eyed, caramel-coloured teddy bear delivered to Nick was big enough to require a seat of his own and the waiter gravely informed them that the bear's name was Kai and he was available for future bodyguard duties. The five dozen long-stemmed red roses presented to Jasmine did not come in a vase – they came in a white beribboned box and the card that came with them brought a glow to her cheeks. The cheap Russian vodka came from John Tey.

'Very good for shock,' murmured Jasmine, and the laughter that followed flowed free.

'What did the card say?' asked Hallie once the chaos had subsided, and Jasmine smiled shyly and passed the little red card over to her.

Happy Valentine's Day, Traveller, it read.
3yrs – 1yr 342days = 388days.
And counting.

THE END

Meet

ON WRITING AND READING...

What do you love most about being a writer?

I'm never bored. There's always something to think about and work on.

What do you like least about being a writer?

There's always something to think about and work on.

Do you have a favourite locale or setting for your novels? What is it and why is it your favourite?

I don't really have a favourite setting or locale, though I do like setting fish-out-of-water stories in South East Asia. I've lived and worked there many times before and feel comfortable writing about the locations and the customs. I like to take my readers on a journey. I love armchair travelling!

What are your five all-time favourite books (with authors)?

WELCOME TO TEMPTATION by Jenny Crusie

NO PLACE LIKE HOME by Barbara Samuel

THE CHESAPEAKE BAY SERIES by Nora Roberts

TO KILL A MOCKINGBIRD by Harper Lee

THE PALADIN by CJ Cherryh

What one specific piece of advice would you give a would-be writer trying to kick-start a career?

Learn—join a writing organisation, an online group, buy how-to books, attend workshops and conferences. Write. Don't give up.

ON ROMANCE…

Describe the ultimate romantic meal.

You mean one I don't have to cook or clean up the remains of afterwards? In that case, I'll have a table set with matching silverware, stiff linen napkins and glassware that hums long after you ting it. I'll have old-fashioned quantities of modern French food, served on fine white china and washed down with chilled white wine. As for music, Yo Yo Ma will be tucked in a corner, sawing away on his million-dollar cello and Nigel Kennedy will drop by for a quick stint on his violin. The room will be lit by candles, of course, and I'll look years younger than I really am. My husband will be my dinner companion (yes, I've decided to let him join me) and he'll make fascinating conversation whilst looking impossibly sexy (he's actually pretty reliable in this regard). We'll slow dance between courses and at the end of the evening he'll tell me he's pregnant.

What is your all-time favourite romantic movie?

Mulan (it's a Disney animated film).

What is your all-time favourite romantic song or composition?

Jimi Hendrix's 'Little Wing'.

What is the most romantic gesture or gift you have received?

A pair of Belted Galloway calves turning up at the back door on Valentine's Day with pink ribbons around their necks. Moo.

How do you keep the romance alive in your relationship?

We laugh a lot. Give a lot.

What tip would you give your readers to make their lives more romantic?

It's all in your mind!

Where is the most romantic place you've ever travelled?

Istanbul was very romantic, but then, I was madly in love…

ALL ABOUT ME…

Besides writing, what other talent would you most like to have?

Er, concert pianist? Without the all-encompassing practice that goes with it.

Who is someone you admire and why?

My mother. She's the most giving person I know.

Do you have a good luck charm or superstition?

Nope.

Share one of your favourite indulgences with us.

Steaming, bubbling spa baths.

What quality do you most admire in a man?

Oooh. Tough one. You mean I can only choose one? Loyalty.

What is the one thing you've always wanted to do, but never had the courage to try?

Skydive. I'm afraid of heights.

If you weren't a writer, what would you be?

Richer.

Sad the story's over? Don't worry, we've got lots of other
fantastic books coming up!

Turn the page for an exclusive extract from

THE NEXT BEST THING

from bestselling author Kristin Higgins,
available in April 2013.

"Um, listen, Ethan, we need to talk," I say, cringing a little.

"Sure. Let me grab another one of these. They're incredible." He goes back into the kitchen, and I hear the fridge open again. "Actually I have something to tell you, too." He returns to the living room "But ladies first." Sitting in the easy chair, he smiles at me.

Ethan looks nothing like his brother, which is both a comfort and a sorrow. Unlike Jimmy, Ethan is a bit…well, average. Nice-looking, but kind of unremarkable. Medium brown eyes, somewhat disheveled brown hair, average height, average weight. Kind of a vanilla type of guy. He has a neat little beard, the kind so many baseball players favor—three days of stubble, basically, which gives him an attractive edginess, but he's…well, he's Ethan. He looks a bit like an elf in some ways—not the squeaky North Pole elves, but like a cool elf, a Tolkien elf, mischievous eyebrows and sly grin.

He regards me patiently. I swallow. Swallow again. It's a nervous habit of mine. Fat Mikey jumps into Ethan's lap and head butts him until Ethan obliges the bossy animal by scratching his chin. Ethan rescued him from the pound a few years back, saying no one would take the ugly beast, and gave him to me. Fat Mikey has never forgotten just who sprung him from prison, and now favors Ethan with a rusty purr.

I clear my throat. "Well, listen. You know, ever since Jimmy died, you've been, just…well. Incredible. Such a good friend, Ethan." It's true. I don't have the words to voice my gratitude.

His mouth pulls up on one side. "Well. You've been great, too."

I force a smile. "Right. Um…well, here's the thing, Ethan. You know that Corinne had a baby, of course. And it got me thinking that, well…" I clear my throat. "Well, I'd like to have a baby, too." Gah! This isn't coming out the way I want it to.

His right eyebrow raises. "Really."

"Yeah. I've always wanted kids. You know. So, um…" Why am I so nervous? It's just Ethan. He'll understand. "So I guess I'm ready to…start dating. I want to get married again. Have a family."

Ethan leans forward, causing Fat Mikey to jump off his lap. "I see," he says.

I look at the floor for a second. "Right." Risking a peek at Ethan, I add, "So we should probably stop sleeping together."

ETHAN BLINKS. HIS EXPRESSION doesn't change. "Okay," he says after a beat.

I open my mouth to brook his argument, then realize he hasn't made one. "Okay. Great," I mumble.

Ethan sits back and looks toward the kitchen. "So seeing your new niece really got to you, huh?"

"Yes. I guess so. I mean, I've always wanted…well, you know. Husband, kids, all that. I've been thinking about it lately, and then today—" I opt not to describe my whisker. "I guess it's time."

"So is this theoretical, or do you have someone in mind?" he asks. Fat Mikey lets out a squeaky meow, then lifts his leg and starts licking.

I clear my throat. "It's theoretical. I just…I just figured we should make a clean break of it first, you know? Can't have a friend with privileges if I'm trying to find a husband." A nervous bleat of laughter bursts from my throat.

Ethan starts to say something, then seems to change his mind. "Sure. Most boyfriends wouldn't like to find out that you've got a standing arrangement with someone else." His tone is mild.

"Right," I say after a pause.

"Is that door still sticking?" He nods to the slider, which leads to the tiny balcony.

"Don't worry about it," I mutter. My face feels hot.

"Oh, hell, Luce, don't worry. I'll fix it. You're still my sister-in-law." For a second, he just stares at the glass door.

"Are you mad?" I whisper.

"Nah." He stands up, then comes over to me and drops a kiss on the top of my head. "I will, of course, miss the smokin' sex, but you're probably right. I'll drop in tomorrow to fix the door."

That's it? "Okay. Um, thanks, Ethan."

And with that, he's gone, and I have to say, it feels odd. Empty and quiet.

I'd thought he might have been a little more...well...I don't know what. After all, we've been sleeping together for two years. Granted, he travels all week, and on the weekends when he had Nicky, obviously we didn't do anything, but still. I guess I didn't expect him to be so... blasé.

"What are we complaining about?" I ask myself out loud. "It couldn't have gone any better." Fat Mikey rubs against my ankles as if in agreement, and I reach down to pet his silky fur.

The evening stretches in front of me. I have seven hours until I head for the bakery. A normal person would go to bed, but my schedule is erratic at best. Another thing Ethan and I have in common: the man only sleeps four or five hours a night. I wonder if we'll still play Scrabble or Guitar Hero late at night, now that we're not...well, we were never really a *couple*. Just friends, and sort of relatives, linked forever by Jimmy. And lovers, though my mind bounces away from that word. *Friends with privileges* sounds much more benign.

In the first year after Jimmy died, Ethan had been one of the few people whose company I could stand. My friends—well, it was hard for both them and me. I'd married and buried a husband when most of my peers weren't even thinking about a serious relationship. A lot of them just sort of…faded away, not knowing what to say or do for a woman widowed at twenty-four after eight months and six days of marriage.

Corinne ached for me, but seeing her eyes well up every time she saw me didn't do much for my emotional state. My mom had a grim resignation to Jimmy's death, almost a *been there, done that, own that crappy T-shirt* attitude as she patted my hand and shook her head. My aunts, forget it. To them, it was my destiny…*Poor Lucy, well, at least she got it over with.* Not that they were heartless enough to say that, but there was sort of a maudlin welcome feeling when I was around them, as if my widowhood was simply a fact of life. As for Gianni and Marie, I could hardly bear to be around them. Jimmy was their firstborn son, the chef in their restaurant, the heir apparent, the crown prince, and of course, the Mirabellis were absolutely ruined. Though we saw each other often, it was agony for all three of us.

But Ethan…maybe because we were almost the same age, maybe because we'd been pals at Johnson & Wales before he fixed me up with Jimmy, but whatever the reason, he was the only one who didn't make me feel worse.

In those first few black months, Ethan was a rock. He found this very apartment, right below his. He bought me a PlayStation and we spent far too many hours racing cars and shooting each other on the screen. He cooked for me, knowing I'd eat Sno-Balls and Ring Dings if left to my own devices, coming down with a pan of eggplant parmigiana, chicken marsala, meat loaf. We'd watch movies, and he didn't care if I'd forgotten to shower for the past couple of days. If I cried in front of him, Ethan would patiently take me in his arms, stroke my hair and tell me that someday, we were both going to be okay and if I didn't stop blubbering on his shirt, he was going to fit me with a shock collar and start using it.

Then he'd head out for another week of traveling and schmoozing, which seemed to be what he was paid so handsomely to do. He'd e-mail me dirty jokes, bring me tacky little souvenirs from whatever city he was in, send pictures of himself doing those stupid daredevil things he did—helicopter skiing in Utah, sail-surfing in Costa Rica. It was part of Ethan's job to show the demographic of *Instead*'s consumers that eating a real meal was a waste of time when such fun awaited them. Which was ironic, given that Ethan loved to both eat and cook.

After the first six months or so, when I wasn't quite so soggy, Ethan backed off a little, started doing the things normal guys do. For about two months, he dated Parker Welles, one of the rich summer folks, and to me, they seemed quite nice together. I liked Parker, who was irreverent and blunt, and assumed Ethan had found his match, so I was quite surprised when Ethan told me they'd broken up amicably. Then Parker found out she was pregnant, informed Ethan and politely declined his marriage proposal. She stayed in Mackerly, living in her father's sprawling mansion out on Ocean View Avenue, where all the rich folks live, and gave birth to Nick. Why she passed on Ethan is a mystery—she's told me time and again she thinks he's a great guy, just not the one for her.

After Nicky came into the world, Ethan and I found ourselves hanging out once more. I guess the privileges part was bound to happen eventually, though neither of us planned on it. In fact, you could say that I was stunned the first time he—well. More on that later. I should think about something other than Ethan.

Looking around my apartment, I sigh. It's a nice place—two bedrooms, a living room, big sunny kitchen with ample counter space for baking. Prints hang on the walls as well as a large photo of Jimmy and me on our wedding day. The furniture is comfortable, the TV state-of-the-art. My balcony overlooks a salt marsh. Jimmy and I were in the process of moving into a house when he died. Obviously I hadn't wanted to live there without him, so I sold it and moved here, Ethan's proximity a great comfort.

I had imagined that Ethan and I would spend more than ten minutes breaking up, and I find myself at a bit of a loss for what to do. It's nine-thirty on a Friday night. Some nights, Ash, the Goth teen who lives down the hall, comes over to play video games or catch a movie, but there's a high school dance tonight, and her mother forced her to go. I could go over the syllabus for the pastry class I teach at the community college, but I'd just be guilding the lily, since I planned that out last week. My gaze goes to the TV.

"Fat Mikey, would you like to see a pretty wedding?" I ask my cat, hefting him up for a nuzzle, which he tolerates gamely. "You would? Good boy."

The DVD is already in. I know, I know, I shouldn't watch it so much. But I do. Now, though, if I really am moving on, if I'm going to find someone else, I really do need to stop. I pause, think about scrubbing the kitchen floor instead, decide against it and hit Play.

I fast-forward through me getting ready, watching in amusement the jerky, sped-up movements of Corinne pinning the veil into my hair, my mother dabbing her eyes.

Bingo. Jimmy and Ethan standing on the altar of St. Bonaventure's. Ethan, the best man, is cracking a joke, no doubt, because the brothers are laughing. And then Jimmy looks up and sees me coming down the aisle. His smile fades, his wide, generous mouth drops open a little and he looks almost shocked with love. Love for me.

I hit Pause, and Jimmy's face freezes on the television screen. His eyes were so lovely, his lashes long and ridiculously pretty. A muscular physique despite cooking and eating all day, the longish blond hair that curled in the humidity, the way his eyes would half close when he looked at me…

I swallow, feeling that old, familiar tightness in my throat, as if there's a pebble lodged in there. It started after Jimmy died—I'd actually asked my cousin Anne, who's a doctor, to see if I had a tumor in there, but she said it was just a classic symptom of anxiety. And now it's back, I suppose, because I'm about to, er…move on. Or something.

The last part of becoming fully alive again—because when Jimmy died, he took a huge part of me with him—would be to find someone new. I want to get married and have babies. I really do. I grew up without a dad, and I wouldn't willingly take on single motherhood. And though I'll always miss Jimmy, it's time to move on. Finding another husband…it's a good idea. Sure it is.

*Can sparkling summer flings ever
turn into forevers?*

Tamsin's ready to spend her summer relaxing, until
Alejandro—the man who nearly destroyed her reputation
—comes back into her life. Now his world of champagne
and scandal awaits her once again…

Sarah's summers are about spending time with her little
girl. She never has a chance to think about herself. Until
an encounter with a film director turns her life upside
down and thrusts her into the exciting world of
glitz, glamour and gossip pages.

www.millsandboon.co.uk

0712/MB380

New York, Hollywood... Pregnant?

If her landlady's cat hadn't gone missing and Connor
Brody had bothered to return her messages asking for
help in the search, Daisy Dean wouldn't have been
sneaking around his garden at night—and he would
never have caught her in her underwear!

But Connor's quite pleased with his scantily clad intruder.
His business deal is about to fall through—maybe Daisy
could make it up to him by accompanying him to NYC?

What's the worst that could happen?

www.millsandboon.co.uk

0712/MB373

Rules are made to be broken this summer!

Midsummer madness has gone to everyone's heads…two new arrivals have blown into Glenmore and life at the hospital looks like it could get tricky for Flora and Jenna.

So, it's time to set some rules.

Flora's summer is simple, avoid kissing Connor MacNeil.

Jenna's summer 'Why I shouldn't fall in love with Dr Ryan McKinley' list is a little more complex…

It's so difficult to be good when temptation is right on the doorstep. But rules are rules.